csc

CW01508200

4 Murders, a Wedding, and a Cruise

-not necessarily in that order

Stuart St Paul

AMAZON BEST SELLING AUTHOR

FOLLOW THIS AUTHOR

AMAZON
https://www.bookbub.com/profile/stuart-st-paul?list=about

BOOKBUB
https://www.bookbub.com/authors/stuart-st-paul

APPLE
https://books.apple.com/us/author/stuart-st-paul/id1632890033

GOODREADS
https://www.goodreads.com/author/show/7960151.Stuart_St_Paul

IMDB
https://www.imdb.com/name/nm0820787/

WIKI
https://emmerdale.fandom.com/wiki/Stuart_St_Paul

WATERSTONES
https://www.waterstones.com/author/stuart-st-paul/7052733

THRIFT BOOKS
https://www.thriftbooks.com/a/stuart-st-paul/2488497/

WEBSITE
www.stuartstpaul.co.uk

ONLINE BOOKCLUB
https://forums.onlinebookclub.org/shelves/author.php?a=255351

ROMANCE OI
https://www.romance.io/authors/657d6086ab9bdf7fce15d84c/stuart-st-paul

CSCI CRUISE SHIP CRIME INVESTIGATORS

This work of fiction references ships and cruise ports and adds a dramatically exaggerated crime. It is all a product of the author's wild imagination.

4 Murders, A Wedding, and A Cruise

- not necessarily in that order

Stuart St Paul

Edition 250114
Copyright © 2023/4   Stuart St Paul
All rights reserved. All rights reserved.
DORIS VISITS CRUISE BOOKS
Northwood, England.

Amazon **ISBN:** 9798301863837
www.DorisVisits.com

THE CSCI SERIES OF BOOKS

CSCI - short for *Cruise Ship Crime Investigations* - is a captivating collection of crime thrillers set against the backdrop of the luxurious yet enigmatic world of cruise ships. These novels combine elements of classic whodunits, modern thrillers, and exotic travelogues, creating a unique genre that appeals to fans of mystery and adventure alike.

Each book in the series is crafted to take readers deep into the intricacies of life aboard cruise ships, from the glitzy public decks to the hidden corners where secrets unfold. The stories often delve into the duality of cruise life - the opulent, carefree atmosphere experienced by passengers versus the complex, tightly managed operations behind the scenes.

They can all be read as stand-alone novels, or enjoyed as a series where the characters really unfold.

Key Themes of the CSCI Series:

1. **Murder and Intrigue at Sea**
   Each instalment presents a fresh mystery, typically involving a crime that takes place aboard a ship or in one of its exotic port destinations. The closed environment of a cruise ship amplifies the tension, making the investigation all the more gripping as

suspects, witnesses, and clues are confined to a finite space. See the rear of this book.

2. **Authentic Cruise Ship Details**
The author draws heavily from real-life experiences aboard cruise ships, infusing the series with authenticity. From insider knowledge about the crew's roles to descriptions of ports of call and maritime regulations, readers gain an immersive understanding of this unique world.

3. **Exotic Locations**
The books transport readers to stunning locations around the globe, with vivid descriptions of iconic and lesser-known destinations. Each port offers its own mysteries, dangers, and cultural nuances, adding richness to the narratives.

4. **Character-Driven Plots**
Central to the series is a recurring protagonist (or team) tasked with unravelling the complex web of motives behind each crime. These characters often face personal challenges that run parallel to the main plot, deepening their appeal and relatability.

5. **Fast-Paced, Suspenseful Storytelling**
With tight pacing and unexpected twists, the CSCI series keeps readers on edge, blending heart-stopping action with moments of wit and levity.

The CSCI books are more than just crime novels - they're explorations of human nature, morality, and the contrasts between appearance and reality in a luxurious, high-stakes setting. They offer a perfect blend of escapism and intellectual engagement, appealing to armchair travellers, mystery lovers, and cruise enthusiasts.

Whether you're a seasoned cruiser or new to the world of maritime adventures, the CSCI series offers a thrilling journey that will leave you eagerly anticipating the next instalment.   (web search result)

8-1 STUMPED
CSCI HQ Miami - Tuesday, Day 1 - afternoon

Netted scaffolding obscures the modesty of Palladium House, a two-story Art Nouveau building with a colourful pastel past. This protected structure, now undergoing long-awaited restoration, sits outside a fashionable zip code, which previously left it overlooked by investors. Its survival wasn't championed by the same influential lobbyists who zealously monitor higher-profile landmarks like the Art Deco Tower at 330 W. 42nd Street (known as the McGraw-Hill Building), the Empire State Building, or the Chrysler Building - architectural icons of the 1920s and 1930s. With no advocates and the high cost of repairs, Palladium House, located west of Little Haiti, had fallen into disrepair.

The building spans an entire block, its sixties-era, Jetson-like design evoking early space-age technology. Its fortress-like exterior, reminiscent of darker times, conceals a central quadrangle entirely hidden from street view.

Dwight Ritter, a large African American man, leads suited executive Dan Creedon through a damaged wing where the floor above has collapsed, and the roof above that awaits repair. Their route is restricted by hazard tape. They turn into another wing where renovations are well underway. This section is fast becoming a sleek ground-floor office for the Cruise Ship Crime Investigators. Circular saws whirr as carpenters cut wood, electricians lay conduits, and

1

ceiling fitters install panels for the new false ceiling. Stacks of furniture, electronic equipment, and screens lie covered by protective sheets, but a massive wooden crate stands conspicuously in a far doorway. Its pristine condition and large courier labels suggest it was delivered recently.

Dwight is surprised to see their night watchman sweeping. "Vinnie?"

"I stayed on to help out," Vinnie says, his Irish-accented voice betraying roots in New York or Boston.

"You've just done a night shift. Go home. You don't need to do this."

"This room's nearly there. You'll see the difference tonight."

Dwight takes the broom from Vinnie and unconsciously uses it as a makeshift walking stick, wincing from pain. He watches Vinnie squeeze past the crate.

"What's with the sarcophagus?" Dwight asks.

"It arrived earlier. I thought it was building materials, so I dropped it on the dolly and fetched it. It's not theirs. Want me to move it?"

"No, it's probably tech. Go home."

Vinnie leaves, and Dwight turns to his guest.

"He came with the building. I think he's worried we'll let him go."

"Will you?"

"We don't rock that way," Dwight says, gesturing to the evolving workspace. "This will be our centre of operations. We started with a much smaller digital HQ and an old unit across town. We grew fast and learned a lot. Two years in, with half a dozen major crimes solved, it's time to graduate."

"You have big ambitions?"

"Go big or go home."

"You must be well-funded."

"We have direction, but we're pacing ourselves. When this is finished, the builders will move into the damaged wing. They'll recreate sections of a ship there."

"You need to build an actual ship?"

"For training security staff. It's a military thing - make it as life-like as possible. We're talking to scrappers about acquiring pieces like a cargo door and a gangway. Maybe even an internal watertight door. But the building doesn't have an opening large enough to bring them in, and the walls are protected since it's on the Historic Register."

"There's a hole in the ceiling back there."

"Exactly. That's why we haven't fixed it yet. The plan is to drop them in and then patch the roof."

"But doesn't that leave you vulnerable?"

"That's why Vinnie's here at night."

"And when the old ship pieces are in, he'll be... obsolete?"

"He'll always have a place here."

"Old ship pieces - doesn't that make training outdated?"

"Principles don't change."

"But technology and threats evolve. What about pirates?" Creedon challenges.

"Pirates! Ha! What would they want with thousands of complaining cruise guests?"

"The buffet wouldn't be the same," Creedon quips.

"You're right. Cadets will need modern defences. We're incorporating LRAD and operational fire hoses."

Dwight nudges the box with the broom. It shifts just enough for him to lead Creedon past it into another room.

Twenty two year old Izzy types at a computer station set on a folding table. "This is Izzy," Dwight says. "She joined as an intern and earned her promotion to junior partner."

"Will training include firearms?" Creedon asks, acknowledging her.

Izzy, eager to contribute, interjects: "Our trainers are top-notch

"Familiar with physical force?" Creedon presses.

"Trained killers," Izzy says with a grin.

"I hope that box isn't for one of your targets," Creedon jokes.

Dwight remains stoic - veterans don't joke about death. His pain is worsening, but he refuses to show weakness.

Izzy realises her mistake. "That came out wrong. Sorry. Ignore me."

"Death's the only guarantee in life. She'll be quoting Voltaire soon," Dwight says, masking his struggle.

"That box isn't for a body, is it?" Creedon asks.

"No. We burn those in the yard," Dwight replies without humour.

Creedon's expression falters.

"We did lose a founding partner recently, but that's not him," Dwight says.

"I'm sorry for your loss."

"We all share the same end game. People die on ships. Hopefully, no cruise guest ever will. But if called upon, our cadets will be ready."

Dwight finally sits, his exhaustion evident.

"With Voltaire quotes?" Creedon asks. Dwight shrugs slightly, signalling the end of the conversation. "It's probably junk for the holiday season. Izzy, show Mr. Creedon the square. Get him a coffee at Wild Mary's. I need to use the washroom."

"Sure." Creedon follows Izzy out. "Call me Dan," he says.

Izzy, pleased with the baton handoff, leads him out of the temporary HQ.

Left alone, Dwight exhales sharply, suppressing a scream. He unzips the leg of his tailored trousers, revealing his prosthetic. The white sleeve is stained with a chromatographic pattern of blood and pus, ranging from red to yellow and green. His motorised wheelchair sits across the room.

"I hope you're powered up, old buddy," he mutters.

He drops to the floor and rolls toward it but stops, dizzy and close to passing out. A figure looms above him.

"Am I interrupting something?" Kieron Philips, his British colleague, asks.

Dwight tries to compose himself, but the pain is too great.

"You order yourself a coffin?" Kieron teases, sliding the box aside and calling out for help.

The workers from next door rush in and lift Dwight into his chair.

"A timely arrival," Dwight says, sweating.

As the workers back out, the box hits a propped sheet of wood, sending it crashing to the ground with a loud clap and a puff of dust.

8-2 GREEN TOMATOES

CSCI HQ Miami - Quadrangle - Day 1 - afternoon

In the quadrangle, Billy is drilling a dozen young recruits, guiding them through basic marching turns. Izzy waits by the rear door of Wild Mary's Diner, watching as Dan Creedon studies the small troop. The recruits demonstrate varying levels of success in following Billy's commands. After a moment, Dan joins her.

"Mind if I take some pictures?" he asks.

"Er... I'd rather you didn't," Izzy says, steering him inside. "I'll get you a sales brochure. The focus was on finishing this diner first so Mary's could open. We can set up the computers anywhere later."

"Why 'Wild' Mary's?"

"Take a seat. You'll see."

The retro diner is nearly identical to Mary's old place across town. They've reused all the sixties-style black and chrome-rimmed tables and the red and beige bench seats. The grill and counter are the same, and her prized Wurlitzer 1250 jukebox stands proudly on a larger dance floor than the one at her previous eatery.

"What are you having?" Mary barks, looming over the table. Dan takes a seat.

"Just coffee, please," he replies with a polite smile.

"Wrong answer," Mary shoots back. "Take a minute to study the house specialties."

"No, really. Just coffee will be fine."

"No, it won't."

Izzy gives Mary a warning look that says, *Behave.*

"Fine. Coffee it is - since you're not staying long," Mary relents, grabbing the coffee pot and two mugs. She swings back around and fixes Dan with a piercing stare.

"I'm not much of a meat guy," Dan says.

"I can see that," Mary replies curtly. "Let me know if you decide to try my fried green tomatoes."

"I will. Thank you, Mary."

In the clean, functional washroom by the yet to be used reception, between the diner and the technical wing, Dwight examines his infected leg. The stump from his above-the-knee amputation is swollen and oozing pus. Gritting his teeth, he tries to clean it with damp tissues, but the pain is intense.

"It's good you can still feel it," Kieron says, stepping inside and glancing down at the wound.

"I can still feel my toes - and they're not even there," Dwight mutters.

"That needs proper treatment."

"I look at it every day. And every day, I relive it - the stupid off-road detour I knew was wrong. Then boom! Before I could even yell 'stop.'"

"This isn't the Middle East, Dwight. You're not on tour anymore. There's an ER just down the road."

"I'm fine. I called you in to take over the meeting with Creedon, the cruise executive. He's at Mary's."

"Izzy can handle that. You're going to the ER. If you don't, you might lose more of that leg."

"I've got my casket ready."

"That might not be far off if we don't go. You don't look too good, Dwight."

After a moment's hesitation, Dwight nods, his resistance faltering. "I ain't exactly full of holiday cheer. Best I go to my clinic. I'll get myself there."

"No. You call them and say we're on our way. I'll drive your truck - it'll be easier."

"I can manage."

"Keys. That's an order, soldier."

Dwight sighs and hands over the keys just as Mary walks in.

"This is the men's room, Mary," Dwight says, raising an eyebrow.

"That looks nasty!" Mary exclaims, pointing at the wound.

"Kieron's taking me to the clinic," Dwight replies.

"I don't like the look of that flake sitting with Izzy."

"Flake?"

"Vegetarian. Same thing."

"Have Billy join her," Kieron suggests.

"I'll tell her she's flying solo," Mary says, shaking her head.

"No, Billy sits in," Kieron insists.

"Why? You want the man killed? Is that casket for him?"

"Billy's gentle with vegetarians," Dwight says with a faint smile.

"Get that seen to," Mary says, walking out.

Left alone, Dwight stares at the box.

8-3 CIA

CSCI HQ Miami - Mary's Diner - Day 1 - afternoon

Billy walks into the diner from the quadrangle and takes a seat next to Izzy.

"Mr. Creedon, I'm Billy," he introduces himself.

"Call me Dan, Bill."

"Billy," he corrects. "The 'y' is always important. Dwight and Kieron have been called away on urgent business. They've asked me to sit in. Izzy can handle everything, but two sets of ears are always better."

Izzy smiles politely.

"I saw you drilling security recruits earlier," Dan comments.

"Potential security recruits," Billy clarifies. "Provided they don't fail the basics or resist command."

"And if they do?"

"We give them their money back and send them packing. A ship runs on the same discipline structure as the military. Newbies need to learn that if their officer says jump, they don't even ask how high. Basic policing."

"But you're not the police," Dan observes.

"No, sir. We're the captain's security team, and at sea, he's judge and jury."

"I didn't expect you guys to be so... physical."

"A ship is physical," Billy says matter-of-factly. "Uncompromising," he adds, when Dan looks confused, wondering why a cruise executive doesn't already understand this.

Dan picks up on his concern. "I guess it is. I don't see much of that side of things."

"They need to be so good you don't *need* to see," Billy explains. "Effortlessly controlling any situation without panic."

"Do you teach them to use force? To be armed?"

"Eventually."

"And run full background checks on them?" Dan asks.

Izzy makes a note on her smartphone - something to add to work within the recruiting program.

"You mean, do we check if they're not on crack before giving them a gun?" Billy asks, with a hint of humour.

Izzy steps in. "We only send people we deem safe and provide a full jacket on each candidate."

"Do they leave with a qualification?"

"Izzy handles the course modules," Billy says. "She works with the cruise companies."

"I'd like us to be more involved," Dan suggests.

"Presidential Cruises are, sir," Izzy replies. "We're in constant communication with your recruitment arm. That's why I thought you were here."

Dan hesitates. "I don't handle staffing. I'm here about a different matter entirely."

"There are two of us listening," Billy prompts, encouraging him to continue.

Dan leans forward. "I was approached by a CIA agent. He warned of a possible terrorist attack."

"Terrorist attack?" Izzy asks, her tone sharp.

"Bomb? Invasion? Hostage situation?" Billy adds.

"I don't know," Dan admits.

"CIA?" Billy asks. "Are you sure he was an agent?"

He is capable of being awkward, special, and dangerous, but for now he is playing the corporate employee and asking a question seriously.

"He showed me his badge."

Billy pauses, leaving space for Izzy to jump in.

"A possible attack? Is there an ongoing crime or clear threat?" she asks.

"No. But as you said, we need to be prepared," Dan answers.

"Prepared for what?" Billy presses.

"The agent had no idea what, when, or how."

Izzy shifts the conversation. "We work through simulations. We're even turning our fourth wing into areas modelled after ship interiors. But to be effective, we need specifics."

"Maybe you could share the bullet points from the CIA meeting," Billy suggests. "Once we've reviewed them, our senior partners can regroup with you."

Before Dan can reply, Mary approaches. "If you're staying, you're trying my fried green tomatoes."

"Alright, Mary. You've sold me," Dan says with a smile.

"Stan! Breakfast special for the man in the suit!" Mary shouts to her husband behind the grill.

"Yes, boss," Stan replies, flipping something on the grill.

Billy refocuses. "When and where did you meet the agent? Did he leave you a card?"

"No card. He said it was informal advice. We met at the Burger Stop on South Beach."

"When?" Izzy asks.

"The day before I called you. Is there a washroom I can use?"

Izzy gestures toward the restrooms at the end of the counter. Dan excuses himself.

As soon as he's gone, Billy leans toward Izzy. "I don't like this guy."

"Why?" she asks, frowning.

"He ain't right."

"What do you mean?"

"He buckled when we started asking questions."

"No, he just ordered breakfast," Izzy defends.

"CIA operatives aren't called agents," Billy says.

"Everyone calls them agents," Izzy counters.

"They don't. They're officers. And they don't have badges or domestic jurisdiction. They work in teams, gathering intel - not one man doling it out."

"This is an international business," Izzy reminds him.

"We're in Miami," Billy retorts. "I'm telling you, he's suspect."

Mary, within earshot, chimes in. "That's what I thought."

Dan returns from the restroom but heads straight for the door. "Stan, cancel that order. I've been called back to the office. Izzy, I'll be in touch."

He's gone.

"He's not coming back," Mary says flatly.

Billy looks at Izzy as he stands. "Write everything down - what he said, what you said."

"Are you giving orders now?"

"Stick to the facts. Don't overthink," Billy says, moving to the window. He catches the registration number of Dan's car as it pulls away.

"We need these cameras up," he mutters, glancing at the hanging wires. "We'd have had him if they were working."

Macey, Izzy's triplet sister, speaks up for the first time. "I don't do jigsaws, but I'm an artist. I paint a little."

Until then she had been ignored, sitting in her painting overalls with her hair in her trademark bun, skewered with brushes. Now, she is grinning like a Cheshire Cat.

They turn to her easel. Macey has painted Dan Creedon, complete with a detailed face and Izzy's outline in the foreground.

Billy snaps a picture of the painting. Izzy's phone pings. So does Macey's.

"Hey!" Mary says, annoyed her phone hasn't pinged.

"That's your network," Billy says, typing furiously. *Croc, wake up. We need an ID on this image, ASAP.*

He holds his phone next to the painting. "The real senior executive of Presidential Ocean Cruises. The real Daniel Creedon. So, what's this terrorist threat about?"

Mary freezes. "Terrorist? You think he put a bomb in that casket?"

"What casket?" Billy asks.

"The one delivered to the office this morning."

Billy bolts for the door, shouting across the quadrangle, "Go home!"

He races into the workspace, spotting the casket. "Clear out! Take the day off - NOW!"

The team scatters, unnerved by his urgency. Billy inspects the box for external triggers before slowly rolling it toward the quadrangle.

8-4 TÚK TÚK

CSCI Mumbai - early morning (still night in Miami)

A world cruise is the ultimate object of desire, symbolising wealth and fulfilling the dreams of many. Before the pandemic, over thirty million people embarked on ocean cruises annually. Post-lockdown, those numbers have been climbing and are expected to surpass previous records. While some ports are reconsidering the value of allowing cruise ships to dock or anchor, plans are underway to construct floating paradise islands - resembling holiday oil rig structures - situated in sunny international waters with multiple berths. These havens already exist in certain parts of the world for gambling and other activities prohibited on land. Decommissioned cruise ships are also being used as offshore hotels catering to niche desires. One thing is certain: the world will evolve, and there will always be those who seek what others find distasteful.

A cruise was never on Winston "Croc" Crocket's wish list, even when he realised he had achieved financial freedom. In the two years since CSCI (Cruise Ship Crime Investigators) opened its first office in Miami, his life has transformed beyond recognition. Once a young Black man arrested for hacking NASA computers, Croc was bailed out by a woman who, he and his sisters later discovered, was their biological mother. In many respects, just in time. His redemption came when CSCI moved into the unit next to her diner, recognising his knack for computing. Overnight, he went from a rescued criminal to a respected data analyst, helping recover millions while solving a high-profile heist.

If Croc's story ended there, it would already be Hollywood-worthy. But he fell in love with Prisha Nah, an Indian investigator at CSCI, and became a surrogate father to her two young children, Lakshmi and Reyansh. Prisha had spent most of her children's lives working at sea, earning money as a crew member in passenger reception to support her family back in Mumbai. With CSCI's backing, Prisha expanded her brother's refrigeration business and established CSCI's Asian office in Mumbai. Within its headquarters is a locked safe containing nearly eight million dollars - proceeds from the cruise ship heist that had inspired CSCI's creation.

Through the metal security grille of his office window, Croc spots Prisha pulling up in their new electric Tuk-tuk. He's outside before she can step out.

The deep blue and red vehicle, with its superhero-inspired yellow flash down the side, is a high-torque redesign of the classic Tuk-tuk, capable of exhilarating speeds of 55 km/h. Its bold colours, chosen by Lakshmi and Reyansh, would turn heads anywhere except Mumbai, where such personalisation is celebrated. "CRUISE DETECTIVE" is painted proudly on the front. While traditional Tuk-tuks are typically yellow, independent owners often paint theirs as vibrantly as their personalities. The modern electric Tuk-tuk, originally a three-wheeled mototaxi with a chugging two-stroke engine, has become a popular urban and tourist vehicle worldwide.

"This is a lot of food," Croc remarks, eyeing the bags of groceries.

"The family won't need to shop while we're away. The freezer at home is full, and Bukka can keep this here. Now, I feel ready to leave for America tonight."

Croc hesitates, and Prisha notices something is wrong.

"What is it?"

"They've opened a new case in Miami."

"That doesn't mean we cancel our holiday."

"I need to identify a face."

"Then do it in Miami," Prisha insists.

"They're asleep there now. I've always handled the night shift. They'll expect an answer when they wake."

"But you're not there," she counters.

"They think it's easier because it's daytime here for me."

"Then solve it before we leave. We must go - we have to tell Mary in person." Prisha hands him the Mumbai Mirror. "Look."

Croc takes the paper and scans the headline: *Ice Queen Prisha Nah To Wed.*

"They called me Ice Queen!" Prisha exclaims.

"They didn't even mention me," Croc says, unimpressed.

"It will be online soon. America will see it. We have to leave tonight. Mary might accept hearing about our wedding secondhand, but she'll want to be the first to know she's going to be a grandmother. And she can get angry."

Croc winces. He knows she's right.

"Upgrade us all to first class. You can work on the plane, and I'll sip champagne - oh wait, I can't drink. I'm pregnant."

Croc's phone pings.

"There - you've identified the face!" Prisha says.

"No. A large item was logged as delivered to the Miami office," Croc replies, confused. "Did they send our present to her early?"

"No. That's impossible," Prisha says.

"What does it say?"

"Large box. Billy called the bomb squad. He's going to have it blown up."

"A Tuk-tuk doesn't come in a box," Prisha says, gesturing at their electric vehicle.

Croc quickly spins through screens on his smartphone. "Our Tuk-tuk is still at the dock. They must have been sent a bomb."

8-5 DODGE ISLAND
Wednesday, Day 2 - 1630hrs Miami

Five large, modern gas-powered ships, each carrying thousands of guests, are berthed in a row along Miami's world-famous cruise terminal. Four generations of any family can enjoy these ships, although they tend to be child-free during school terms. Each ship boasts theme-park-worthy features, ranging from electric go-kart tracks and top-deck water slides to sky-ride tracks with caged bicycles hanging beneath.

At the foot of the gangway, officers are dismantling the shore stand while Kieron Philips and Ronni Cohen wait. Both tower over the adjacent driver of the waiting executive limousine. Models may be tall, but Ronni exudes an air of athleticism and military precision alongside her charm and poise.

The real Daniel G. Creedon descends the gangway, trailed by his personal assistant. Creedon is in his late fifties or early sixties. Though not in a suit, he is immaculately dressed, his well-groomed mop of white-blond hair and Scandinavian tan enhancing his air of wealth and success. A highly accomplished businessman, Creedon was born in Denmark, earned a scholarship to Harvard for business and law, and stands in stark contrast to the cheap impersonator who appeared at the new Miami HQ the day before.

"I'm Daniel Creedon. I believe you're Ronni Cohen," he says, introducing himself.

"Yes, sir," she replies.

He turns to Philips, whom he does not recognise.

"Kieron Philips, sir," the former special forces commander announces.

Creedon shakes Philips' hand but focuses back on Ronni. "Sad to hear you've left the ships, Ronni. Tell me about the man who's been impersonating me."

Kieron shows him the picture Macey produced.

"I've never seen him."

"Can I leave this with you?" Kieron asks. "Others in your organisation might recognise him, but we'd prefer no one be alerted to why you're asking."

"How do I ask without showing the picture?" Creedon inquires.

"Try not to let anyone take the picture or probe too deeply into why you're asking," Kieron advises.

"Should I be worried?" Creedon's tone is serious.

"We don't know yet, sir," Ronni responds.

"I'd like to know what's going on," Creedon insists.

"So would we," Kieron says. "But unless he comes back, all we know is that this man visited our Miami office yesterday, pretending to be you."

"What did he want? What did he say?"

"The meeting wasn't recorded because it seemed informal, but those who met him are summarising everything he said," Ronni explains.

"I never got to see your old office, despite all the news coverage you've had. I didn't realise cruise crime required an outside agency. Now you're expanding?"

"Our old office danced with a wrecking ball," Ronni says. "The new CSCI headquarters aren't officially open yet, but you're welcome to visit."

"It seems I already have. I want to know what I supposedly said."

"We'll pass you the notes and leave the decision with you," Kieron says.

Creedon nods, moving toward the open car door. "When? I don't like someone thinking they can impersonate me."

"Tomorrow at the latest," Kieron promises.

"And Ronni, if you ever want a job back in the cruise world, call me. I'll find a place for you."

"I'm in the cruise world," she replies.

"You know what I mean. This ship's decorated for the festive season. You'll miss all the fun," he says, stepping into the car.

"We're here to help if you need us," Kieron reiterates.

"I'm concerned," Creedon admits as the door closes, signalling the end of the meeting.

As Kieron and Ronni walk away, the gangway is stowed behind them. The executive car swings around and departs, its darkened windows concealing the passengers. The bustling terminal is quieter now, with thirty thousand guests having disembarked earlier and another thirty thousand boarding for their holidays.

Kieron glances at the first ship, where noisy side thrusters ease it from its berth. "Do you think he recognised his double?" he asks Ronni.

"No. He has a family. He'll be worried about their safety."

"Will he hire us to investigate?"

"If I were him, I'd want to know why someone's pretending to be me. But do we let this go if he doesn't contract us?" Ronni asks.

"We don't need the money."

"But someone came to our office and left a bomb."

"Creedon's support gives us access. For that, we need to be hired."

"You like this game too much to let it go. Hired or not, your special forces instincts won't let this drop," she teases.

Kieron smiles as they reach their car, where Macey stops sketching on her pad to snap their picture.

"You two. How do you put so much emotion into no expression? Pure art," Macey quips. "Now, what's going on? Are we hired?"

"What if this imposter is targeting us? The whole act could be a setup," Ronni suggests. "Let's call him Ghost."

"You sound more CIA than marine biologist. Explain," Kieron says.

Macey flips her sketchpad to a new page, drawing the layout of the dock, the ships, and the overhead road.

"You're suggesting that CSCI is his target?"

"Maybe," Ronni muses. "But remember, the messenger often gets blamed for the message."

"By reporting this, we've already spread panic," Kieron adds. "If that was his aim, he's succeeded."

"CSCI is his weapon," Macey speculates, snapping another picture of them. "So why leave a bomb at our office?"

"It was a bomb?" Kieron asks sharply.

"No," Macey smirks. "Bomb squad cleared it an hour ago. Izzy says the recruits thought it was a training exercise."

"Do we report this to the police?"

"No bomb, no crime," Ronni suggests.

"What about the FBI?"

"They handle threats to society - mass shootings, assassinations, serial killers," Ronni explains. "They're to the police, what we are to on board staff cruise security."

"Homeland Security?"

"No. They are domestic issues - drug and weapon smuggling, intellectual property crimes."

"That leaves your mob," Kieron says.

"I don't have a mob," Ronni retorts.

"CIA?"

"I'm not CIA. They gather intelligence overseas."

"But if Ghost is CIA…"

Macey climbs into the back seat, resuming her sketching. "One of you can drive. I'm no chauffeur."

Kieron takes the driver's seat, mulling over her words. "Would they? Could he be CIA?"

"That's not quite how the lyrics rock. And Streisand wasn't singing about the CIA," Ronni says.

"And if he is, who's pulling his strings?"

4 MURDERS, A WEDDING, AND A CRUISE

"Follow the money," Macey murmurs, looking up at their reaction. "That's what Hunter used to say."

"God rest his soul," Kieron says quietly.

"Oh, and the box is from New York," Macey adds. "It's for Bedřiška."

Kieron frowns. "That box."

8-6 HOSPITAL
Day 2 - 2000hrs Miami

It's early evening in Miami, and a low sun blasts through Dwight's room at the Prosthetic and Amputee Rehabilitation Unit. Sitting up in bed, hooked to a pain drip, Dwight answers Izzy's questions while she types on her laptop from a nearby chair.

"That's all we talked about - the building, CSCI's ambitions. He never explained himself or mentioned any job. I called Kieron in because I was feeling ill," Dwight says.

"I'll go back to the office and add in the conversation Billy and I had. Everything else is up to date," Izzy replies, switching to the main company screen.

Dwight opens the laptop lying on the sheets in front of him, syncing to the same shared screen Izzy has been updating.

"This keyboard is too small for my fingers," Dwight complains.

Izzy opens a dropdown menu and selects Message To All: First one in from the office, please bring Dwight a remote keyboard.

"No idea why I sent that - it'll probably be me," she adds.

"I'll get used to this," Dwight grumbles.

"I know. You're grumpy."

"I hate hospitals."

"No, you don't. You loved it here."

"That was when I had hope of walking."

"The job in hand," she reminds him.

"Yeah. Great work, Izzy."

"I had a good teacher - calm, considerate, helpful. Know anyone like that?"

Dwight just grunts in response.

Izzy checks the screen. "Croc's section is still empty - nothing on the facial recognition."

"The cloud works in India, but only for what he posts. We don't get to see his machines working like when we shared a room," Dwight says.

"He should've at least made a comment or an update. Always chase people. And where's Bedřiška?"

Dwight's laptop starts dialling.

"You're calling Croc? He'll be asleep," Izzy says.

"It's time to wake up in Asia. We can't work without information."

Just then, Kieron, Ronni, and Macey enter the room.

"Planning to stay long?" Kieron asks, eyeing the two intravenous drip bags hanging from the drip stand.

"Antibiotics. I should've come in sooner," Dwight admits.

"We didn't come from the office, so no keyboard," Macey says.

"I've got the office covered," Izzy replies, watching Dwight scan the screen. "He only has to read."

"I want to keep my eye on the little things that slip by," Dwight insists.

"Rest and get well," Kieron says, checking the chart at the foot of the bed.

"Are we calling the perp *Ghost*?" Dwight asks.

"Yes. Why?"

"Creedon's middle name - initial G."

"Don't tell me it stands for *Ghost*."

"No, it's Gifford. But the connection could be dangerous and linger," Dwight explains.

"Well, he's *Ghost* for now. You calling Croc?"

"Yeah. Tell him to be vigilant sitting on that money."

Prisha, Croc and the two children are flying business class. The hull window blinds are being closed, and the lights on the plane are dimmed so that passengers can sleep. Working at his laptop, Croc can see the screen flashing, Call from Dwight Ritter. He waits for the inflight announcement to finish.

"If you wish to continue reading, then please use the overhead light. We advise you to keep your seat belts fastened at all times. We will wake you with a light breakfast two hours before we are due to arrive in Miami," an air host concludes.

Croc blocks all his surrounding background with a green colour and he answers. "Hey. How are you?"

"Alive. Where are you?" Dwight says.

"Out and about. Where do you want me to be? In a zoo, at the top of the Burj Khalifa, in a cave or in a plane."

Dwight watches Croc's background change. "Kids can do that on their smartphones. They grow up knowing more than you had to learn."

"Croc, CSCI might be 'the' terrorist's weapon of choice. Us 'spreading' and 'inducing' fear for them," Ronni says.

"We need a name to the face Macey sketched," Dwight says.

"Still running. No results so far. I can give you a screen share to that search," Croc says, via Dwight's screen.

"The internet is bursting at the sides with pointless stuff; let's not add to it," Kieron says.

Macey settles down with her pad looking at the team members in deep thought. "I love it when you guys are serious. Your faces are so expressive."

"We are supposed to be the unknown, undercover investigators. Not the subject of your art gallery," her sister suggests.

"But their expressions demand I paint them, and I never wanted to be a portrait artist. That guy Creedon was lying, so I painted him."

"You saw he was lying?" Dwight asks.

"His face was transparent, and then Billy's was excited, but I didn't paint him."

"Why not?" Kieron asks.

"He's creepy."

"Croc, can you build a space for Macey's intuition into the system," Dwight says. "Macey's creepy analytics."

"I thought the internet was overloaded with pointless stuff," Izzy says.

The sisters exchange a look often rehearsed in adolescence.

"It's only what AI does," Kieron adds.

"But quicker, right?" Izzy adds.

Macey fires Izzy a seriously disapproving look. "I'm better than a computer, sis. AI learns from creatives like me."

"Intuition on another level. Let's see how it works out," Dwight says, looking tired.

"The Macey effect," Macey boasts. "I'm in the system. Finely tuned, sis."

"The system is always learning," Croc says.

"The system ain't learning too much about that face," Izzy fires.

"Well back at Dodge Island, Kieron looked well worried, and Ronni was stoic."

"She's a better poker player," Izzy says.

"A trained biologists, joining the dots, and I was listening," Kieron says.

Dwight takes a deep breath and blows at the bull that is circulating the room.

"Biologists?" Izzy asks.

"Yeah. Ronni was a marine biologist; she was never in the CIA."

"Look, I'll get back to y'all when I know who owns that face," Croc says.

Dwight's screen goes blank, then flicks back to the company data. Izzy's jumps back to the data screen. Croc has left the meeting.

"If that Ghost, Creedon two, never met a CIA agent, what's he pitching?" Dwight starts.

"Let me check my picture," Macey says, playing her expanded theme up. "He's lying, and he's listening. Inquisitive," she throws in.

"What if he is the CIA," Kieron adds, not lingering on her input.

"So, he wasn't inquisitive; he was instructing," Izzy formally corrects. "Picture diagnosis was wrong."

"No." Macey shows her original picture that is still in her pad. The one that got copied. "What's it say? Lying and listening. If he was instructing, it was just the occasional bomb he dropped in."

"His name was simply enough, because we are moving, we are building, we are embryonic, and we never checked," Kieron says.

"Vulnerable. Just when you hit a target," Dwight says. "We failed."

"He doesn't look CIA," Ronni says.

"Did you meet them all when you were in the navy lab?" Kieron asks, deep in new thoughts.

"What's your thinking, boss?" Dwight asks.

"Cut the boss, we are all partners now," Kieron says.

"Not until Elaine agrees. She owns Hunter's estate, which is our ass."

Kieron almost nods, but can't be distracted by the problems his deceased CSCI partner is bringing the company. "If he's not CIA, then he's a terrorist."

"Billy said our visitor got everything about the CIA wrong," Izzy says.

"Sure. Billy's good, but I was his commander for a reason. What is it Kieron? What's your intuition?"

"Does everyone get an intuition box on the platform?" Izzy says.

Kieron looks at Ronni and pauses. She is a mystery who has flown under the radar like a well-trained intelligence officer. "The heist was documented in my daughter's book, but that was done with the cruise line, and for public consumption."

"Why are you looking at me?" Ronni says.

"It was crafted not to mention any money other than that sent to the children's mission in St Vincent."

"That's how we're building a great base in Miami and have an office in Mumbai with millions in the safe," Ronni says.

"That's how I'm in the best vets clinic and not homeless on the street," Dwight adds.

Macey is sketching everyone's face.

"Ronni Cohen was never mentioned in the book."

"You just said, every reference to money was washed away," she says.

"But you were never mentioned as one of the players."

"Where you going with this?"

"You, as a very smart marine biologist, built like an athlete, controlled your omission from the story like someone who had previously worked in intelligence."

"This is not about me," Ronni says, feeling betrayed.

"CIA love to get other people doing their jobs, right? I am just suggesting that we all ask around old CIA friends to see if they are involved?"

The silence in the room stagnates and the focus is on Ronni, the only one with an unknown past.

"You suggesting the CIA fed us the story?" Dwight asks Kieron, to break the silence.

"Just asking if we might all show Macey's picture to old friends to see if it gets a hit," he says, still appearing to direct his remark to Ronni.

"If I do, that will open a case file," she offers. "They have to document everything, even off-the-record enquires."

"Can't hurt to have the CIA on board," Dwight says.

"If we are chasing a terrorist, they should have a heads up, and maybe can do some of the work for us," Kieron agrees.

"You want to play this card even if it's some lazy assed agitator who's using us?" Ronni checks.

"Just because the Ghost might be using CSCI as his current weapon of choice, does *not* mean he's lazy. Or stupid. Or that he doesn't have a second move," Dwight says.

Izzy sums up as she is working point at the office.

"Possibilities. One, Ghost is reporting a tip-off of a terrorist attack. Two, he is the terrorist, using us to engage fear and panic. Or, three, he is CIA inviting us to do his work."

"Or four; Ghost has a beef at Creedon and wants to get at him and his family," Macey adds.

"Five; he's after disgracing CSCI, or after our money," Ronni adds.

"Is that five, or five and six?" Izzy questions.

"After our money?" Kieron asks.

"Anything's possible for eight million dollars," Ronni says, as she and Kieron share a look. "You brought up the money. Not me."

"Bullet the money as number six," Dwight says. "Now, I'm getting tired, but thanks for the concern, the flowers and stopping by."

"How many cruise ships does Creedon control?" Kieron continues.

"Sixty-plus working under five different banners," Ronni says. "He's an obvious target."

"Goodnight," Dwight says.

"We still need to create a report based purely on the perp pretending to be Creedon. Enough for Creedon to engage us," Kieron offers.

"Why frighten him?" Ronni asks.

"He targeted Creedon."

"Just list the facts. There is only one. Someone is pretending to be him, end. The rest is unsubstantiated conjecture. That's all we have and I can write that up in the morning," Dwight says.

"In the meantime, we ask Croc in India to tighten security on our money pot," Ronni suggests.

"If you guys don't mind. I'm tired now."

They all fist bump and leave, Izzy is the last at the door.

"Izzy. There is always something else. Always something left off a report, because it didn't seem relevant. There's always something an agent doesn't tell you. Look for trouble, dig deep, demand more. And lean on Ronni; she was the compliance officer on cruise ships for years, she knows this industry inside out."

Izzy smiles as Dwight sinks into his pillows fighting the need to sleep. "Ronni Cohen, CIA," he mutters. "Has everyone forgotten there's a bomb in our building?"

"Sleep!" Izzy leaves quickly.

8-7 FIRED UP

Day 2 - 2100hrs Miami

Izzy's car pulls up outside Wild Mary's, the lone source of light breaking through the scaffolding on the quiet industrial estate. The diner, however, is alive, buzzing with energy.

Macey leans over from the passenger seat, past Izzy, to snap a photo of the strange scene inside.

Through the glass, two bomb suits - each clearly occupied - flank a dining table. Around them, a lively crowd cheers as though witnessing a high-stakes game.

"What the hell?" Izzy mutters, unbuckling her seatbelt.

"That ain't a bomb," Macey says, snapping another shot.

"I can see that," Izzy replies as the crowd inside erupts in celebration, sending one of the suited figures toppling over.

The sisters exchange a glance before climbing out of the car and charging into the diner. The bell on the door jingles as they push through the crowd.

Izzy finds herself beside Stan, clad in his white chef's coat and hat, while Macey trains her phone camera on the scene. Billy is helping one of the cadets, Craig, out of the helmet from the Explosive Ordnance Disposal bomb suit.

"No bomb!" Izzy shouts at Billy, who's entirely at ease among the chaos.

"Nope, just an exercise. Jenga with fries," Billy replies, grinning. "She lost."

Craig fingers his hair free, as another cadet steps up. Nick, eager for the next turn.

31

"It's a new module for training," Billy explains.

"It takes 42 weeks to qualify for this badge," the actual engineer says, helping Craig, the cadet out of the bulky suit. "But these kids aren't learning this skill. They're not headed for the hurt locker - they'll be on cruise ships."

Izzy blinks, caught between disapproval and curiosity, while the cadets laugh and cheer. She glances up at Stan for guidance.

"Can't remember the last time we had this much fun," Stan says.

"Never?" Izzy offers sceptically.

"Maybe back when we threw that sixteenth birthday party for you, your brother, and your sister. Mary dressed up as a clown. None of you laughed."

"She wasn't funny."

"You were, though. Still remember the looks on your faces."

Izzy stares at Stan, caught off guard by the warmth of his memory. Her feelings about him - Mary's husband yet not her father - are complicated, especially after learning Mary is her biological mother.

"What're you two giggling about?" Mary interrupts.

"You as a clown," Izzy replies dryly. "World's worst children's entertainer."

"I laughed," Stan says, smirking.

"I was the consummate performer!" Mary retorts indignantly.

"No, you weren't," Stan counters, grinning.

Mary rolls her eyes. "You both better suit up if you wanna survive the shrapnel I'm about to send your way."

Izzy shakes off the moment, turning her attention back to Macey, who's snapping more photos.

"You taking pictures for the catalogue or your art?" Izzy asks.

"Either."

"Billy, do they even have bomb suits on cruise ships?" Izzy asks.

"No idea. Ask Ronni," Billy says.

"Why is it always 'Ronni this, Ronni that'? She's not the only one with a clue!" Macey snaps.

"Ronni's here. Prisha's in India," Billy shrugs. "Now Hunter's gone, they're the two who worked the ships."

The sisters exchange an exasperated glance as Billy leads them out into the yard and toward the office.

Ronni and Kieron were thrown together on his first ever cruise, which was the money heist out of south America. The ex-Commander expecting to have a quiet holiday noted how astute she was, as the danger unfolded. None of the other CSCI staff were there. Ronni has only just retired from sea and her special knowledge makes her invaluable to CSCI. However, her share of money and of both CSCI Miami, CSCI Mumbai, and the freezer company have yet to be determined. No one kept score in the whirlwind of so much money, and staying on the ship with the hidden cash to herself, guarding the chest, she lived very well. Hunter being killed on the diamond mission has meant that Elaine, his wife, technically owns half of a completely unknown and undocumented fortune. Now that it has been removed from the ship and is hidden in Mumbai she has left working at sea. If and when they are asked,

CSCI Miami was seeded by money from an Indian benefactor, one affluent enough to restore the very dilapidated but special building.

Inside the ops room, the lights flicker on, revealing an unexpected centrepiece: a coffee table, its flat surface the contorted back of a woman on all fours. Her shredded clothing clings to a bloodied body.

"What the hell is that?" Izzy recoils. "That's disgusting. Get it out of here."

Macey steps closer, circling the table.

"No...this is incredible," she murmurs. "It captures pain, abuse, survival."

Her words falter as she gets a clear look at the face. She freezes, staring at Billy and Izzy.

"Turn the lights off. Get rid of it," Izzy says, her voice sharp.

"No, wait," Macey counters. "Billy, did you even look at the face?"

"No. I'm not into art."

Izzy stiffens as realisation dawns. "That's Bedřiška, isn't it?"

Billy moves closer, his jaw tightening as he recognises the face.

"This is sick," he growls.

Macey picks up a crumpled sheet of paper tucked beneath the table.

"It's from Anoataly Istov in Russia. Sent here via Ouch Gallery in New York."

"I don't care where it's from. I'll kill whoever made this," Billy snarls.

"It's a self-portrait," Macey whispers. "Bedi made this in therapy - to process her trauma."

"She what?" Billy stares in disbelief.

"She held her face in wet plaster," Izzy recalls softly. "She wanted it to be perfect. She didn't even breathe."

"When? Why?!" Billy's voice cracks.

Izzy looks at him, her expression heavy. "You need to talk to Bedřiška."

Billy grips the edge of the table, his knuckles white. "Tell me."

"Call her," Izzy says.

8-8 PICK UP
New Day . Thursday, Day 3 - 0800hrs Miami

Croc's mind churns with the new reality that has reshaped his once solitary life. On the plane, seated beside him, are two children he is now responsible for, and their mother, Prisha - a woman he knows remarkably little about. His own past offers hardly anything in terms of guidance: a father he never knew, a mother who died of an overdose and a life spent avoiding the idea of home.

The woman who once guided him at the diner, Mary, turned out to be his biological mother, though her husband isn't his father. The other two waitresses? His sisters. Family, as a concept, feels foreign to him.

And now, Prisha is carrying his child. He intends to stand by her, but will anyone care about his resolve?

He glances at his phone. It switches to his US network as the plane lands and taxis toward the sprawling expanse of Miami International Airport - twice the size of Mumbai's.

Croc dials a number.

"Kieron, it's Croc. I've been thinking. If the fake Creedon is using us, he'll want to know if we've done what he's after. He might've been watching you and Ronni meet Creedon at Dodge. Can you get the dock security footage? I still don't have a hit on Macey's likeness."

He ends the call and shares the message with the office.

Prisha stirs beside him. "Did you tell him we're back?"

"No, he didn't pick up. Just left a voicemail. Someone in the office should handle it. I need to check if our ride's waiting."

Prisha peers out the window at the planes docked at their gates. Then she turns to the children.

"Lakshmi, Reyansh, wake up. We're in America."

"I'm hungry," Reyansh grumbles.

"You slept through breakfast," Prisha teases gently. "But don't worry - you're about to brighten Nanny Mary's life. Guess where she lives? A diner. A restaurant that makes food for everyone."

"Is she our other nanny we've never met?" Reyansh asks, rubbing his eyes.

"She's a new nanny, yes. And we're bringing her a present," Prisha replies.

Meanwhile, Croc makes a call. "Hello. My name's Winston Crocket, account name Cruise Ship Crime Investigators Mumbai. Shipment number HR7245C97. Can you confirm where at Miami Airport I can collect it?"

Prisha watches him with curiosity as he speaks.

"They said it left Jacksonville just after midnight," Croc explains, ending the call. "But they haven't confirmed if it's arrived in Miami yet."

"Why didn't it ship straight here?"

"Vehicles from Asia go to Jacksonville for customs testing," Croc says. "They must've enjoyed testing ours."

Prisha snorts. "Well, I hope Mary enjoys driving it. This isn't India."

"Mary's loud. She'll love it."

Prisha turns back to the children, ruffling their hair. "And she'll love you two."

"Do we call her nanny, nanny-gee, or grandmother?" Reyansh asks.

Prisha glances at Croc, seeking guidance.

"You're gonna have to ask her that," he says with a wry smile.

Meanwhile, at the CSCI parade ground:

Billy watches the recruits jog the perimeter as he paces, phone pressed to his ear.

"Bedi, it's me again. Pick up. Message me. You didn't come home last night, and this...thing arrived. We need to talk. I get you. We're the same. Come home. What's going on?"

He hangs up, glances toward the office, and peers through the window. Empty.

In the office:

Izzy leans over the desk, listening to Macey's phone call on speaker.

"Good morning, Mr. Creedon," Macey says briskly. "I just spoke with Miami Port Authority about obtaining security footage near the gangway where you met Ronni Cohen and Kieron Philips yesterday. We suspect your stalker may have been watching. Unfortunately, they've said they don't usually release footage without a warrant."

She pauses, listening to the reply.

"I thought you might have some pull, sir."

Another pause.

"Yes, the transcript is ready. I'm sure one of the senior partners will get it to you."

Macey hangs up and sighs, glancing at Izzy.

"Kieron went to voicemail, and Dwight is unavailable - minor surgery, apparently. Nothing serious, they assured me."

"So, what do we do? No one's answering. Should we call Croc?"

"Hell no," Macey says firmly. "He's not senior to us. Send the transcript to Creedon. What harm can it do?"

Izzy hesitates but nods. "Fine."

Macey presses send.

Immediately, the room is filled with the blaring chaos of alarms.

8-9 UNEXPECTED

Day 3 - 1000hrs Miami

Outside Wild Mary's, pedestrians pause to admire the pink tuk-tuk festooned with vibrant garlands. Horns and sirens blare, and Prisha and the children wave enthusiastically. Wild Mary storms out, her expression thunderous.

"Did you take the wrong road?" she snaps.

Croc jumps down, a grin stretching wide across his face, and gestures proudly at the vehicle.

"I can see it. What the hell is it?" Mary demands.

"Hello, Nanny! These are for you," Reyansh says, stepping forward with a large bouquet of flowers.

"Nanny!"

"Or should we call you Granny?" Lakshmi teases from her elevated perch on the tuk-tuk, tossing a garland over Mary's neck.

Mary recoils at the title as though it's a spider. "Granny?"

Izzy and Macey appear, rushing out to embrace their brother. Reyansh separates briefly to make introductions.

"Rey, this is your auntie Izzy, and this is your auntie Macey. And this is Reyansh," he says, pointing to his stepson, "and my daughter, Lakshmi."

"Auntie," Izzy says, pointing at Macey.

"Auntie," Macey echoes, pointing at Izzy.

Then they both point at Mary.

"No," Mary says firmly.

Ignoring her protest, the girls hug a child each.

"Daughter? Is Croc your daddy?" Macey asks Lakshmi.

"He's going to be. Mummy and Croc are getting married."

"Married?" Mary shrieks.

"We were going to wait for the right moment to tell you," Prisha says, stepping down from the tuk-tuk to face Mary. "But I guess this is it. Mum."

"That's kids for you," Croc says.

"I am not old enough to be a grandmother!" Mary declares.

"Mummy's pregnant," Reyansh announces cheerfully.

All eyes turn to Prisha, who nods with a small, proud smile as she wraps her arm around Winston Crocket. His pride is evident, though it's quickly interrupted as his sisters envelop Prisha in a jubilant hug.

"Any more surprises before I rush to the ER and get my heart checked?" Mary asks, her voice trembling with mock exasperation.

"Yes. This is yours," Croc says, steering her toward the front of the tuk-tuk.

Where his version of this vehicle reads *Cruise Detective*, Mary's new pink ride bears the label *Nanny-G*.

Izzy pulls Prisha aside, her gaze sharp. "Are you sure it's Croc's?"

"What do you mean? Of course, it's your brother's," Prisha replies, her tone defensive.

"You slept with your old boyfriend on the ship just days before you and Croc got together."

Prisha's face drops to one of concern as she contemplates the worst.

8-10 OUCH
Day 3 - 1103hrs Miami

Kieron and Ronni rush out of JFK Airport, still wearing yesterday's clothes and carrying no baggage. They look tired and sombre as they join the fast-moving queue at the taxi rank. Before long, they're in a cab heading into the city.

"Welcome to New York. Where to?" the driver asks.

"Ouch Art Gallery, Central Park West," Ronni replies.

They both settle into their seats, gazing out the window as the city whirs past.

"Where's home?" Kieron asks Ronni, his voice devoid of emotion.

"Home? University, military, cruising... Where is home? Not here," she answers.

"You don't like New York? Thought it was so good they named it twice."

"Who are *they*?"

"Now there's a million-dollar question. You'll never know who's really giving the orders or sending the messages. The circle."

The taxi pulls up outside a sleek, double-glass-fronted art gallery. The minimalist space inside features large art pieces sparsely displayed on pristine white walls. At the far end, a desk is staffed by a poised assistant who stands to greet them as they approach.

"Good morning. May I assist you?"

"Tell Mr. Crouch we're here," Kieron says.

"Do you have an appointment?"

"He didn't have one when he visited me on Cocoa Beach."

Before the assistant can respond, Crouch emerges from a concealed door in the white wall. "You received the table?"

"Obviously," Kieron says. "And the message," he adds.

Crouch hesitates, calculating the implications of their visit. He decides to offer clarification.

"I forwarded the table as soon as it arrived here. All I did was the import paperwork for Istov. He sent no message, so I included no paperwork - just followed his instructions."

An uncomfortable silence follows.

"I didn't clean it," Crouch finally says. "Was that blood on the table?"

"The message wasn't in the box," Kieron responds coolly.

Crouch frowns, sensing the gravity of the situation. "Was it Bedřiška's blood?"

"Doubt it. From what I remember, Anoataly Istov was bleeding when Bedi bent him over the table and threatened to kill him," Kieron says.

"So it was Istov's blood. He sent the table as it was. I didn't touch it. I have no idea what it means. Probably a Russian thing - she might understand it."

"Oh, she got the message," Kieron says.

"Which is why we're here," Ronni interjects. "What's going on?"

"I have no idea," Crouch replies.

"Who's the guy impersonating Creedon, and what does he want?" Kieron asks.

"Or has he already gotten what he wants?" Ronni adds.

Their determination is evident, and Crouch realises the seriousness of their questions. He leans forward, emphasising his stance.

"I know nothing."

The tense silence is broken by Kieron turning to the assistant. "You can take an early lunch."

The assistant glances at Crouch for confirmation.

"Go. I'll see you in an hour," Crouch says.

The assistant gathers her things and leaves in a hurry.

"In case she calls the police, let's move this along," Kieron says sharply. "Creedon, Anoataly Istov, Bedřiška - what do we not know?"

"It sounds like you know as much as I do," Crouch says defensively. "Shall I call Anoataly? Because I've never heard of anyone called Creedon. What did Bedřiška say?"

"She said nothing," Ronni replies.

"Ask her again. She always knows what's going on."

"I went into the office late last night," Kieron says, "because this whole Creedon thing was bugging me, and I saw the table."

"She opened it?"

"No. One of our team flagged it as suspicious and called the bomb squad. They opened it."

"But it was clearly marked as art from this gallery."

"Sure. But who sent the message?"

"What message?"

"Who killed Bedřiška?"

8-11 NICE VILLAGE
Day 3 - 1130hrs Miami

Croc has rented a sleek, modern house just north of Miami Shores and south of North Beach, with a stunning view overlooking the sea and Surfside across the water. The pink tuk-tuk sits conspicuously in the driveway, adding a splash of colour to the otherwise conservative neighbourhood of just over three thousand residents.

On the lawn, the two children play happily in a sandpit. The bi-fold doors are wide open, letting in the sea breeze as Prisha unpacks furiously, trying to keep up with the bags Croc brings in. This will be their home for the next few weeks.

Croc's phone buzzes.

"Kieron. Hi, Boss. Where are you?"

"Izzy told me you're back in Miami. Who's guarding our nest egg in Mumbai?"

"That's fine. I brought back another ten grand - the limit without paperwork - and paid for my rental and your builders online before I left."

"And the picture of our Ghost. Who is he?"

"No hits yet."

"Well, keep your head down and don't broadcast being back. State police called me late last night. Someone killed Bedřiška."

"What?" Croc says, stunned. "The Ghost? He killed her?"

Prisha looks up from unpacking, alarmed. Her eyes dart instinctively to the children playing outside, then back to Croc, searching for answers.

"Don't know," Kieron replies, his tone heavy. "But we need to ask him some questions."

Croc slowly sinks into a chair, the weight of the news hitting him hard.

"Who?" Prisha asks, her voice tinged with worry.

Croc lowers the phone from his ear. "Bedi."

Prisha's face falls, and her first response is reflexive. "She taught me to drink champagne."

Croc ends the call, his hand trembling slightly as he sets the phone down. His expression is a mix of shock and sadness.

"I saw her take out a whole army of street soldiers in Overtown," he says quietly. "Never seen anything like it. She was a machine. I thought she was invincible. Superhuman."

"Who would do this to her?" Prisha asks, her voice thick with disbelief.

"My guess? Plenty of people would've wanted to. The question is: who was capable? She was a killer who'd survived other killers."

"Could it be the gang she killed in your slums?"

"No," Croc says, shaking his head firmly. "She didn't leave a single one of them alive."

8-12 WHO LET THE DOG OUT?
Day 3 - 1230hrs Miami

Overtown isn't just the worst part of Miami; it has been described by U.S. presidents as the worst place in America. British footballer David Beckham dreams of replacing it with a football stadium, but for now, it remains a no-go zone. Unless you live there, you simply don't enter - not even the emergency services. So, a bright pink tuk-tuk powering through its streets is an undeniably bizarre sight.

Croc, feeling entitled to the intrusion because he grew up there, drives fast until he skids to a stop outside a more impressive mid-terrace house guarded by two street soldiers. They glare at the garish vehicle as if a spaceship had just landed.

"Watch my ride," Croc says, as he jumps out and strides toward the building.

"Ain't watching that. Park it someplace else, like in another state," one of the guards retorts, poking the "Barbie Mobile" with his gun.

Big Dogg appears at the top of the eight steps leading to the house. Dressed in a dark suit over a white shirt, his outfit is as out of place in the slum as Croc and his tuk-tuk.

"You can't come here in that," Dogg says.

"Only wheels I've got."

"You drive all the way from India?"

"Why you still living here, bro?"

Big Dogg hugs him like a brother. "You can take the street out of the boy, but you can't take the boy out of the street."

"I think that's supposed to go the other way around," Croc says, smirking.

"You and your detectives only come by 'cause me got an army. The mayor only invites me to dinner 'cause I can talk to people who don't listen to him. Me leave here, and I got nothing. Come inside - I can't be seen with that."

Dogg leads Croc into the house.

"What's with the Pero-look?" Croc asks, gesturing to Dogg's suit.

"City function. What you here for?"

"Our girl's dead."

Dogg's broad grin vanishes instantly. He had known there must be a serious reason for Croc's visit.

"Who?"

"Bedřiška. There's a big hole in CSCI."

"You calling 'cause there's a vacancy to fill?"

"No. Someone needs killing," Croc replies.

"Who did it, bro?"

Croc pulls out his phone and shows Dogg the picture of Creedon's imposter.

"Drop it over," Dogg demands, holding out his phone. Croc sends the image, and Dogg circulates it immediately. "He must be a nasty dude if he could waste that queen."

"We need to find him."

"Aren't the police all over it?"

"Above ground zero, sure. The gangs of Miami can see in the dark. We need this."

"Respect for Bedřiška - that's a shock. I was her wingman in Eastern Europe on your art theft job."

Croc nods.

"What d'you know?" Dogg asks.

"I can't find a name for this face. A ghost. I've looked everywhere."

"No one a ghost in my town."

"He might not be from here. Might be Russian."

"I dodged a couple of them on the Tallink Ferry," Dogg says, studying the picture. "He don't need to live here. He only needs to eat, sleep, or call a cab, and me will know. What was his style?"

"Knife across the throat."

Croc bumps fists with Dogg, then clasps his hand in a firm grip. "Be careful."

Dogg nods solemnly, understanding the gravity of the warning. "Now get that out of here and give that pink shit back to Miss Robbie."

8-13 ASSASSIN OF LOVE
Day 3 - 1745hrs Miami

The recruits file into Wild Mary's diner for their end-of-day coffee and debrief. Until the new facilities are built, it's the only large meeting point available. It also makes the diner appear like a bustling, successful addition to the local community and it needs that leg-up to kick start its planned success.

Mary notices that today's new recruit, Wanda, hasn't been shown the ropes and is sitting as if she expects to be served.

"Coffee pot's on the counter next to the mugs. You won't get served on a ship," Mary snaps.

"I thought cruise ships were full-service luxury," Wanda replies.

"This ain't a ship. And when you're on one, it's you who'll be doing the serving," Mary shoots back. "Okay, everyone, give me your best cruise smile."

Some smile; others ignore her.

"A good smile is the main requirement of the job," Mary says.

"Is that why you're not on a ship?" Nick jokes, earning a few laughs from the other cadets.

"I ain't the employer, just the messenger. You wanna work on a ship, teeth bleaching needs to go well."

"We're required to bleach our teeth to get employment on a ship?" Wanda asks, seemingly miffed despite her good teeth.

"Not if you're working in the engine room," Mary quips. "Actually, I ain't sure about that exemption."

Macey and Izzy walk in just in time to catch the end of the exchange.

"What are you on about?" Macey asks.

"Just telling them they need good teeth," Mary replies.

"Don't wind them up. We've got enough problems. Ask Billy to join us when he comes in," Macey says before she and Izzy head to the far end of the diner, beyond the jukebox and dance floor.

Billy eventually enters from the courtyard, where he had been trying to call Bedřiška again. He addresses the twelve cadets.

"Tonight, I want each of you to write a detailed report, as close to word-perfect as you can remember, about what was said and done when Commander Kieron Philips passed by the class yesterday morning. Include times and specifics. Think of it as a statement for court - no conferring. And if you're wondering if this skill will ever be needed, trust me, it will. I had to do just that last night."

Billy grabs a fresh coffee from Stan behind the counter, fist-bumping him on the way.

"I don't know if any of these are gonna make the grade," Billy says to Stan and Mary.

"Two more new ones tomorrow," Mary informs him.

"We should stop there."

"Why? You need a good one, right?"

"We can't keep restarting every time someone joins. The girl is finding it tough. Tomorrow will be harder to catch up."

"Wanda? She just hasn't settled in yet. She's a little abrasive."

"Another reason future applicants will have to join Course Two."

"Our girls want you," Mary says, pointing at her daughters. Billy heads over to them.

"That doesn't look good, Stan," Mary mutters.

The departing cadets freeze as Billy lets out a deathly scream, fuelled by anger. The sisters try to console him, but it's no use.

"Guess that wasn't good news," Mary says, watching. She ushers the cadets out. "Class is over. Go home."

"Do we need to stay? Is he okay?" Wanda asks.

"Thanks for your concern, Wanda, but you go home now. Tomorrow's another day."

As the cadets leave, Kieron Philips enters, back from New York. Ronni Cohen is tucked behind him, she naturally stays invisible.

"You picked a bad time," Mary says, nodding toward Billy, who is too distraught to be consoled.

Kieron walks over. "Sit down, soldier," he says, putting a hand on Billy's shoulder and easing him into a seat.

"Who killed her?" Billy asks.

"Don't know," Kieron replies. "We thought it was an old Russian nemesis - she had a few - so we went to New York to question the art dealer who exports there. He swears he has no knowledge of their involvement."

"Russians? Why? And what's that table about?"

"Bedi was abused as a child prostitute in Russia but escaped. The table was a self-portrait of her struggle. She joined the KGB determined to fight child trafficking, maybe also to find her sister, who was lost in the system."

Billy is stunned. This was a side of Bedřiška he never knew. Their relationship was still new, and

Kieron had only learned this history because they were very close.

"She found the Russian system corrupt and killed many officers involved in trafficking. Bedi became a target and fled Russia to stay alive - before she could find her sister."

"I'll kill whoever did it," Billy vows, trying to rise, but Kieron gently pushes him back into his seat.

Stan brings over a bottle of whiskey. Billy takes a deep swig until Kieron grabs it from him.

"How did she join CSCI?"

"She worked on cruise ships, trained in security, and took over from Hunter on the ship we left. We recruited her to CSCI. We all loved her."

"I loved her."

"You two made a special couple, I know. I'm sorry for your loss. We're all grieving. This hurts me, too. I'll find who did this. If I get to them before you, I'll try to leave a little life in them so you can make it ugly. But we need to be calm, collected, and figure this out."

"You don't think it's the Russians?"

"I don't know. Maybe the Ghost is working with them. You met him - was he an assassin?"

"No," Billy says, thinking. "I know killers. No. But..." He pauses, shaking his head. "He can't be."

"Sure?"

"Sure. Anyone can kill, but he wasn't good enough to kill Bedi. How was she killed?"

The bell jingles, and Daniel G. Creedon enters. Scanning the room, he spots Kieron and Billy at the back and heads toward them. Ronni intercepts, leading him to the counter.

"I've got the CCTV footage from the docks," Creedon says.

"We'll scan it and let you know if he's on there," Ronni replies, sensing it's not the time for conversation.

"You don't think I checked first?"

"Is he on there?"

"I saw someone. He doesn't look like me, but I could tell it was him from the likeness."

Billy, who only knows Creedon from his picture, watches him hand something small to Ronni.

"You think he's involved?"

"This ghost might be. Looks can be deceiving. Hopefully, Creedon can help us find him," Kieron says, leaving Billy and signalling to Izzy and Macey to look after him.

8-14 ISTOV

Day 3 - 1755hrs Miami

Four workers have joined forces to lift a large glass screen up to ceiling mount slung from a low beam just above the false ceiling structure. A fifth man bolts it into its bracket with minimal guidance from Croc, whose arrival has sped up the Miami technical installation.

"That's going nowhere now," Croc says, dismissing the workers. As they jump down, he pulls a cable along a duct above the false ceiling and connects it. Stepping down, he looks up just as Kieron leads Daniel G. Creedon, Ronni, and Billy into the now dramatically improved room.

The two-meter-wide glass screen commands attention, looking as if it has always belonged there.

"We got security footage of the dock," Kieron announces.

Croc powers up a rack of workstations and places two cordless keyboards and a pad onto a desk. "Five minutes. Less if it works first time."

The screen comes alive with the CSCI logo.

"Beautiful," Kieron remarks.

Croc takes the pen drive from Kieron, plugs it into the rack, waves his hand over the pad, and quickly locates the files. In no time, the available camera angles are displayed on the huge screen.

Creedon steps forward. "That camera pointing at the wall?"

"That's the back of his head," Izzy says, entering the room.

"Spool on - he's watching us meet. When I leave, he turns to go. On this camera, he gets into a waiting car. Someone's driving, but I can't see who. They actually drive off while you're talking around your car - here."

Croc fast-forwards through the footage, stopping to piece together the sequence. Returning to the turn, he hunts for the clearest frame, zooms in, enhances the image, and saves it in one smooth operation.

"We miss these skills here, Croc," Kieron says.

"I can do this from India."

"But you're not *here*. You do things instinctively because you gel with the team. No instructions needed."

Croc lifts a desktop widescreen onto an adjacent table and plugs it in. In another second, it's live. "The Mumbai desk," he says, sitting down and multitasking. "The new mugshot of the Ghost is in the system, but Macey's picture was good, so don't expect much. This guy is either new and unknown or very good and deeply hidden."

"No beginner kills Bedřiška," Billy says. "And probably not alone."

"Agreed. It's someone intentionally untraceable," Croc concludes. "Which makes this job tough."

Phones across the CSCI team begin to ping as the image is distributed.

"Can I get that?" Creedon asks.

Like a trained soldier deferring to a superior, Croc glances at Kieron, seeking permission. At Kieron's nod, Croc initiates a scan of all smartphones detected in the room, their details appearing on the large screen.

"Is that yours, ship one?"

Creedon nods, and the image is sent to his phone.

"Can I get that too?" a worker asks.

"No," Croc says, smirking. "But I *could* factory reset your phone, wipe it clean, turn it off, and leave it for dead."

All the workers clutch their phones protectively, looking unsettled.

"And I could do that from India."

"If you can…" one worker begins.

"Others could," Croc interrupts. "Be worried as to what you use it for."

"Let's get back to work," Ronni suggests.

"I'll get these screens up while I'm here," Croc adds, trying to redirect the workers.

But Creedon stops them, pointing to the main screen. "Before you do, there's someone else hiding in the dark. Look at the shadows move." He points to an unexplored camera angle.

Croc rewinds the footage, zooming in on the shadows. The picture lightens in stages. Kieron and Billy lean closer to the screen.

"That's Bedřiška. She's following him," Billy says.

Kieron turns to Izzy.

"I got acknowledgments that the job notification was delivered to her device - same with each report I posted - but she never responded or came back to me," Izzy says. "I didn't chase her as we have been busy."

"Bedi never gets back unless she has something to say," Kieron adds.

"She never said she was attending. I assumed she was waiting for instructions or information," Izzy says.

"She went to the meeting as back-up," Billy concludes.

"And saw us being followed," Kieron says. "She was on the job. Her report and movements are what we need." He glances at Croc, who is already working. "But she never had time to send them."

The large screen now displays a map of Miami-Dade, slowly zooming in.

"Her phone took a direct route, stopped here, and is now at this police station," Croc says.

"It'll be in an evidence room, waiting to be sent for technical analysis," Ronni adds.

"It self-switched off - the battery level is low."

"I see what you mean about having him around," Daniel says.

"This room will be fully operational within hours. It'll feel like I'm right here, no matter where I am," Croc says, his attention still fixed on the task.

Commander Kieron Philips's phone rings out. The call is answered, and Anatoly Istov's face fills a box on the screen.

"I was expecting your call after Crouch told me of your visit," Istov says.

"We're pinging you a picture. Who is this man?"

The ping in Russia is audible in Miami. Istov glances at his device.

"I do not know him."

"Well, the finger is pointing at you, Istov," Kieron says. "And you know we can get to you."

"Trust me, I did not do this. If I did, I would own it."

"I smell a Russian connection."

"I do not know everyone in Russia who wanted her dead."

"But you can ask around."

"If I do, I will be dead."

"If you don't, you'll be dead. Twenty-four hours," Kieron says, cutting the call.

"I've never seen that side of you, English boy," Mary says, holding a coffee pot and mugs.

Croc continues working. A new box appears on the screen showing the car the Ghost used to leave Dodge Island. Croc zooms and sharpens the driver's image until a face emerges.

"That's the new girl who started today - Wanda," Mary says from the back.

Billy steps forward. "I've been teaching Bedřiška's murderer all day!"

Billy is ready to explode, but Kieron grabs his arm firmly.

"And you'll teach her tomorrow," Kieron says. "Because she'll lead us to whoever wanted her dead."

"And you may discover why they so pointedly involved me," Creedon adds, concerned.

8-15 CLOSED
Day 3 - 1815hrs Miami

Mary walks through the empty diner, where Stan is closing down the kitchen. She reaches the main door, spins the hanging 'open' sign to 'closed', and throws the locks.

"Stan. You'd better fire up that grill. I think we're in for a long night."

Stan pulls his hat on again. "We're getting back to normal," he says, enjoying the ride.

"That new girl, Wanda. You think she's a murderer?"

"She murdered one of my burgers at lunch," he says, laughing.

"Yeah, but could she murder Bedřiška?"

Stan stops laughing and looks up. His face is one of shock at having lost one of his own 'family'.

"Yep. That's what's being discussed back there," she says, heading back to the new ops room.

In the new operational room, the team stares the large screen, which shows the on-line application that Wanda Renton filled out to join the security cadets.

"That won't be her real name," Izzy says.

"Then how does she expect to pass training and be hired on a ship?" Creedon asks.

"Maybe what they're up to doesn't happen on a ship," Mary offers, imposing herself on the group.

"I've got a feeling it might be her name," Ronni says, making herself the centre of attention, with Kieron frowning and Croc beginning to investigate.

Mary breaks the moment. "She's gone. They all gone. The diner's empty, locked up, and Stan's fired up the grill. We're all gonna sit, eat, and take this slowly. You-all get dangerous when you're angry." She looks back at the screen. "Wanda Renton, you disappoint me. Guess you won't be back tomorrow."

"She'll be back, Mary," Kieron says. "She has no idea we've linked her to any of this. No reason to suspect, and we mustn't give her one."

"Oh," Mary grunts. "I need to know what you're all eating."

"I ain't hungry," Billy says.

"I never asked if you were hungry. In fact, don't answer. I know what you eat. I'll go do my thing then call you all. Mr Creedon, sir, what would you like to eat?"

"I'll leave that to you, Mary."

"Man got style," she says, leaving.

On the screen, Croc slides a new box: Wanda Renton's Minnesota driver's license.

"No way," Billy whispers.

Kieron turns from the screen to look at Ronni. "I'm gonna do an adult education course in... what was it you said you were? Magician? Mind reader? Marine biologist?"

"You can cut that right now."

"And what does it mean, she's an enhanced driver?"

"She's not. The license is. It's a compliant form of ID. Like your passport. Some states add a little star top right, some states use a flag bottom right."

"It means, she's on line. We know everything about her. School, employment, address, parents…" Croc says. "She certainly ain't a marine biologist."

Ronni puts her hand on Croc's shoulder, her fingers push gently into the carotid artery in his neck, making him feel faint. She's made her point.

"Whatever's going on, she didn't kill Bedřiška. She's a grunt, a recruit, someone who has been groomed. But, she could lead us somewhere," Ronni says.

"So, from this job being hard, it's becoming easy," Izzy says.

"All investigations and missions go from puzzle to result, but we're not there yet," Kieron says. "Our Ghost is still invisible."

"Deliberately," Croc adds.

"Correct. She needs to lead us to him."

"How do we do that?" Izzy asks.

"We need to follow her."

"But she knows all of us."

"She doesn't know me," Prisha says. The CSCI's Indian agent has slipped into the room. Reyansh and Lakshmi round the team and sit with their new step father, Croc, who is at the gadgets they want to play with.

"No. No. No. You know what she did to Bedi," Croc says, avoiding words he does not wish to distress the children with.

"That wasn't this kid from Wayzata High School, Plymouth, Minnesota. I want him," Billy says, pointing at the Ghost's picture. "Her. She comes later."

"Prisha, you can't do this."

"I am a CSCI agent."

"You're pregnant."

The shock announcement makes her the centre of attention.

8-16 KILL MISSION

New Day. Friday, Day 4 - 0730hrs Miami

Billy walks into Dwight Ritter's room at the private clinic but doesn't stop him eating breakfast.

"Ain't exactly a field hospital, Sergeant."

"Billy, what you doing here?"

"Came to see you, boss."

"Appreciate that. Now, wazzup?"

"They got Bedřiška."

"Who got Bedřiška?" Dwight stops eating.

"Maybe our perp that claimed to be Creedon, but we think the Russians are behind it."

"She's dead?" Dwight says, trying to digest that, and pushing the food away on the wheeled tray.

"Yeah. That didn't get posted. Not sure it's sunk in. Damn sure Izzy has no idea how to report it."

"Dead?"

"Hard to believe. We did countless tours and we're still above ground. She gets hit in Florida."

"I feel sick. That ain't right. She wasn't meant to go. She was invisible."

"Copy that. What's happening with you, Sarge? You taking a holiday?"

"They opened up the wound, cleaned the puss out. Now the antibiotics might have a chance. I was lucky."

"Lucky?"

"Pop your head around the gym on the way out, soldier, and you'll see how lucky we both were. Ask Bedřiška who's lucky. Ask Georgie, ask Hunter, or the ones we lost to a serial killer."

"I'm going to Russia. Find her killer and her sister. Zack's taking over the school."

"If you want to stay in one piece, forget that idea."

"I'm not frightened of dying. Just being respectful and telling you. I'm going off grid," Billy says, nodding as he leaves.

Dwight grabs his cell phone and dials.

"Zack. I hear you're on the way in to train our recruits. Someone hit Bedřiška and Billy's seeing red mist. He's after the killer. He's not in the right frame of mind. Report to Kieron; I'm getting out of here as soon as I can."

8-17 PROSPECTIVE CADETS
Day 4 - 0845hrs Miami

Inside the diner, the new recruits grab coffee and biscuits as they pass through, heading past the toilets, through the empty reception area, and the temporary office where Izzy and Macey are gathering their things. They finally enter the impressive multi-screen

61

control room, which has been worked on all night. Croc is still at the centre, where two workers are in early, fitting window blinds. The low ceiling is complete, and the mood lighting is working. The inspiring technical setup now boasts many smaller screens scattered around: cameras, keyboards, and small trays everywhere.

"On a ship, space is a premium. Square footage is currency," Croc explains. "They don't have a big control room like this; it's squashed down to cabin size. We'll build one like that next door." He turns to face them. "You're gonna need to know your way around cameras, data, recording, copying, keeping."

"Thanks for mansplaining. I did film editing in high school," Carol, a recruit snaps.

"What are these?" Wanda asks, pointing to some small trays. "Too small for documents."

"We don't do paper," Croc says. "For coffee cups and liquids. We keep liquids away from anything electrical."

Kieron and Billy enter the room at the back. Billy watches Wanda closely. Kieron leans in and whispers.

"Any over-interest will be noticed and give away the only lead we have."

"She ain't noticed."

"I did. Others might. And we don't know if she's working alone. Who else in this room is involved?"

Billy straightens up and scans the recruits, eyes narrowed.

Kieron walks to the large screen and adds the CSCI logo. "That's all I've learned to do. But I never worked in security. Your room next door will be ready before the end of your course, and you'll get time in it. Croc heads up our office in Mumbai and has worked all night on this room."

"When night came, it was still daytime in India," he offers.

"Now it's daytime here. When are you going to sleep?" Wanda asks.

"I'll sleep when I'm dead," Kieron jokes, but the wide grin drops as he realises it's not funny.

"What are you doing in Florida if you run Mumbai?" Wanda presses.

Croc pauses, considering his response. His previous remark had been too flippant, lacking control.

"Tech. Then I fly straight back."

"That seems like an unnecessary journey. There must be people in America who could do this."

Croc continues working but now slower and more precise, considering the weight of Wanda's involvement. He can't blow Prisha's cover; he can't let anyone think she's here in Florida. Even being seen in the office is reckless. He feels guilty and worried.

Kieron shifts focus. "You've met. Let's introduce ourselves. Two new recruits today: Abigail."

"Abi," she interrupts, the same girl who accused Croc of mansplaining.

"And Carol." Kieron gestures to the second recruit. The two girls offer the expected slightly embarrassed smiles and waves.

"Why do you need all this?" Abi asks.

"As well as training security staff, the company is developing software for the shipping industry. At least, I hope it does."

Zack appears at the door to the yard and waits.

"Now, this course is full. No more restarts. Newbies, go to the next block after the holidays. Today, you step up to work with Senior Instructor Zack, another seasoned veteran who has served his country," Billy announces.

"Coffee cups in the trash. Assemble in the courtyard," Zack says firmly, with no invitation for backchat.

As the room clears, Kieron follows them and closes the door behind them. He looks at the workers, pointing toward the window. "Are the blinds working?"

Kieron is handed the remote and closes the internal shutters. The room is now dark, lit only by lamps and screens.

"Would you two mind connecting all the cameras inside and outside Mary's diner next?"

The workers leave, and Kieron closes the yard door behind them.

"Croc, check for listening devices. Assume this room was just compromised, just like on a mission," Kieron orders.

"We are on a mission," Billy says.

Kieron moves towards the door that connects to the next room. He invites Izzy and Macey in. In seconds, his actions set an active command level.

"Billy, I want you to manage a unit that will follow Wanda tonight."

Billy looks at him, intrigued. "Prisha? She's my one-man unit?"

Croc waves a hand-held detecting scanner over every part of the room, listening intently. His glance shows that he wants to step in and stop Prisha from being used, but he restrains himself. He knows Kieron is an astute commander.

"No. We have other assets - street soldiers that need schooling. We can't afford them to put a foot wrong. Croc, I want you to set up an offsite control centre. You're gonna need a machine, a screen, whatever. A mobile version of this. Prisha can stay in the background. You work point for Billy out in the field."

Croc smiles with relief. "I'll take everything I need." He looks around the room that he's so painstakingly created.

"No, leave all this. We need to build a separate satellite unit that can be moved and set up anywhere, fast. Even at sea. Let's think about this. Purchase the right equipment and build it properly. Light, mobile, ocean-ready."

Billy and Croc now both focus, engaged in the task.

"But before that consumes the rest of your day, and Izzy and Macey start to work in here, let's backtrack. Losing Bedřiška was a diversion. If she hadn't followed him, would she still be alive? Why did he impersonate Daniel Creedon? What's he up to? How dangerous is he? Why is he a ghost?"

"I have a list of possible types of terrorist attacks a cruise ship is vulnerable to," Izzy says, sending it to the big screen.

"I want to find who killed Bedi." Billy interrupts.

"Exactly. Why she died, and how this connects," Kieron commands.

"A cruise ship has more chance of being disrupted by a storm," Billy says.

"Sure," Izzy agrees. "But Kieron asked for a risk assessment. Even though a terrorist attack is unlikely, I'm adding it to the training program."

"The murder of Bedřiška jumps this terrorist threat up from 'unlikely' to 'in progress.' This is now very real," Kieron says.

8-18 CRIME SCENE
Day 4 - 1015hrs Miami

Ronni drives past the main building of the Miami Biscayne Blue Motel, not because it's small, but because she can see the blue flashing lights of a police car in the car park just beyond. As she turns in, she spots CSCI's brown compact utility car, which Bedi drove, still parked outside the main building. She continues towards the two black cars with darkened windows and parks next to the patrol vehicle. Ronni gets out and walks toward a body being wheeled on a gurney toward an open coroner's van, but she is stopped by a uniformed officer.

"Let her through," a man in a suit shouts. She meets him at the back of the coroner's van. "Miss Cohen, it's been a while."

She shakes his hand. "Ted."

"Did you know her?"

"If it's Bedřiška Kossof."

"That's the name on her driver's license," Ted says, unzipping the bag.

Ronni sadly acknowledges the body is hers. The agent zips the bag closed and allows it to be loaded.

"What's your connection?" he asks, leading her to the only open orange door in the row of four rooms at the far end of the motel. Getting no answer, he continues. "She was found here, in room five. Pretty sure the killer checked in to lure her into a kill zone, then left through the open rear window. He used a false ID, no bags, bed never slept in, left no prints. But I guess you know that."

"I don't know anything. What name did he use?"

Ted looks to Lenny, his assistant, who checks his pad. "Signed in under the name John S. Owens."

"Left as a ghost," Ronni mutters.

"He's on camera. We'll match him."

"No, you won't. We've already run his face through the system," Ronni says, looking around the inside of the room. The blood pool is just inside the door.

"Our system might find him."

"We looked in your system."

She opens the door just behind her and looks at the small space between the door and bare wall. Just enough to hide.

"He hid behind the door, slit her throat from behind as she entered," Ronni offers.

"We thought she was a hooker; Russian name."

"Except she was ex-KGB. She didn't make mistakes."

"Are your mob going to demand jurisdiction?"

"I haven't been with the agency for years. And she was out of Russian service, working in the cruise industry."

"Then why are you here?"

"I was asked to identify the body. Give me your card and I'll send you her jacket."

Ted hands Ronni a card. "And yours?"

"I don't have one."

"So, who are you with?"

"Until very recently, I was working and living on cruise ships. We worked on the same ship for a while."

Ted looks confused.

"The state boys called my new partner last night to be told she'd been found murdered. Our office was closed; he picked up the divert. Since he's out of town, he asked if I would ID her."

"Where do I find you?"

"CSCI."

"Who are they?"

"Cruise Ship Crime Investigators. They do exactly what it says on the can. I was about to join them, but if life on land is this dangerous, I'm going back to sea."

"Cruise crime investigators?"

"Just moved into Palladium House."

"I saw it was being renovated."

"Long job. This might slow it down."

"Why? Was she doing the building work?"

"No. The guy who might have killed her swanned in there pretending to be Daniel G. Creedon, saying he'd been warned of a future terrorist attack on a cruise ship. No details. He vanished and you know the rest."

"Did he show you ID as this Creedon guy?"

"I wasn't there, but I hear it was an innocent visit, so no need. What ID did he use to get the room?"

"Driving license."

"Minnesota?" Ronni asks.

"Yeah," Ted's sidekick says, as he checks his notes.

"Pure conjecture. What's the chances?" she says, cheekily.

"One in fifty," Ted replies, knowing she didn't guess.

"Russian victim, killer from out of state. Is the FBI replacing the state police?"

"Just casting an eye. Is CS…"

"CSCI."

"Are they investigating this too?"

"I'm new."

"Can't have them treading on toes," Ted says.

"Come by anytime," Ronni offers. "Just don't tell them anything about me. I'm on probation."

Ted looks at her as if that's unlikely. "Probation? You?"

Ronni steps over the blood and into the room, past the washroom, and looks out the rear window. The fire escape route is a path back to the road.

"Check for a dark blue sedan out front. He had someone waiting for him, unless they joined him. Bedřiška must have thought he'd been dropped here for the night. Check her blood work for drugs. If she wasn't off her game, then he's special."

"You don't happen to have the number of that sedan?"

"No. As I said, pass by CSCI, bring us what you got."

"Right behind you."

"No one's there today. But tomorrow, I'm sure Commander Kieron Philips will share."

Ronni strides out of the motel room, but stops and turns back. "Nice to see you again, Ted. Well, not in these circumstances. She was a friend."

"You both worked on cruise ships?"

"No stress, no death threats, travelled the world, ate great food, watched a show most nights, drank in swanky bars, shopped in the world's best cities, laid on famous beaches. Where did it all go wrong?"

"We both know, something always goes wrong."

"Only on land, Ted."

"You'll be going back to sea?"

She looks down at the blood and back to him with an expression that asks, what do you think? "Throat slit from behind?"

"Don't go without saying goodbye."

"Goodbye, Ted," Ronni says, and she leaves, stopping and turning back Columbo-style. "Why was the body still here?"

"System's back up. It's the holidays."

"Not 'til next week."

Ted's partner has consumed every word. "You know her, then."

Ted shakes his head. "A lot less than I thought I did. And that wasn't much either."

8-19 KILL ZONES
Day 4 - 1035hrs Miami

Standing on the corner of the first-floor balcony of the motel, Kieron, Billy, and Croc watch Ronni leave, shadowed by the two FBI agents.

"Ronni didn't exactly kiss them goodbye, but she seemed to know them," Kieron observes, turning back along the balcony. He steps inside the corner room the team has rented. Croc is setting up technical equipment while Billy rips the packaging off a new monitor.

"If the killer comes back, God bless me with restraint," Billy says.

"Show some restraint, and we'll get them all. Here and in Russia," Kieron replies.

"You mean that?" Billy asks. "All of them?"

"I'm all in. Every last one of them."

Billy offers him a fist bump, and Kieron hopes his words have hit home.

"My rental's walkable from here," Croc says.

"Good, because that pink truck might as well have a spotlight on it," Kieron quips.

"I could take Bedi's car," Croc suggests.

"They know that car," Kieron says firmly. "And if we're sure they're not watching us watching them, we need to take it back and analyse it. You should walk in and out like you work here - maybe take a bus one stop and loop back."

"Yeah. Never take a direct route home, and always watch your back," Billy advises.

"I don't think they'll return," Kieron says. "But don't get seen."

"So, if they're not coming back, why are we here?" Billy asks.

"Let's give it a day. When the police leave, we need to check reception's room log for the last three or four weeks. Look for anything odd - names we know, Minnesota IDs.," Kieron explains. "This is as good a place as any to build a field station. We can move if needed."

"It's a good kill zone," Billy comments, nodding toward the crime scene.

"Any motel on a main road would be," Kieron counters. "But I think they knew they were being followed and acted immediately to remove the tail."

"Thought she was FBI?" Croc asks.

"Or they didn't care," Billy offers.

"Or they were in a hurry to get where they're going and didn't want to give away their base," Kieron says. "Whichever it is, this was just a waypoint. If it was planned, we need to know why. Tonight, after work, we follow Wanda."

"But," Croc interjects, worried, "they spotted the last tail and executed her. Prisha shouldn't be anywhere near this; she doesn't have the skills to defend herself."

"Billy knows what he's doing," Kieron says firmly, emphasising the team's safety.

"I don't like this," Croc says, unconvinced.

"You got the bug sweeper?" Kieron asks.

"Yeah. I swept the room. It's clean."

Croc holds the hand held device up, Kieron hands it to Billy.

"Scan Bedi's car," Kieron instructs, watching the coroner's van leave, followed by the two dark FBI cars. "Just a patrol officer left. He's busy. Probably waiting for the cleanup team. Take Bedi's car back. I'll tail you to make sure you're not followed."

"Should I grab a hotel trolley and pretend to clean up? I could go over the crime scene," Croc offers.

"No. That could blow our cover here," Kieron says. "If Ronni suspected something, she would've asked us to do that. Set up point here."

"It's done, look," Croc says, turning his focus back to the active monitor. "Izzy, can you see me?"

"Yeah, I see the whole room, so don't do anything nasty," Izzy teases, her voice coming through the screen.

"I'm about to get married. You're about to be an auntie," Croc says.

"I like that, but I'm not sure Mary's used to the grandma tag yet. Woman probably needs therapy," Izzy jokes, clearly visible in the corner of the monitor.

"What time do I leave?" Croc asks, exasperated.

"You say that like we have a lot of staff," Kieron replies, moving to the side window overlooking the crime scene.

Kieron watches Billy cross the motel drive and get into the car Bedřiška had arrived in. As Billy pulls away, Kieron heads down to ground level, moving toward the CSCI car he had used to settle the team at their mobile station.

Back in the room, Croc sets up a pair of binoculars on a stand, aimed at the crime scene.

"'Kill or be killed,'" he murmurs to himself. "I'll never forget you, Bedřiška. 'Do unto others as they might do to you.' You definitely had a very different version of the Bible than my church." He pauses, reflecting. "But then, there were dealers waiting on the steps, selling drugs to the congregation. That was a kill zone. So, I have no idea how this world works. Or who's supposed to be watching over it."

8-20 DEATH SENTENCE
Day 4 - 1245hrs Miami

Although four blocks of offices form the Palladium House complex around a quadrangle, the fortress's weakness lies in the gated drive at the rear block's centre. Once a commercial factory, the yard likely served as a parking lot for workers commuting from residential areas. Few commercial units remain occupied, and none are ornate enough to qualify for the National Register of Historic Places - unlike the buildings on South Beach or nearby.

The damaged, rotten wooden gates creak as Kieron and Billy force them open. Zack orders the students to assist, freeing Billy to return to the waiting brown compact car and drive it into the yard.

Kieron pretends to film the car entering but instead captures Wanda's reaction. Her face betrays recognition of the vehicle - the one she must have known was following her. The same car she lured into the Biscayne Blue Motel, just before the Ghost killed Bedřiška. If they were the kill team.

Once the gates are securely closed, Billy turns to the students. "Stay clear. This is a crime scene now. It stays that way until it's worked for clues and evidence."

With the students settling back under Zack's command, Kieron heads for the operations room.

"Doesn't bringing Bedi's car here blow our cover as software developers?" Macey asks as he enters.

"Anyone who looks past the initials of our name figures out what we do," Kieron replies.

"These recruits joined to become security operatives," Izzy interjects.

"Or to get their claws into CSCI?"

"Macey, keep recording Wanda," Kieron says, sitting at a workstation in the semi-functional operations room.

"Abi too," Izzy adds.

Macey works the joystick controlling the cameras hidden in the yard's corners. Billy steps in and peers over her shoulder at the screen. "Dead man walking," he says.

Macey stiffens, realising the weight of her task. She knows Billy's reputation - he's a killer. She's known it but compartmentalised it, comforting herself that he works for the "good guys." Her entry into CSCI had been through an art theft case, which gained her recognition as an artist. The promise of her own gallery in one wing of Palladium House was her real motivation. Now, she's directing a killer toward his target.

"What's up? This is Florida - a death penalty state, isn't it?" Billy asks, his tone sharp.

"Oh, right," Macey stammers. "You mean we'll arrest her, and she'll get executed at Florida State Prison."

"That's OK?" Billy teases. "The state can kill her, but I can't? End result's the same."

Macey swallows hard. Billy's taut cheeks and intense eyes show he's serious, his tone laced with dark banter.

"We help the proper system," she manages to say.

"Macey, help the poor girl out," Billy says, feigning magnanimity. "She doesn't want to wait in line for years. There must be hundreds in front of her. That's no way to treat one of our own cadets. Zoom in, get the evidence, and I'll move her right to the front."

"In England, we call that 'jibbing in'," Kieron says.

"I didn't think England had the death penalty," Izzy comments.

"Not by the state. Just by teenagers with knives," Kieron replies, his voice tinged with irony. "We deferred state power to them. But 'jibbing' means skipping the queue - forcing your way to the front."

"I thought 'jibbing' meant stopping," Macey says nervously.

"That's the other definition," Kieron says.

Billy smirks. "We don't need her being that rude. We can help her out here."

"I'm not sure I like this job," Macey mutters.

"Neither did Bedi," Billy counters.

"Or Hunter, or his wife Elaine, or his daughter," Kieron adds grimly.

"Or Georgie," Izzy offers.

"Such a stellar success rate for a new company," Macey says.

"That's not even the full list," Kieron says, his tone biting. "There were the two seconded to the serial killer case on the Pacific crossing."

"We didn't know them," Macey protests. "Like we didn't know the gang members Bedi killed in Overtown."

Billy raises his hand. "Time-out. Focus. These killers are planning a terrorist attack on a cruise ship."

"They haven't done it yet," Macey says.

"They killed Bedi. How many more deaths will it take for you to switch from a police objective to a military one?"

"We are not the military!"

"And we ain't the police," Billy fires back.

"OK, enough!" Kieron cuts in. "Izzy, what's the list of potential cruise ship attacks?"

"They're rare," Izzy begins, pulling up a file. "But here's what I found:

One: Boarding. Hostages or the ship itself could be seized. Example: the PLF hijacking of the *Achille Lauro* in 1985."

"That's specialised, like 9/11," Billy notes.

"Go on," Kieron prompts.

"**Two: Pirates.** Not Johnny Depp," Izzy says dryly. "Somali pirates have targeted ships for ransom payments."

"They'll be armed," Billy adds.

"**Three: Bombs.** Either planted on board or explosive-laden boats driven at the ship."

"Or drones," Billy interjects.

"Correct," Izzy continues. "Recent targets included merchant ships in the Red Sea. Patrolling destroyers intercepted drones, especially near Yemen."

"That won't end soon," Mary says, entering with a tray of coffee.

"You're right, Mary," Kieron agrees. "CSCI reacts to situations - we're not philosophers."

"Our Ghost wasn't CIA," Billy insists. "They wouldn't kill Bedi."

"It was a specialist. She was slit from behind," Ronni counters. "No ID check. They acted fast."

"Let's keep an open mind," Kieron says. "If the CIA's involved, there's a reason. And if we've been dragged into this, there's a reason for that too."

"FBI was at the scene this morning, not the CIA," Ronni explains. "They have nothing, and they'll be here tomorrow if not before. They asked that CSCI not step on their toes."

"But would the FBI know of CIA involvement?" Kieron asks her.

"No," Ronni says, with a little too much fun and confidence showing a bias that only someone inside might show. It is the first time she has offered a 'tell'.

"Look, I'll give you that our Ghost may have been some skinny sensei with super powers. We've all met them."

"I haven't," Macey throws in.

"But he ain't a CIA field operative," Billy insists.

"Nice phrasing. He could be a desk junkie, tipping us off because no one will listen at the farm," Ronni adds.

"Like our sex trafficking case when two young executives, too scared to ever say boo to a goose, used us to come in," Kieron adds.

"Games get played," Billy says, sipping coffee. "Don't like it when one of my own gets killed."

"Lot of people don't like the way America supports and interferes," Macey says.

"What the hell did you have for breakfast?"

"Let's calm down," Kieron says. "The Ghost came in pretending to be Creedon - there was a reason. The girl who drove him away, is outside training with us - there is a reason. Bedřiška followed them - there was a reason. Someone killed her, maybe those two - there was a reason. FBI are involved - there will be a reason. CIA might be involved - there will be a reason. Lastly, we have been involved - what is the reason?"

"Did someone write all that down?" Mary says, thinking the list was quite a mouthful.

"Yeah, I'm recording it training purposes," Izzy says, evoking a momentary silence.

"Like you said, we're damned if we do, and damned if we don't. CSCI have been used to foster fear. Should be a board game; Foster Fear," Billy adds.

"Izzy. Is there any more on your terror attack list?" Kieron asks.

"**Four:** The realisation that a cruise ship is a high profile and newsworthy target. It's not as flexible as taking a plane and weaponising it. Ships are slow, you would have to control thousands of guests and half as many crew, who are not seated in neat rows with belts on. A ship is slow and not easy to hide, damage, or sink."

"But, newsworthy. I like that. Everyone who picks up a pen is at war," Kieron says.

"Get you," Mary says.

"That wasn't my wisdom."

"Voltaire?" Izzy asks.

"Yeah. Carry on."

"On the newsworthy angle, Cruise ships are of a highly iconic nature. They can be seen to reflect a type of explicit materialism and affluence that many dislike, and I don't mean just Bin Laden–like extremists," she adds.

"It can't be easy to attack a cruise ship," Mary adds, thinking. "Unless they get someone on the inside. Like one of them Nick Cage type movies. He does those kind of films, right?"

"Extremists like Wanda," Billy says. "Maybe I should talk to her."

"You leave it with me, Billy," Mary says.

"Bedřiška tried to follow her."

"I don't want you spreading her blood all over my new diner. I bet you're glad you asked me to this meeting. I'm gonna go keep me an eye on those recruits," Mary says, leaving.

"I don't think Izzy's finished yet," Kieron says.

Mary stops at the door and listens.

"This is a lot of types of terrorist attacks," Macey says, exhausted.

"This is a great training module, our next segment will be what?"

"Weapons," Billy offers.

"We'll do that, last. But our training block, after listing the types of terrorist attacks should be how to spot them. And we have not achieved that yet. Carry on Izzy, I'm sure the best is yet to come."

"**Fifth method of attack**: contamination of the water, air, or food supplies," Izzy says. "Those areas are constantly tested and systems can be shut down fast. So, my personal worry is six: a virus outbreak. It is far less controllable than all those I have mentioned."

"Ships are used to dealing with Norovirus and others regularly. They have systems in place," Ronni says.

"Well, **six**: Virus worries me," Izzy says.

"But what just hit you is fear," Kieron says. "But that is a great expanding syllabus. Let's add seven, people planted on board. Like Wanda. But don't use the name."

"And she'll be wanting her lunch any minute. That girl can eat. Not like Abi, one of them vegetarians, Wanda not got a problem eating anything," Mary says, leaving.

8-21 PINK ON PINK

Day 4 - 1630hrs Miami

"Auntie's here to babysit!" Macey announces brightly as she steps into the Biscayne Park house Croc and Prisha have rented.

"We're not babies!" Lakshmi protests, her voice defiant.

"You're my babies," Macey teases, pulling her into a hug. "This family hasn't had little ones in forever."

"What, no kids at all?" Reyansh asks, wide-eyed.

"Nope. Now, who wants to walk along the beach?"

"Do you know the way?" Lakshmi challenges.

"Of course I do. I live here, remember?" Macey hugs them both again, ruffling Reyansh's hair. "But first - sun hats and cream!"

"We're used to the sun," Reyansh says, with an exaggerated sigh.

Prisha's small, uneasy smile catches Macey's attention. Something isn't right.

"You don't have to do this," Macey says softly.

"What, have the baby?" Prisha replies, slinging a bag over her shoulder. "A bit late for that, don't you think?"

"That's not what I meant. Are you feeling okay?"

"It's not my health."

"Then what is it?"

Prisha hesitates.

"Big Dogg has plenty of crew to keep an eye on Wanda," Macey says, to ease her concern.

That does not help.

"It's not about the job either, is it?" Macey presses.

Prisha shrugs, looking away. "Ask Izzy."

Macey frowns, frustrated that Prisha would drag their sister into something unrelated. Before she can ask more, Prisha is already heading for the door.

"I'll walk," Prisha calls over her shoulder. "You can take the tuk-tuk."

Macey glances at the pink, three-wheeled vehicle with a mix of horror and disbelief.

"Great! Can we drive to the beach?" Lakshmi asks, bouncing with excitement.

"You want me to drive *that*?" Macey points, incredulous.

"Yes!" Reyansh shouts, hopping in.

"Mummy says you're a great painter," Lakshmi adds.

"I'd like to repaint this thing," Macey mutters, sliding reluctantly into the driver's seat.

"Yeah! Paint us in the tuk-tuk!"

"That's about as likely as me painting a pony with pink hair," Macey says dryly, starting the engine.

"Yeah! Paint us a pink pony!"

"No, the pony is brown. It just has pink hair. And it's a *nightmare* I have."

Reyansh grins. "Paint us a pink pony, Auntie Macey, please?"

"Someone already did. They beat me to it."

"Does that make you sad?" Reyansh asks.

"Can't say it does," Macey replies, steering the tuk-tuk out of the driveway.

"Where did Mummy go?" Lakshmi asks, as the tuk-tuk bounces along.

"To work with your new daddy in his office."

"Can we drive there?" Reyansh asks.

"Is that where the pink pony is?" Lakshmi adds, leaning forward.

"No, the pink pony is on the ship," Macey says, as the horizon comes into view. The sea sparkles under the sunlight. "That's another image I'm never likely to paint - pretty as it is."

"Which ship is the pink pony on?"

"Every ship. That's the problem."

"How can it be on *every* ship?" Reyansh asks, sceptical.

"Smart kid. You'd think someone else might've asked the same question."

"So, it's everywhere?" Lakshmi says, her eyes wide with wonder.

"Yeah. And thanks to you two, I might never get the image out of my head now."

"You're welcome, Auntie Macey," Reyansh says, with a cheeky grin.

8-22 FEAR IS THE KEY

Day 4 - 1700hrs Miami

Croc steps away from his desk at the Miami Biscayne Blue Motel to greet Prisha with a hug and a kiss as she enters his new office. One look at her face tells him she's not herself.

"Wazzup?" he asks gently.

Prisha shakes her head.

"You don't have to do this," Croc offers.

"It's not that," she replies. "I didn't like leaving the kids. It's... everything. But I'm okay. What's the plan?"

"Hopefully, nothing," Croc says, though they both know it's unlikely.

Prisha gives him a look that says she's waiting for her orders.

"Big Dogg's crew is following Wanda," Croc explains. "They'll keep you way back in the procession. If she stops somewhere and goes inside, they'll watch, and you'll do nothing. If she stops and walks, you'll need to join the team tailing her."

The door opens, and Doc, one of Dogg's crew, Raul, enters. Dogg is a tall Black man with a prominent scar on his face, he carries the distinct scent of sweet colitas. He fist-bumps Croc.

"Hey, bro. She my package?"

"I'm your package," Prisha says, stepping forward. "No smoking. I'm pregnant."

"Me don't smoke. Just some 'erbs that'd do the baby just fine."

"That's exactly what I mean," Prisha says firmly. "Do you have a driver's license?"

"Me licensed," Dogg replies with a grin.

Prisha raises an eyebrow at Croc, challenging the casual dynamic.

"Kinda like Mumbai," Croc shrugs. "Welcome to Miami."

"I've been here before, Winston Crocket."

"Not my Miami."

Dogg fist-bumps Croc again before turning to the door.

"My name is Prisha," she says pointedly.

"Call me Dogg. I medicine man."

Croc watches them leave, heading to the rental car.

"What did I do to get called *Winston Crocket?*" he mutters.

"Welcome to married life," Dwight's voice chimes in from a nearby screen.

Croc turns to him. "Sorry, man. Forgot you were there. So, you're not getting out today?"

"I'd discharge myself if this infection didn't need a solid whipping."

"We've got it covered."

"You've got no leads, so nothing's covered," Dwight counters.

"Hey, I was in India, you were in the hospital, and the B-team got nowhere. We'll figure it out. If you're stuck there, I'll move the mobile ops centre to you."

"Not sure they'd like that, but I'll think about it. Tomorrow, though, Palladium House could be a no-go zone."

"Why?"

"Reports suggest the FBI will swarm it by morning. We can't let them spook our recruits."

"Unless we crack it tonight," Croc says.

"Get to reception and snap some recent pages of their register. I'll call ahead, tell them to expect a good-looking FBI agent."

"That'll land me three years inside."

"Prisons are full," Dwight quips.

At the motel reception, Croc admires a Christmas tree decked with presents.

"We need to get our tree up," he says to himself. "That looks good."

"Makes it feel homely," the receptionist agrees. "Family-time."

"Yeah, looking forward to that," Croc says. "Mind if I take a quick look at your register?"

The receptionist laughs and spins the book around. "Been expecting you."

"Not me," Croc replies firmly, sitting at the coffee table and flipping through the pages. "You psychic?"

"Nah," the receptionist says, amused. "Got a call."

Croc snaps photos discreetly as he works backward through the register. "Not from me," he says absently.

"Your office called."

"I don't have an office. Just looking for a buddy who owes me money."

The receptionist frowns. "You're not FBI?"

"No way. You see a black guy in beachwear posing as the FBI?" Croc quips.

"Someone called, though. Asked to see the register."

"The FBI wouldn't ask," Croc says, handing the book back. "Way too polite. You think they ring my mom when day gonna stop and search me? A call

4 MURDERS, A WEDDING, AND A CRUISE

gives you time to rip pages out. Must've been a prank. Dial star-sixty-nine and see."

The receptionist tries the call-back. "It's a hospital."

Croc pauses on his way out. "Hospitals are full of cranks."

The receptionist shrugs. "Weird, man."

At the Miami ops room in Palladium House, the scanned pages of the register appear on a large screen.

Izzy scrolls through the names. "What kind of attack worries you most?" she asks the team.

"Messing with food or water," Mary answers, eager to contribute.

"Controlled IEDs," Kieron says. "Targeting each section of the ship."

"Sections?" Mary asks.

"Ships are built in units that can isolate damage. Most have five to ten sections. But hitting all at once is easier now with digital drones."

"An attack on another one of us," Billy says quietly, lowering the room's energy.

Mary notices cadets filing into her restaurant. "School's out. Not that they ever spend money."

She takes the internal route, passing through construction areas before entering the diner, where Stan is decorating a tree.

"No one's gonna see that there. Should be by the door," Mary says.

Abi and Wanda confront Billy about the evidence car in the yard.

"Why do we have that car?" Abi asks.

"It was involved in a crime."

"Why not hand it to the police?"

"You mean NCIS," Billy says.

"That's a TV show," Abi says, sceptical.

"It's also a real agency."

"CSCI handles civilian ships; NCIS is navy," Kieron says as he joins them.

"Maybe the driver was navy," Wanda fishes.

"If the injured officer dies, NCIS will take over," Kieron says.

"Dies?" Wanda asks.

"That always causes a jurisdiction battle," Billy adds. "Who knows, maybe NCIS parked it here to keep it away from the FBI. If that female officer doesn't make it, everything will kick off."

Kieron opens the door and holds it for the cadets filing out. "Have a good evening," he says, addressing them pointedly before heading to join Billy who has gone to the grill.

After a moment, Billy turns to check, seeing the last two students - Nick and Craig - waving goodnight. He nods in acknowledgment. The door closes.

"Fear is the key," Kieron says quietly.

"The ball's going to get kicked upfield," Billy replies. "You think we should be handling tonight's business ourselves?"

"No," Kieron says. "We can't risk being made. We have to trust Big Dogg and Prisha."

In the ops centre, Izzy is leaned forward, concentrating hard, manoeuvring the joystick the joy stick to move the new outside cameras. The live feed follows the students as walk away from the diner, fragmenting into pairs and singles. The picture of them is clear under the amber glow of streetlights.

Kieron enters. 'That's not a video game."

Izzy does not look away from the screen. "No, but it's just as addictive. Look, have we got a problem. Two of them are lingering. Are they watching us?"

"When I said 'fear is the key', I meant for them to be afraid," Kieron says, looking at the screen. "Vinnie is going to love playing with this on the nightshift."

The girls appear to rudely refuse to talk to the male students and as the party breaks up Nick and Craig are left talking.

"They are not very pleasant girls, are they?" Kieron asks.

"Nick and Craig are not exactly the catch of the day."

8-23 IMMINENT
Day 4 - 1730hrs Miami

The team gathers in Dwight's private room at the clinic. Kieron and Billy nearly block the door, while Ronni stands by the window behind Izzy, who is seated with a screen open, ready to explain Croc's progress report. Though they could all access it on their smartphones, they prefer the group setting.

"The ops centre looks amazing. Like a real TV spy centre," Izzy says.

"Hate to break it to you, but television spy centres are not real," Dwight says. "They're normally a tent in the desert, or a derelict warehouse."

"Well, ours is like they are in the movies."

Mary places food parcels and a plate on Dwight's tray.

"They do have food here, Mary," Dwight says, unwrapping the silver foil to reveal a stacked burger. He takes a huge bite.

"See? You're ravenous. I've never seen a man fade away so fast," Mary says.

"They said I gotta lose some weight," Dwight replies, taking another bite.

"You need these?" Mary asks, holding up cutlery.

"Not unless you brought salad."

"Not like you ever see rabbits eat with utensils," Ronni quips, showing her lighter side.

"You're a great addition to CSCI, Ronni. I hope you stay on the team," Kieron says.

"I haven't joined yet."

"Oh, you have," Izzy says flatly.

"Look at that - he just inhaled it. Didn't leave a fingerprint of waste. No one cooks a burger like my Stan," Mary says.

"Bed bath?" Ronni jokes, handing Dwight a towel.

He wipes his hands and turns to his screen. "Work. Wazzup, Lizzy?"

"Wanda, Abi, and Carol from the cadet course are in a compact. Raul's in a drop-top with four of Dogg's men, partying. They look nothing like law enforcement."

"They never heard of blend into the background and not be seen?"

"In a word, no."

"They should leave the game," Dwight mutters. "Do they have a unit following their own girls?"

"Negative."

"Because they might not be partying like is 1995."

"I wasn't born in 1995."

"Trust me. Watch for another female unit. Be scared. Female soldiers are less likely to take prisoners," Dwight says.

"There's no data to back that," Ronni corrects him.

"Not published data. I was out there sending intel back, and I know not all the beans get counted."

"What are you implying?"

"Just telling you: history, numbers, data - it's all recorded the way it needs to be told."

"Like how you never hear that one in five soldiers are female?" Ronni counters.

"Wow," Izzy interjects. "Is that true?"

"Not in the marines," Dwight adds.

"A unit of five female IDF soldiers on border guard was one of the first Hamas killed on October 7, 2024," Ronni says. "Women are out there changing the face of the military."

"Copy that, Ronni. But if America goes toe-to-toe with Russia and we're invaded, stats say more will run than stand and fight," Dwight replies.

"I'd love to keep debating," Kieron says, creating a pause.

"But?" Mary prods. "You going for a spray tan and manscaping?"

"They've turned off 95 at Golden Glades and taken the 826 to North Miami Beach. Croc's team has swapped the first tail and are returning to the rental."

"Get them to pull over and drop the passengers. Only needs a driver to swap the car," Kieron says.

"A new unit is tracking Wanda. Prisha and two other cars have also turned off," Izzy continues.

"Tell me about Golden Glades," Kieron asks.

"Ten miles north. Nice suburban area in Jacksonville. Predominantly Black, with good schools. Most are homeowners," Izzy says.

"And North Beach?"

"Mixed community, including Asians. Medium-price neighbourhood with expensive waterfront properties. Tourist-heavy with Everglades airboats."

"A place where new faces wouldn't be noticed," Kieron suggests.

Izzy nods. "Croc says they've split. Abi's team has turned into a mall."

"I'd stay on Wanda and post a unit at the mall. Odds are they've gone for supplies," Dwight says.

"What kind of supplies?" Ronni asks.

"Let's see what they buy," Kieron says.

"I thought you were going for a dark spray tan?" Mary asks.

"It could be taken the wrong way, and I'd hate to offend."

"Croc's switched the tail again. A delivery van is following Wanda into North Beach. Prisha and one other car are on standby. Used units are being swapped out," Izzy updates.

Wanda's car pulls onto the expansive driveway of a two-story white house. The fenced property has a wide-open gate, arched porch, three garages to the left, a bay-windowed room to the right, and balconies with black wrought-iron railings. Terracotta tiles top the roof, while a pool maintenance van parks at the edge of the drive. An engineer works on the side of the house.

Dogg's van drives past. Two hundred yards away, it pulls into a marina's car park. One of his many street soldiers, Stax exits, looks back at the house, and snaps pictures.

"Last house on Marina Drive. Over a dozen rooms and a pool behind the fence," Stax reports. "We should have a car here."

A small dog runs to Stax's feet. "Hey, little guy." He picks up the dog and tosses it into the truck. Scattering sweets inside, he closes the door on the excited animal.

A woman weaves through parked cars, calling, "Chick! Chick!"

"Have you seen a small white dog?"

"No, ma'am."

Stax jumps in the van and drives away.

At the end of the street, Prisha stirs awake in her ride when Croc calls from the command centre.

"Prisha, you've found a dog. Walk it back to the marina; its owner's looking for it."

"I'll take photos of the dog outside the house," Prisha suggests.

"Not unless there's something we need. That property's listed as an Airbnb. Everglades Marina Mason - a twenty-bedroom rental unavailable until January sixth. We now have a time window for the attack."

"That's soon."

"Hi, Prisha. It's Kieron. See if the marina is hiring, especially if the job comes with a room."

"Assume it's an active cell, Prisha. Be very careful," Ronni adds.

"So, I won't see my kids tonight?"

"Maybe I'll bring them down for dinner," Croc offers.

8-24 Killers
Day 4 - 1845hrs Miami

Ronni, Kieron, and Billy step into the mobile command centre, a cramped but well-equipped RV parked inconspicuously at the Miami Biscayne Blue Motel. Inside, Croc is monitoring multiple screens, each displaying live feeds, maps, and data streams.

"Anyone been back to the crime scene?" Ronni asks, settling into a corner.

"Not that I've seen," Croc replies. "No forensic team, no reporters. It's like it's already been forgotten."

"Good work on the tail," Kieron says, glancing at the feeds. "But let's not jump to conclusions. We're not sure who these people are, what they're planning, or even if they're the right targets. This could just be a family holidaying in a big house because their daughter is training for cruise ship security."

"In a twenty-room mansion with private access to Biscayne Bay and Dodge Island?" Croc retorts, flicking a key on his keyboard. An aerial photo fills the main screen. "I sent up a drone. Take a look."

The picture shows the sprawling property, complete with a long wooden jetty extending into the water. Two sleek boats are tied up on either side of it.

"Those two boats are identical," Ronni observes, leaning closer.

"They're rentals," Croc says. "Dogg's guy, KooBaa, is already on his way to rent one for us. I'll have the ocean exit covered."

"Do they need a license for that?" Kieron asks. "In the UK, it takes two weeks to get a Day Skipper certification."

"Here? I got a Temporary Navigation Certificate in fifteen minutes," Croc replies. "Cost me ten bucks, and no photo required."

"No records, no control," Kieron says grimly. "Anyone could rent those boats, load them up with explosives from supplies bought at malls all over town, and drive them straight into a ship docked at Dodge Island."

"That'd be a disaster," Billy says. "Shut down the cruise industry for days, maybe weeks."

"And make headlines," Ronni adds. "That's always the point of these attacks."

Croc leans back in his chair. "Those cadets you're training don't exactly scream 'fanatical suicide bombers.' Some of them wouldn't even eat a burger."

"They don't need to be fanatical," Billy says. "Just point the boat, lock the course, jump off, and get picked up by another vessel."

"Like dropping a toxic comment online and never facing the backlash," Kieron mutters.

"That sounds like the cadets I saw," Croc agrees.

"Or anyone with a grudge and a keyboard full of hate emoji," Ronni adds.

Kieron crosses his arms. "We need hard evidence. Croc, have your boat pick us up. We'll plant remote cameras on the property without blowing our cover. Meanwhile, trace the names of everyone who rented that make of boat and look for unusual purchases in the area."

Ronni shakes her head, her expression sceptical. "What I don't get is why they're even doing a cruise ship security course. It doesn't match this attack scenario or the timeline. Something's off."

"We need more intel," Kieron says, his tone firm.

"And the FBI's passing by tomorrow," Ronni adds.

"Why are they interested?" Billy asks. "This doesn't scream organised crime. Bedi wasn't a state official. It's not a hate crime or a mafia hit."

"I invited them," Ronni admits. "It gives us today to act without interference. Besides, it's Saturday tomorrow. Let's see how eager they are to show up; Agent Ted has a kid in Little League."

"That's a lot of hoops for a marine biologist to jump through," Kieron says, his brow raised.

"I was curious why they were even at the crime scene in the first place," Ronni counters.

Kieron nods slowly. "So, what did Bedřiška know that got her killed?"

"Let's hope Prisha hears something useful at the marina," Billy says.

Croc spins his chair to face them. "She's got kids to take care of back here."

"Then move the command centre to your place," Kieron suggests, "so you can be with them."

Croc shakes his head firmly. "And put my kids at risk too? Not happening."

Ronni sighs, looking between them. "We're all taking risks. But if this escalates, we'll need to act fast. No room for mistakes."

Croc turns back to the screens. "Then let's make sure we're ahead of the game."

8-25 BAR STAFF
Day 4 - 1930hrs Miami

Betty bursts into the bar area of the Golden Glades Ocean Marina, clutching her toy-like dog, Chick.

"I've found him, Scott. I've found him. You can all stand down."

"Stand down, everyone - the dog has been found!" Scott, the bar manager, shouts to the other non-existent staff as he places clean glasses back on a shelf.

A chef appears at the kitchen door. "And I was sure Chick would be in my kitchen looking for food."

"No, Chick is very well-fed."

Prisha stands in the doorway, taking in the small bar sparsely dressed with tinsel and garlands.

"What's your name?" Betty asks.

"Prisha."

"Prisha found her."

"Thank you, Prisha."

"You're welcome, Scott," Prisha replies, matching his undisguised sarcasm.

That makes Scott look up and smile. The chef smirks and retreats into the kitchen.

"Would've been a poor Christmas if you'd lost your dog," Prisha adds.

"Yeah. Bet his presents are already stacked under the tree," Scott says, more to Prisha than Betty.

Prisha pretends to appreciate the humour.

"Scott, will you save me my table tomorrow?"

"Yeah, that's fine, Betty," he replies without consulting any system.

Betty leaves, and Prisha steps further into the bar.

"I was going to ask if you needed any bar help. But from the speed you checked reservations, maybe not."

"Oh, we are busy. Pre-Christmas is always mad, and just when staff want time off. Big party in tomorrow, but even if we're full, I'll find a place for Betty and her dog."

"You could offer her the chef's table," Prisha suggests, ensuring she's liked.

"I hadn't thought of that, but it's a great idea."

There's a crash from the kitchen.

"Shoot!" the chef shouts before reappearing at the door. "My table just collapsed."

"What are you looking for - bar or kitchen?"

"Bar or waitress."

"You're hired. We serve, then clean up as we go along."

"Got experience?"

"I work on the cruise ships."

"And they let you go when they're busy?"

"They're always busy. I only have a few days before I sail again. They're so busy I can pick my ship."

"Probably why we can't get staff," Scott mutters, disappearing into a back room.

"They have no dogs and offer the chance to travel the world with bed and board."

"I can offer you a board to sleep on," he calls from the back.

"Then I'm definitely interested."

Scott reappears and throws her a shirt.

"It's about to get busy. I'll show you the room later."

She steps aside as a group of four enters.

"You can change back there."

"I walked past some beautiful houses. The last one looked empty," she says, stepping behind the bar.

"Marina Mansion. It's a rental - big families, bachelor parties, wedding celebrations. It's rented otherwise I'd put you in there. We have a party booked in here tomorrow."

In the backroom, Prisha starts texting a report.

"You don't have time for a shower!" Scott shouts.

Prisha, keenly aware of her new employee status, rushes to type her message as she talks to herself.

"I hope this is for one night only, Winston."

She heads back to the bar.

"You worked a tech-pad order system?"

"Yeah."

"Great. Orders go to the kitchen. You get pinged when they're ready."

"So, there is a party tomorrow?"

"No. No. I meant the all in the house were coming for lunch."

8-26 NIGHT SWIMMING

Day 4 - 2125hrs Miami

KooBaa, one of Dogg's lieutenants, captains the rented twenty-foot Sea Ray Sundeck 200. He idles the boat, allowing the three frogmen to roll off the back into the dark water, blind to the shore. Staying close together, they swim away, constantly scanning for threats.

Saltwater crocodiles aren't found in these waters, but the American Crocodile has been spotted on

Miami beaches and in Biscayne Bay for decades. With fewer than a thousand remaining, encounters offshore are rare, though they can be active at night. The beaches in Biscayne are open to swimmers at all hours, but lifeguards only work during the day. Alligators, which rarely venture into saltwater, normally remain within the nearby Everglades. Not that anyone under attack ever worries which species is doing the biting.

The boat turns and heads toward the marina, blending in among the many others docked there. KooBaa is armed and ready, waiting for a signal to return.

Keeping their black thermal balaclavas and masks on, the swimmers pull themselves onto the jetty. They move carefully, inspecting the Nautic Star boats without rocking them. Both appear undisturbed - nothing removed, nothing added. Ronni attaches a tracker to the first boat, then to the second. Kieron mounts a 360-degree camera atop the arch at the start of the jetty, while Billy checks the fuel cans and other stacked accessories.

They exchange glances and nod. Time to move.

"Cameras?" Kieron whispers.

"Light," Billy says, pointing to one mounted high on the house wall, just under the roofline. "Stay at the edges."

They crouch low, moving stealthily along the perimeter. Halfway down the fence, Kieron photographs the back of the house. Through the partly drawn curtains, he can make out a few people, some of whom he recognises as his security cadets.

Billy enters the pool shed, photographing the chemicals stored there. Ronni heads for the garage, which runs from the front to the back of the house. It's large enough to store a boat or mower but is securely locked.

Suddenly, the garden light trips on, flooding the pool area with harsh light. Billy and Ronni flatten against the walls, but Kieron is exposed and dives to the ground, relying on a few skinny shrubs for cover.

The light switches off. Unsure what triggered it, Kieron signals for Billy to retreat first. Once Billy is back at the jetty, he signals Ronni to move. She is only ten steps from the house when the light blazes on again. Dropping flat, she crawls forward with practiced precision, her movements deliberate and confident.

Kieron watches as a figure - *the Ghost* - approaches the bi-folding doors. He snaps photos before pressing himself into the grass. The key turns and the door slides open.

Ronni rolls into a flower bed, no doubt damaging it in ways that will be noticed come morning. For now, it conceals her.

The Ghost steps onto the patio, scanning the swimming pool. He marches left and then right, and looks again. He checks the rear garage door, then looks out at the garden again. Taking a few steps forward he looks at the swimming pool before retreating back inside.

From across the garden, Ronni signals her intent to move. Kieron gives the go-ahead. She pulls a claw stamp from her pack, pressing gator prints into the soil as she makes her way back.

Kieron installs a hidden camera in a crack in the side fence, then turns to leave. His gaze lingers on the pool, where he notices a dark rim at the far end.

Slipping silently into the water, he swims to the deeper end. He duck dives down and feels the bottom of the pool. His fingers find a gap between the pool's side and a false wooden base painted sky blue to match the liner. Beneath the base is a deep hopper. Although the base is cable-tied down, he manages to lift it just enough to shine his flashlight inside. Rows of large plastic jerry cans - like those used for fuel or chemicals - fill the space. Kieron takes several photos before having to surface for air. He waits at the pool's edge, checking all around him, before climbing the step ladder and leaving dripping a trail of water. He fixes one last spy camera focused on the pool. Then, sprinting to the jetty, he dives into the sea, where the others are already waiting.

"KooBaa's on his way," Ronni says.

They begin to swim out. Once safely on board, the boat carves through the dark ocean, its wake foaming with white horses.

"Well?" Ronni asks.

"The deep end of the pool is covered by a false floor," Kieron says. "Aerial photography wouldn't spot it."

"Guess what's under it?" Billy adds.

"I think our algebraic equation is turning into an aquatic one," Kieron replies, scrolling through photos on his camera. He pauses at an image of the house interior, taken through the bifold windows.

"I've missed working with you guys," Ronni says, high-fiving Billy. "We got away clean."

"This one didn't," Kieron says, beckoning them to the camera. With two wet fingers, he zooms in on a figure tied to a chair, a hood covering their head. "What was Prisha wearing?"

Ronni studies the screen. "Is that... a prisoner?"

"We have to go back," Kieron says firmly.

Billy shakes his head. "I wanna kill them as much as anyone, but we're not equipped for an assault. If this turns into a gunfight, Prisha's dead."

KooBaa offers them his gun.

"I'm not into sharing; there's three of us," Billy says.

"They killed Bedřiška, but not Prisha," Ronni says. "There's a reason she's still alive."

Kieron takes the gun from KooBaa, his jaw tight. "We can't just leave her there."

"At this moment, we have to," Ronni replies. "Even with more guns, we'd need snipers and protection. This needs a plan." She takes the gun from him and gestures for KooBaa to continue driving.

8-27 WHERE IS MUMMY?
Day 4 - 2245hrs Miami

Croc carries equipment into his Biscayne Park rental and drops it carelessly. KooBaa, Kieron, Billy, and Ronni follow, hauling the remainder of the mobile control centre inside.

"Where is Mummy?" Lakshmi shouts, leaping up from Macey's lap on the sofa in the living area, where they'd been watching TV. Reyansh, more drowsy, is too tired to fully wake.

"She's gone to dinner with some old work friends," Croc says, picking her up. "Bedtime."

Macey stands, lifting Reyansh. "You're a heavy little man."

"Mummy reads us a story," Lakshmi says.

"And so do I. I read you stories too," Croc replies.

"Can we paint a picture?"

"We don't have the materials," Macey interjects, as they climb the stairs.

"We can use yours."

"My paints are real oil," Macey explains. "You'd make too much mess. Tomorrow we'll find a craft shop and get you a painting kit."

Downstairs, the senior team is left alone.

"Croc?" Kieron calls out.

"I'm putting my kids to bed. Go home," Croc shouts back from upstairs.

"He doesn't mean that," Ronni says, moving to explore the downstairs. "Here, let's set up in this den."

She strides into the small room, pulls the curtains closed, and begins setting up. As the equipment is laid out on the coffee table, she plugs it in. Kieron flicks the power on, and the screen comes to life.

Macey reappears in the doorway. "He's upstairs lying on the bed, cuddling two kids who are fast asleep. What happened to him?"

"He became a father. He'll be down," Kieron says.

"I'm not sure he will," Macey replies. "I've never seen this side of Croc before. Croc the father."

"Big Dogg's men have the marina house surrounded," Kieron says, focusing on the equipment. "The lights are off, and they're sure everyone's in bed. They don't see any prisoner."

"You need to get Prisha back," Macey says.

"Prisha's fine," Croc says, descending the stairs and shutting the door behind him. "She just called to say goodnight to the kids. She's working in the marina bar next door and hasn't had a minute to herself."

"Then who's the prisoner?"

Kieron shares the photo with the team, the image popping up on the screen as a notification. He opens it, zooming in clumsily but deliberately. Croc watches silently, letting him work.

"Judging by the shoulders and body size, it looks like a young woman," Kieron observes. "But with the hood over their head, it could be anyone. That's Wanda in the background, and Abi. I don't see Carol, and Creedon isn't in this picture either. We should get Prisha away from the area."

"She says the whole house is booked into the marina restaurant tomorrow," Croc says. "She's got a room there and is staying the night. But this isn't funny - she's a mother. Of three to be." His voice hardens. "There's nothing more we can do tonight. Let's discuss it in the morning."

Croc grabs a cold beer and sinks into the sofa, ignoring the team. One by one, they file out. Macey stays, sitting beside him. He puts his arm around her.

"We were happy when we had nothing, when we didn't have a mother," he says.

"Were we?" Macey counters.

"Before we were brother and sister."

"We lived in a ghetto, watched our neighbours get hooked on drugs. We could've gone the same way. We could've been in gangs, fighting our own habits."

Croc looks at her sceptically.

"We have a real mom now," Macey continues. "She cares. We know she does. We have friends. We've started seeing the world."

"I have a family now," Croc says, after a pause. "I'd give up all my money for those kids. Their mother should never be put at risk."

"She never saw them before she joined CSCI," Macey reminds him. "She worked on cruise ships to send money home."

"That was brave," Croc admits. "But she doesn't have to do that anymore. *I* don't have to anymore. Prisha is fine. Tomorrow, someone can talk to her. Tomorrow morning, we start fresh. I'm okay now. You can stay, but you should go find Richard - you haven't seen him in days. Don't give your whole life to CSCI. It might end up being shorter than you planned."

"How do I get back?" Macey asks.

"Take the tuk-tuk."

"It's okay. I'll walk." She stands and leaves.

Outside, KooBaa is waiting with a car.

Kieron swings the door open. "Squeeze in. How is he?"

Macey climbs into the back with Kieron and Ronni. Billy rides in the front passenger seat.

"He'll be fine in the morning. He had a shock," she says. "How was your evening?"

"Good. We went for a swim," Kieron replies.

"Maybe we should all have a drink," Ronni suggests.

"Someone's still being held at that house," Billy says.

"The house is sleeping, and it's being watched," Ronni replies. "It can wait until morning."

8-28 EVERYBODY HURTS
New Day. Saturday, Day 5 - 0740hrs Miami

Croc drags two heavy bags of equipment from the pink tuk-tuk parked right outside Wild Mary's Diner. The children each carry a box of gear and some cables. As he opens the door to Wild Mary's diner, the familiar bell jingles. He stacks the bags just inside.

"Don't leave that in my restaurant!" Mary snaps.

"You got customers I can't see?" Croc retorts.

"Saturday. It's slow, but it's coming."

"It's empty."

Mary hits the intercom. "Come through and clear your junk!"

Croc takes the last bundle of cables from Reyansh and Lakshmi. The children light up when they can run to Mary.

"Granny!"

Mary turns in surprise but finds herself wrapped in their eager hugs.

"You two must be hungry," she says, ushering them to the counter. "Stan! Feed these kids. And you two, don't fall off the stools!"

Mary turns back to Croc, hands on her hips, ready for a showdown.

Kieron enters from the adjoining reception area, pausing at the sight of the gear, Croc's grim expression, and Mary's annoyance.

"Good morning. What's going on?"

"I'm out," Croc declares.

"Out?"

"There's your equipment. Whatever else you need, I'll sort it. Whatever I owe you, I'll pay back. Just tell me how to get out."

Kieron frowns. "When?"

"As soon as I collect Prisha. Then we're heading back to India."

"You're leaving? You just got here."

"Prisha and I came back to tell you we're getting married. To plan the big day. Have any of you asked about it? No. None of you."

"What?" Mary blurts. "Married?!"

"Exactly. You screamed, told me you were too young to be a granny."

"Nanny, you are old," Lakshmi pipes up, helpfully.

"I was in shock!" Mary protests.

"We even brought you a present - your own wheels. And you love pink."

"I said, I was in shock!"

"'Thank you' would've been nice," Croc snaps. "Maybe asking when we're getting married. Or when the baby's due. But nothing."

Kieron sighs, guilt etched on his face. "Croc, I'm sorry. We got swept up in this case. I should've asked."

"You should've," Croc says coldly. "Instead, you sent a pregnant woman out into the field."

"I asked her. She wanted to go."

"You know she'll always say yes. That's how you treat people - you push, and they follow."

"You're not employees. You're partners," Kieron says defensively.

"Until we're killed," Croc shoots back. "I spent the whole night trying to talk sense into Prisha."

"Croc, we're a team. Let's talk about your wedding," Kieron starts.

"Yeah. Let's sit down and talk this out over breakfast," Mary offers.

"No. I'm done. It's always the same. Manipulation."

Mary bristles. "Manipulation? Can I remind you, you were a hacker who got himself into other people's computer systems and made them do what you wanted. You broke into the brain at NASA and wondered why you got arrested. Who bailed you out? I did. Me. Your *mother*."

"Mother?!" Croc explodes. "You almost told us too late! And couldn't even be bothered to tell me who my father is."

The room goes still. Mary struggles for words, but when they come, they hit like a thunderclap.

"I was raped," she whispers.

Silence swallows the room.

Stan pushes two plates of diced potatoes and eggs towards Lakshmi and Reyansh. "My new dish. Crispy potatoes with bell peppers, chopped onions, garlic, and paprika with eggs on top."

"I think Crocket is upset," Lakshmi says.

"Is mummy going away on the ships again?" Reyansh asks.

"No, she's making you a little brother or a sister."

"Do you have any spicy sauce?" Reyansh asks, after tasting.

"That ain't hot enough?" Stan says, rounding the counter. He lifts his fingers in a raised hand gesture that gets Croc's attention. Stan never says much, but when he does he is listened to. "Kids be a little concerned you be upset." He takes a bottle of brown sauce from a table and places it on the counter.

"This be as spicy as it gets here, if it works, and you eat everything, I might be able to find some ice cream."

Lakshmi tips the sauce on her plate and tastes it. She nods. "Good." She then tips a considerable amount more and mixes it in.

"That'll do it," Stan says, watching Reyansh copy.

Stan looks up at Croc, he may be giving him permission to continue, but his look instructs Croc to be mindful of the children.

"I'm getting married. I wanna tell my father. Who is my father, because it ain't you Stan, is it?" Croc says, sniffling.

Mary's voice trembles but grows steadier as she continues. "That man, Stan, most certainly is your father. That man stood by me. Kept me sane. Made sure I stayed in touch with all of you. You want to know what a father is? Look behind the grill. That's love. Pure love."

Tears streaming, Mary storms into the courtyard.

Croc clenches his fists, his own composure crumbling.

Before the tension can settle, or questions be answered, the outer door swings open. Two suited FBI agents stand there.

Ronni fixes them with a sharp look. "Ted, your timing is always the worst."

"The main door at the front was closed."

"It's always closed," she says, pointing to the internal door that leads to the ops room via reception. "Pick up a box and follow, Ted."

She takes a box, Ted and Lenny take boxes.

Kieron puts, an arm around Croc, "Your work doesn't go unnoticed noticed. Sometimes, Stan's does."

Croc walks towards Stan. "Sorry." He turns to his children. "Kids, I'll be back when I've fixed this up for them, then we'll go and get mummy."

"Yey," they cheer.

Croc and Kieron saddle up the rest of the gear and walk out, past the toilets and into the empty reception where Kieron pauses.

"Your new baby won't be here for a while. Your wedding won't be this week. But Bedřiška, who was one of us, was murdered on Wednesday. It's only Saturday. We're in a murder investigation, the FBI have arrived for a sit down. Let's talk after that."

In the ops room, Ronni places the box down, the others follow and she turns and addresses them. "We've got a problem."

"Just one?" Kieron quips.

"There's someone being held hostage in that house. Pretty sure that's an FBI thing, isn't it, Ted?" Ronni says.

8-29 SOMETIMES

Saturday, Day 5 - 0810hrs Miami

"Playbook page one: arrive when it's least convenient," Ronni teases.

"They have to teach you how to do that at Langley," Ted boasts, in a well-oiled inter-agency banter.

Ronni ignores him.

"Is CSCI licensed to investigate?" he asks.

"Under maritime law? To work at sea?"

"You're operating on US soil."

Ronni fires the picture of a hooded person in the middle of the room onto the large screen for Ted and Lenny.

"Yesterday, one of our cadets was helping to find a lost dog. No idea what's going on here, but it looks like she accidentally stumbled onto a hostage situation."

Ted looks at her, accusingly, suspicion flashing in his eyes. He feels like he's being played.

"I instantly thought: Bureau. Then remembered you were due in this morning. So I'm handing it straight over."

Ted snaps a photo of the screen.

"Looking for a lost dog?" he asks, knowing he's being played in.

"Called Chick. Owner's name is Betty. Lost at the Golden Glades Ocean Marina yesterday. She will be there for lunch should you wish to interview her."

"You investigate lost dogs?"

"Which license do we need?"

"Where's this property?"

"Next door to the Marina. Everglades Marina Mansion. Oh, and I'd check the pool."

"For the dog?" Lenny asks.

"No, Betty has the dog back. For hidden chemical containers in the deep end."

Ted nods, waiting.

"Shocked at seeing that," Ronni continues, "she backed away from the house and fell in the pool."

"The dog? The woman? Your agent?"

"Our agent."

"With her camera going, I hope?"

"As luck would have it, yes."

Ronni flicks through prepared pictures. The false base of the pool, then large jerry cans.

Ted looks at her.

"If they were to load a couple of boats with explosives, and drive them up Biscayne and into a ship at Dodge," Ronni starts, changing the screen to a picture of the jetty with two boats. "But the kid is only a cadet. There's probably a simple explanation. She was shocked."

"Can we talk to her?" Ted asks.

"No idea where she is. No school today; it's Saturday."

Ronni changes to the last picture, the one of the Ghost standing on the patio.

"Who is that?" Lenny asks.

"No idea. I wasn't there, and she never said that he looked just like the killer of the victim at the Blue Motel. Or I would've told you that."

"What are the chances?" Ted asks.

"Fifty to one."

"I think I'll do this by the book. Write it up, find a judge, get a warrant signed, book a team, then investigate."

"That sounds like a plan, Ted," Ronni says.

"And it's all mine," he mocks.

"Do you want breakfast before you go?"

"Maybe coffee."

In the stockroom of the diner, at the back of the grill, Stan is still talking Mary down.

"It's all good. Everything's out now. Valve open, pressure released."

"I ain't a steam cooker," she retorts.

"You were. Now you can be one of them new multi-thermomix cookers, with controlled heat."

"You saying I'm not controlled?"

"I'm saying you're totally in control now."

"Croc's after answers. He's changed."

"He's grown up. He's a man now," Stan says.

"You know what the next question's gonna be? Who raped me?"

"That question doesn't have an answer."

"Stan, you can't see the problem."

"'Cause I choose to close my eyes sometimes."

"What do these guys do? Investigate!"

"So they'll look."

"Then what's gonna happen?"

"Can't change the past," Stan says, heading for the door back to the grill.

"What if he finds the guy? Croc's an angry young man, and Billy just loves killing bad people."

The diner now has a few breakfast customers sitting at tables, and Macey is taking orders. Kieron and the two children are still sitting at the end of the counter, but safely out of earshot. Ronni, Ted, and Lenny are at the hatch end, where the coffee pot is. Izzy is filling take-out cups, and they've heard Mary's last line.

"Who likes killing bad people?" Ted asks.

"My old dad," Stan says. "Always wanted to put the world right. God rest his soul."

Croc enters from the yard.

"You ain't this guy's dad, are you?" Ted asks the young man.

"No, he's my dad," Croc says, putting his arm around Stan.

"Don't I know you?" Ted asks.

"Yeah. You arrested me a long time ago. I was the kid who broke into NASA."

"You work here?"

"No. I live abroad now. Just home for a wedding."

Ted and Lenny leave with their coffee, and Mary comes out, sheepishly looking at Croc.

"Sorry, Mom. I was out of order. Sometimes I get a little hot-headed," Croc says, and she flings her arms around him.

"Me too. Now listen, we've got the wedding covered, son. Reception's here. Stan's doing the catering."

"That ain't how Indian weddings work, Mom."

"You ain't Indian."

"So, to not upset either family, we want to get married on a ship. The cruise industry brought us together, we want it to marry us," Croc says.

"Fine by me. And by the way, I love my truck. The pink thing. 'Might even take up golf."

"It ain't a golf cart. It's a proper vehicle. Fast enough to get you a ticket."

"Proper, eh?" she asks, eyeing it. "I might need some instruction on how to fly it."

"Your grandkids can do that."

"They can, can they?"

Izzy approaches Macey by the dance floor to take the first of the orders from her.

"Stan's back, grill's hot."

"How is Croc?"

"A mess."

"What is he going to be like if it's not his kid she's carrying?"

"It has to be."

8-30 STARS

Saturday, Day 5 - 0930hrs Miami

Croc is plugging in the last of the monitors in Vinnie's security room when he hears the whir of an approaching motor. "I know that sound."

"One you thought you'd never hear again," Dwight Ritter says, as he powers in on his electric chair.

"Still got the gun fitted underneath?"

The nozzle of an Uzi rises and edges forward from low between the wheels.

"Don't point that at me."

The nozzle retracts.

"Looking good," Dwight says.

Kieron enters from the ops room.

"The kids done a great job," Dwight congratulates.

"Come and see this," Kieron encourages.

Dwight powers next door, Croc follows him. "Wow. Just how I planned it."

Kieron laughs.

"Gonna finish up, then head back to India," Croc says.

"Why so fast? I thought you'd come for the holidays," Dwight asks.

"I'm not sure CSCI is a good fit for a family man."

"How'd you come to that conclusion?"

"I don't like Prisha being out on the front line."

"My wife never minded that, but she didn't like it when I came home with no legs."

"What's the prognosis, big man?" Kieron asks.

"I got the weekend off. Monday, they'll see if they've healed enough to put the legs back on."

"Then you'll be running around?" Croc asks.

"I'm gonna be back here, getting you to do loads of extra things before you go remote."

"See? You all use people."

"Why? You think you're different from everyone else in the world and don't need to work?" Dwight asks.

"I don't mean that."

"Good, because that's the kind of thing a rich kid would say."

"I offered to give all the money back," Croc says. "I just want to get married, have a family, and be normal."

"Then you need a job," Dwight explains. "Normal people have a job."

"Croc and Prisha want to get married on a ship. I reckon we can lean on Creedon to sort that out," Kieron says.

"A ship?"

"Ships brought us together. It's the perfect venue."

"But now you want to leave them all behind?" Dwight asks, turning to Kieron. "Who are we gonna send out to take over Mumbai?"

"Bukka and Prisha will still run the refrigeration business. You don't need an office there." Croc walks to the window overlooking the yard, watching the two children kicking a ball around with Macey and Izzy.

"Sounds to me like being a dad is scaring the pants off you," Dwight says. "It did me."

Dwight and Croc built the first CSCI headquarters together, and he can berate Croc as one old partner to another.

"I've got two kids," Croc says.

"Ain't the same as having your own. When your wife is pregnant, it sends you crazy with responsibility," Dwight says, wheeling up next to Croc. "Nice kids. You've done well by them. But you're about to become a real dad. That's freaky."

"You ever get to speak with your daughter?" Croc asks Dwight.

"No. The dragon's poisoned her view of me. She's gone. I guess the real job you've got is making sure you treat those two right when the new one barges into their world and steals their mother."

Kieron stays back as Dwight connects with Croc in a way he cannot. All three are completely different fathers. Croc turns to Kieron.

"You ever speak with your daughter?"

"Yep, but not enough. She's not really my daughter."

"She is," Dwight insists.

"I was a temporary fix after she lost her family in the war in Syria."

Slowly, Croc processes everything that was said, then fist bumps Dwight.

"Now we've got a job," Dwight announces.

"Arrange our wedding?" Croc asks, eagerly.

"Okay. Two jobs."

"But the ship is going to arrange your wedding. Check out my new idea: I want a screen as a table."

"A table?"

"Flat screen as a table top. So it could be a map, or the plan of a village, or a ship's deck. An aerial view of anything."

"I like the idea of a second big screen that makes the brain work differently," Kieron adds.

Croc nods. "Anything else?"

"As you've asked, I want a star wall."

That changes the tone of the conversation, and the moment's silence is broken by a question.

"Without names, like the CIA Memorial Wall at Langley?" Kieron asks.

"We don't need to hide names, do we?"

"No," Croc says, solemnly, still thinking. "Bedřiška Kossoff. Died in action at the Miami Biscayne Blue Motel."

"Don't think we need the details, Croc," Dwight says.

"Where?" Kieron asks.

"The blank wall, opposite the security screens in Vinnie's room," Dwight replies.

"No one will see it there. How about the reception? There's nothing planned for that area, and we won't be having a desk with someone sitting behind it, waiting for customers to come by."

"Sure. But is that the right image? They come in with a job, and they see that people die when they engage with us."

"That's why they employ us," Kieron says. "Crime is dangerous. Officers die. It's why they pay bullet money."

"That's why we've got to get Prisha out!" Croc says.

"Can you smell panic again?" Dwight asks, in military banter that reduces Croc's request for concern.

Kieron sniffs.

"I've smelled worse fear. I don't think anyone's quite shit their pants yet."

Croc smiles. He likes being the centre of banter.

8-31 WHO LET THE GHOSTS OUT?
Saturday, Day 5 - 1000hrs Miami

"Good morning, Vietnam!" Big Dogg shouts from his hire boat, steered by KooBaa. Two of his street soldiers crouch at the bow, ready to board a moored boat off the shore of the Golden Glades Ocean Marina in North Beach, out on Biscayne Bay. The stationary boat has fishing rods propped at each end, a weak attempt at disguising its purpose. The guards on board, however, are fast asleep. Dogg scoops up a bucket of water and drenches them.

"Are you two high?" he growls.

"No, boss," one mumbles, shaking off the water.

"The whole of Miami can smell it!"

"It's spooky out here in the dark, boss," the other says defensively.

"Fish are beaching themselves thinking they can walk. You're supposed to be watching."

"Watching what? Nothing's happening," the first guard retorts.

"I'll tell you what's happening: this place is gonna get swatted by Five-O and the suits."

"We can go home?"

"Get in here!" Dogg demands.

The exchange of guards is swift, and KooBaa's boat powers away. Dogg shouts a final order over his shoulder: "Unless Five-O moves you on, I want a live stream of the show!"

The mansion remains quiet, with no signs of SWAT.

Further along the waterfront, Dogg's second unit watches from a rental car in the marina parking lot. An SUV pulls up behind it, and Dogg's men, Emo and DRK, step out to relieve the night-shift pair, who climb into the rental and leave. Raul guns the SUV down the road, stopping a few hundred yards past the target mansion, where another white rental van is parked. The guards there are swapped, and Raul drives off again, heading home.

KooBaa's boat approaches a landing area to rendezvous with the SUV. Big Dogg leaps to the dock and climbs into the vehicle, followed by the two men from the fishing boat. The pungent aroma of their earlier activities fills the cabin.

"You been watching the detectives, or getting anaesthetised?" Raul, the SUV driver jokes.

"Ghosts out there, man. Pirate ghosts. Dark, misty, and spooky," one of the guards slurs.

"Good thing nothing happened, or you wouldn't have seen it," Raul mutters, keeping his eyes on the road.

Big Dogg is already on his phone. "Fresh teams, no movement in the house. No sign of SWAT."

"Did you see Prisha?" Croc's voice crackles over the speakerphone.

Dogg looks to his men for answers.

"The marina café was open for breakfast. I went in for coffee, and she was serving," Raul replies.

Meanwhile, in Vinnie's security room, Dogg's face fills a central screen. Croc stands transfixed, his gaze darting across the wall of monitors, many showing live feeds of the Everglades Marina Mansion in North Beach.

"Can you fix a camera on the marina so I can watch Prisha?" Croc asks.

"Do we look like an AT&T crew?" Dogg snaps. "My boys are the eyes. They can walk in to eat anytime."

"Have them do that. Feed them up. Ain't nothing happening in the house, and I can see that from here."

In the ops room next door, Dwight, Ronni, and Kieron analyse photos from their night raid.

"Yeah, Big Dogg. Let them take a break," Dwight says loudly, hoping to ease Croc's nerves.

"The FBI should be handling this. Prisha should be back here with the kids," Croc yells, still pacing.

"Let her finish the lunch shift. She might overhear something about the ship attack. We need that intel before we pull her out. The FBI might stop this attack, but we need to prepare for another attempt," Kieron responds.

"Ted's probably still working out how to type his report. Without it, he can't request a warrant or a tactical team. The raid won't happen until this afternoon. And since it's Saturday, most of the team will dodge the call to watch a game," Ronni explains.

Croc appears at the doorway, unimpressed. "You mean they're with their kids?" he snaps.

"It doesn't happen as fast as in the movies," Ronni replies.

"And how do you know that?" Kieron teases, attempting to pry into her past.

"It might not happen until tonight," she admits.

"We could go in now," Croc suggests. "Prisha could be here, enjoying time with Mary and planning our wedding. Isn't that what you two are supposed to be doing in there, while I'm stuck building your tech den?"

"We protect ships. We did the right thing handing this over to the FBI," Kieron says, firmly.

Izzy enters the room. "The kids are taking Granny for a test drive in her new ride. They expect us all to be there."

Croc looks ready to repeat his mantra, but Kieron cuts him off with a glance. Ronni and Kieron walk through the security room, joined by Croc, and stop in the reception area. The space is clean and minimal, with pastel lilac walls. Kieron gestures to two walls.

"The Memorial Wall has to be here and here," he says. "Using the wall by the washrooms would be

123

disrespectful. If we use the wall in security, no one will see it."

"Two walls," Ronni suggests.

"But they should all be together."

"CSCI members on the private wall; allies on the public wall," Dwight adds.

Kieron touches the agency wall. "Hunter and Bedřiška go here."

Ronni lingers, her hand pressed against the wall as though mourning.

Dwight places his hand on the public wall. "And my old buddy Benny here."

"Who's Benny?" she asks softly.

"A data analyst. He would've been in our ops room."

Ronni looks at Kieron for clarity. "What happened?"

"Benny was a solo cruiser helping us track a killer. He was so good, the killer took him out," Kieron explains. "She even killed Sally, the ship's photographer."

"She? A female serial killer?" Ronni asks, inferring such a thing is rare.

"Yeah. Technically she was not a serial killer. They are normally men. She was a spree killer," Kieron explains, moving his hand to Benny's proposed position. He then moves along one. "Sally. Sally was a pointless cruel killing. The ship's photographer."

"She killed everyone to get what she wanted," Dwight explains.

"What did she want?" Ronni asks.

"This job," Dwight replies bluntly.

The room falls silent. Croc, Macey, and Izzy stand quietly by the washrooms, absorbing the gravity of CSCI's history.

"People do die," Croc murmurs, following Dwight and Kieron to the diner.

8-32 PINKMOBILE
Saturday, Day 5 - 1000hrs Miami

Raul pulls up outside the diner in the SUV. Big Dogg and his night shift soldiers jump out and look at the pink Tuk-tuk framed perfectly by the opening in the scaffolding that surrounds the building which is edged with festive lights.

Croc, Dwight, Kieron, Izzy, and Macey all stand outside the diner watching Mary being shown the vehicle's controls by the two children.

"Mummy takes us to school in her one," Lakshmi says.

"That school in India, right?" Mary barks, from the sidewalk, a safe distance away.

"Get in nanny," Reyansh shouts.

Mary moves forward and sits in the passenger seat, but they climb around her and push her to the driver's seat.

"Those children wrap her around their finger in a way we never could. I love them," Izzy says to Croc.

"You should have some."

"Fat chance," Izzy says. "I'm married to work."

"Heads up; this place will consume you."

"Only when there's an investigation."

125

"Sis, you invented the training. It gonna get bigger and you're inviting the devil in. Why?"

"We want to help those who served find a new meaning."

"That ain't who you got. These cadets have never served. They never would, they would run from trouble."

"Dis is the first course. It'll be right."

"You'll become old and single before you know it"

"Then I'll need to find me a single dad with a ready-made family."

"One whose wife went off in the line of duty and never came back?" Croc fears.

"You gotta stop saying that."

"Yeah. I know. I ain't gonna be one of those single dads."

Mary screams as the Tuk-tuk jolts forward. Croc sees that at last she is in the driving seat. Raul runs to the SUV and moves it away.

"Its instant!"

"You press the pedal and it does what it's told. Kids, jump out. Watch nanny from the sidewalk wid me."

"Who's coming with me on my test drive?" Mary shouts.

No one steps forward.

"Big Dogg, get in here. Show them what real men are made of."

"Real men don't sit in a pink mobile."

"Real men do what they told!"

"No. I ain't getting in that."

He is mocked by his men, and threatened by the look from Mary. Big Dogg steps in as everyone's cameras are up taking pictures.

"You the black Ken and Barbie," Raul shouts.

They whip off at speed.

"That might not have been a good idea," Croc offers, looking at his smart phone, which has the street security cameras on. He can watch her speed around the building. "Clear the way. She's coming back!"

The tuk-tuk skids to a stop. Dogg is nodding slowly.

"That is fast!"

Mary sits back and breathes out, but Dogg is already on the pavement.

"She might get the hang of it, but her foot's a little heavy on the gas."

"It can accelerate, right?" Croc says.

Dogg agrees.

"Where's Ronni?" Macey asks.

Croc and Dogg look around, but she is not amongst them. Macey goes back in and heads towards the washrooms. Croc follows, worried that something is wrong. Dogg follows, because he is instinctively drawn to trouble.

Just beyond the washrooms, Ronni is sitting on the floor in reception, staring at the blank Memorial Wall. Macey is quiet and looks on in fear. Dogg cannot get a handle on what is going on. He shrugs, requesting information.

"It's our memorial wall," Izzy says.

"Ain't nothing there," Dogg says.

"Hunter, Bedřiška, and Georgie," Croc explains.

"There's someone else here," Macey says.

Ronni smiles. "His name's Curt."

They all stay respectfully quiet, and Izzy and Croc edge back into the space outside the washrooms with Dogg.

"Heavy," Dogg says.

"The other wall is going to be for those who worked with CSCI, but were not staff."

"Which wall do I go on?"

"Hopefully neither," Croc says.

"And this wall, opposite the washroom. Is that for the turds we shot."

Croc looks at the wall. "No, we'd need a bigger wall. Just for the ones Bedi wasted."

Macey joins them and edges them back towards the team at the tuk-tuk. "She needs some time."

"Who's Curt?" Dogg asks, as they pass through the diner.

"Who is Ronni?" Croc adds.

8-33 LUNCH TIME
Day 5 - 0930hrs Miami

The sun is fully featuring the tables laid outside Golden Glades Ocean Marina, and they are filling fast. Prisha may have started in service on the cruise ships but she quickly moved to the reception team which required less physical exertion. She found last night exhausting, and then all the guests were inside. Today, they are outside, and the walk to deliver drinks and food is that much further. She also has to run orders to the boats berthing in the marina. The one table she wants to focus on is not technically within her service area, and the only way she can get near to them is to come back that way empty handed.

"Sofia. You want me to take dishes back with me?" she shouts to the other server.

Sofia is only too glad of the help, but before either can engage, Abi has lifted her plate and holds it up to Prisha with total disregard for the server. Within seconds, Prisha is loaded with plates and approaching The Ghost at the top of the table. On one side of him is Heather Frost, a woman nearer to his age than most around the table. She is a sophisticated but arty lady. The other side is Wanda.

"Would you mind taking a picture?" Wanda asks, offering her smartphone to Prisha.

With a smile that would be compulsory on a cruise ship, Prisha agrees, putting all the plates down in one neat stack on the next table which is empty. Prisha takes the camera and frames the whole table. Then another one. Wanda puts her hand up for the return of the phone, but Prisha checks her work.

"No. One more, I need to do it again. Move in closer and smile," she indicates, but she is concentrating on dropping the picture from Wanda's phone to her own. Her own phone bleeps. "One moment." She looks at her phone and pretends to disregard the message, but what she has done is accepted the picture. Then before retrieving the stacked plates, she moves the condiments back to the centre of the table, leaving a miniature microphone bug. She lifts her pile to go.

"Can we order ice cream?" Carol asks.

"I'll have your server come right over," Prisha says, leaving.

"We're agreed, Christmas Day," The Ghost says.

The whole table agrees. Prisha hears no more, but she knows the team in the van will be receiving everything they say, and Croc and others will be listening in the ops room. Her work is done.

After dumping the plates at the hatch, Prisha pulls up a bunch of dessert menus and hands them to Sofia. "They're asking for these."

Prisha picks up her next order from the pass, looks at the ticket, and heads out taking it to a boat on the marina.

In the ops room, Croc turns around to Kieron and Ronni. "Whatever it is, it's going down on Christmas Day."

"That doesn't make sense," Ronni offers. "There won't be any ships berthed at Dodge Island on Christmas Day."

"Then the target is not a ship," Kieron adds.

The picture of the group around the table pings onto the large screen.

"That's Wanda, Carol, and Abi," Billy says, pointing them out. "Just three. Don't know the others."

"Big Dogg's team are reporting the FBI arriving at the mansion," Croc announces.

Seeing the agents approaching, The Ghost excuses himself from the table early and heads inside to the washroom. Prisha is on her way back to the building with dishes, and follows him in. She puts the dishes at the hatch and heads around the bar. The Ghost has bypassed the toilets and gone out of the other door. She stands at the side of the building watching him go to another boat. She speaks into her smart phone.

"The Ghost has left and is heading to another boat. Big one. Blue hull and a white cockpit type driving area."

"Roger that," KooBaa says, urging the single-lever, dual-function power control forward. His boat is still sitting out in the bay and his twin outboard motors have dropped into gear and begin to power the boat forward. Two twenty-six foot Fluid 780 rigid inflatable boats approach from at speed heading for the jetty of the mansion. "Two police patrols inbound to the mansion. I'm on our man." KooBaa is moving in the same direction as The Ghost's boat, but offset enough not to be suspected.

Prisha has crossed back through the restaurant, and observes Ted and three other agents offer their badge to the ten diners from the mansion. No one moves. They all stay very calm and inquisitive.

"FBI Special Agent Edward Cronkite. Sorry to disturb your festive celebrations, but we have a warrant to search Marina Mansion, grounds, and pool."

"Its not our house," Heather says.

"I understand you are renting and I don't wish to inconvenience you, but if you have personal effects inside, you might wish to be there."

"How do you search a pool?" Abi asks.

"With divers, mam. Divers and a crane."

The ten collect their things. Sofia edges in quickly with a card machine to take payment.

"I'll get this, we can split it later," Wanda says, and they all leave in a very civilised manner.

Prisha continues her report. "They are heading back to the house with the agents. Very calm, not at all like worried terrorists. I think you need the man in the boat."

Uncomfortably close to Dogg's two men in the rental car, Emo and DRK, the side fence of the mansion has been taken down. A crane is being reversed up to the pool, and divers drop into the water.

The two inflatable patrol boats settle back into the water and drift up to the two small leisure craft on the mansion's jetty. The police board the jetty and begin to search the moored craft.

SWAT officers are checking every outhouse in the grounds.

The drive at the front of the house and the road are filled with three black Lenco BearCat Humvees, a GM sedan, and an explorer SUV. It is a much bigger presence than was at the Miami Biscayne Blue Motel for Bedřiška's body.

"Can we clear now, 'blood'?" Emo asks, using his cell from the car, that is so close to the FBI team working the pool that it is almost part of the operation. "The feds nearly climbed over us to take the fence out."

"Negative, Emo," Kieron replies. "You will report back to us quicker than they will. When they leave, collect Prisha and return."

"Ten-four."

DRK steps out of the rental. "Going for some relief and eats." He walks towards the marina.

8-34 SEARCH WARRANT

Inside the Marina Mansion house, Ted offers the warrant to the women again.

"Why do we wanna see it? We don't live here. Carry on," Heather encourages. She appears to be a leader.

"Hey. That's my stuff, its not from the house." Wanda screams, following an FBI agent who has her knapsack. "You can't open that."

The agent looks towards Ted. Ted turns to Heather with the warrant.

"Sure you don't want to look at this?"

"No," Heather says. "What's the point?"

Wanda snatches her sack from the agent.

"Wanda. They have a warrant," Heather states.

"To search the house. Not our stuff," Wanda insists.

"We're in the house, we can be searched. Don't worry, we have nothing to hide."

The agent takes the sack back and tips all of Wanda's things onto a table.

"I'd like a female officer to look through my things!"

The agent puts the bag down and takes a step back. He has instantly complied. With a wave, Ted assigns a female officer and the male agent rejoins the general search.

"What's your name?"

"Heather Mathers," she answers, handing Ted her ID and a business card.

"Water colour instructor," Ted reads. "You teach painting?"

"Yeah. This is my art class. I'm working on a ship over the holidays, and a few of my pupils decided to come to Miami early."

"Working over the holidays?" Ted asks.

"As required. The schedule is up to the entertainment manager."

"On the ship?"

"Yes. I report to the 'ents' manager."

"What do you paint?"

"It's not a case of what I paint. It is more what can I get the guests to paint."

Ted gestures that he wants more. "I ain't ever been on a cruise, or painted."

"If I have people who have never painted, I might start with three circles and turn them into a duck."

"And you get paid for that?"

"I am a guest employee. I don't get paid, but I am allowed to further my business there. Guests will sign up to my classes online, like these students once did."

"An online course to turn three balls into a duck. How do I join?"

"I also do seascapes and landscapes."

"You do portraits?"

"Sometimes. I'm not really a portrait person."

"Is that why you put a bag over their heads."

"What?"

"There's an internal security camera here. Because we have the place under surveillance as a possible link in a major drug smuggling syndicate, we dropped in on the camera. We saw someone in a chair, with a hood over their head. Kind of rang alarm bells. We had to move in."

"Hood? When?"

"Last night. We had noticed two boats outside for days and had started to take interest."

"A hood. No. We had a meal," Heather stops. "The girls played games."

"Games?"

"They played a wizard-like game."

"A Harry Potter-type thing?" Ted delves.

"It's called Keeper of the Keys," Wanda explains.

Heather lets Wanda take over.

"You've attacked us because we had some drinks and played a game?"

"We have not attacked anyone, but your stance has been noted. Please tell me more."

"Someone is blindfolded and sits on a chair, and the others sit around in a circle. Under the centre chair is an object we have to steal. It should be keys, but it can be anything."

"That's a game?"

"It doesn't sound so much fun when you're sober, but yes. If the blindfolded player hears someone trying to steal the keys, they name them."

"And you're going on this cruise?"

"We all are."

"When?"

"Tuesday," Abi says, as she joins the group around Ted. She shows Ted her booking. "If the keys are taken, the players all hold their hands behind their backs and the middle person has to take their hood off and guess who stole the keys."

"These two didn't explain that part. Now I see the fun," Ted says, walking away and towards the bifold doors and out into the garden.

The crane is lifting the jerry cans from the water. One has already been cut open.

"We can get this tested, sir, but I think they're just filled with concrete. There might be something hidden inside, but I doubt it. It's a way of filling in the deep end. Many modern pools are all the same depth. Patio pools, no deep end. Especially in rentals. A pool is more fun if it's the same depth."

Ted turns back to the women.

"I'm sorry we disturbed you ladies. Even more sorry we have hit this drug drop when it's not being used," Ted says. "We're gonna get out quickly and hope they won't know we were here."

Wanda and Abi deliberately look at the damage the FBI have caused outside.

"Heather, look."

"We put a deposit down against damage," Heather says.

"That'll all be made good before you leave."

"You mean you will be disturbing our vacation?"

"I'm giving you things you can paint."

"That game you liked, officer. Take the idea home. It's sometimes played at wife swapping parties," Wanda says, to tease him.

8-35 SECURITY ROOM

Watched by Kieron and Bill, Ronni ends a phone call that she has kept to herself. They are keen to know all the details as it was with Special Agent Edward Cronkite, or Ted, as she knows him.

"Ted's not happy. He says there was nothing at the house and they are tourists."

"No they're not," Billy says. "Bedřiška's been killed."

"They are part of an art class and all about to get on a cruise together. Tuesday."

The mention of an art class causes Macey to show interest. She was helping her brother Croc create his magic with the technology by holding a wire he is feeding under a desk in the ops centre, but he is now on his own. Macey became very well known in art circles when she was needed as a plant on a ship while the team investigated art theft and forgery on another cruise line.

"Three of them are on a course here to be security officers," Croc says.

"Art class. I should be there," Macey says. There was a time that her hair was always up in a bun, with paint brushes through it like a sea urchin, but not so much while she has been busy with the move into the new building. Her chance to paint has been limited, but she has been promised her own exhibition area.

"Ted said he couldn't arrest them for threatening to go on vacation over the holidays," Ronni explains.

"I don't care what Ted thinks, something is going down, and it's planned for Christmas Day," Kieron states. "Why two boats?"

137

"For going out to look back at the shore and painting it. They go off hire on Sunday evening."

"I don't buy it," Billy says.

"Why would anyone want to paint the shore?" Macey adds.

"I agree. They don't. The Ghost who pretended to be Creedon vanished from lunch as the FBI swooped in," Kieron says.

"Ted doesn't know that," Ronni adds.

"Where is The Ghost now?"

"In the wind," Dwight says. "KooBaa lost him on land. He left the boat by a market and vanished in the crowd. I'm waiting for an update."

"KooBaa should be careful, Bedřiška was killed tailing that guy," Billy says.

"If they are joining a ship, and planning something for Christmas Day, it is happening at sea, not here," Ronni states.

"Are those security candidates here at CSCI just to figure out how to get gear onto a ship?" Billy asks, making everyone think.

"We have to be on that ship," Kieron.

"Which ship?" Macey asks.

"Us boarding will cause panic. Is that what they want? Us doing their dirty work?"

"So we let it sail with the potential of unknown danger?" Billy asks, rhetorically.

"Did Ted say which ship they were joining?" Dwight asks.

"No," Ronni says, redialling on her smartphone.

"Five ships in Dodge on Tuesday," Croc adds, studying the Port of Miami schedule on a screen.

"If Ted won't tell us, get the passenger lists of all ships leaving Tuesday."

"Ted," Ronni says into her phone. "Are you dictating that report?" She holds the phone away as she mouths to her team. "He's not happy." After giving him a moment she goes back to the phone. "Ted, do you have the names of everyone in that art class and what ship they are joining?"

"Why?"

They all heard that shout from Ted.

"Because Wanda, Abi, Carol, and maybe others that are on our cadet course training to be ship's security officers, might be on it. Does that help you excuse actions in your report?" Ronni stops, looks at her phone, then turns to the others. "He hung up. I think he's on the way here."

"How do we get on that ship along with this art group?" Kieron asks, looking at Macey.

"Don't ask me, I can't sign up for an art class. They'll recognise me."

"You've been waiting tables and serving all week. Have they recognised you?"

"No. Coz they're not artists. They're enthusiastic amateurs."

"You just ain't that famous, sis," Croc enjoys adding.

"I have pieces in galleries all over, and was in all the art press," she fires back at her brother.

"That is a good point. Why did they not recognise a newly heralded American artist recently discovered by the cruise industry?" Ronni asks.

"They may not be artists," Macey starts. "But someone on the ship will blow my cover. You need another excuse to get more than just me on the ship."

"How? They know every one of us. Almost as if that might have been their intention. Now, they see us coming," Croc says.

The door opens and in walks Big Dogg with Izzy and Prisha.

"Look who's home," Izzy announces.

Croc hugs Prisha. "That's your last ever mission, mummy."

"You two still wanna get married on a ship?" Kieron asks.

"Yes," they say together.

"How about Christmas Day?"

8-36 JURISDICTION
Saturday

"Saturday night gonna be jive night. This dance floor is going to be alive. But for now, I'll allow you all to sit and eat without dancing," Mary says, standing in the aisle between tables, handing out menus.

Izzy, Macey, Croc and Prisha sit at one table. Dogg, Ronni, and Billy are at another, and Kieron sits at a third with Dwight in his chair. The two children, Reyansh and Lakshmi sit with Stan at the counter.

The familiar doorbell chime announces Ted and Lenny, who walk down and sit at the table for four in the square.

"Explain," Ted asks Ronni, looking at the menu. "Let's see if what you got is good enough for my children's father to keep his job."

"A man we are calling The Ghost impersonates cruise CEO Daniel G Creedon and warns of a terrorist attack. Our agent Bedřiška follows that man away from Dodge and is found dead at the Miami Biscayne Blue Motel. The Ghost may have been driven away from Dodge by CSCI security candidate Wanda Renton, who you discovered at Everglades Marina Mansion in North Beach. You searched the property and found an art group boarding a ship on Tuesday for the holidays. A CSCI agent reported overhearing plans for something happening on Christmas Day. However, you found no evidence of wrongdoing."

"We don't get to go to sea."

"Which is why you are continuing a relationship with CSCI."

"No, we are investigating a murder. The tip you gave us gave us does not yet connect the two."

"Except Wanda Renton," Kieron says. "What ship is she getting onto?"

"Heather Frost is getting onto one of Creedon's ships, but it doesn't fly an American flag. Whilst we have a duty of care to American passengers, at this moment in time no crime that we are aware of has been committed by Miss Frost."

Macey holds up her cell phone, which shows a painting landscape painted by Heather Frost. "I disagree. Have you seen her paintings? Look."

"Do you have the names of all the artists at the mansion?" Kieron asks.

"Alleged artists," Macey adds.

Ted ports the list to Ronni's phone.

"That's Heather Frost's ship, and the names of those in her group. I don't have enough to detain Wanda Renton."

Ronni ports the list to Croc.

"Heather Frost is a registered travel agent, and she sells the cruises she appears on. She gets eight percent of the ten guests' booking fees. The American dream," Ted says.

"There's a reason for everything, and it's normally money," Billy says. "Money or power. Either way, they're fanatics."

"They're all on the same cruise. The ship's sold out, apart from a couple of suites," Croc announces gaining everyone's attention. "None of them has a wrap-sheet, although Wanda has been on a watch list. College stuff. Demonstrations and the usual campus trouble with local police. She has no criminal record."

"He's quick. We could do with him working on our system," Ted says.

"I am on your system," Croc says.

"Ignore that, he's messing with you. How can we work together, Ted?" Ronni says. "I'll give you the links; you can take the credit."

"The Russian woman, Bedřiška Kossoff, worked here. How do you know she followed someone?"

"Port authority security tapes. We'll give you the date and time stamps. You'll need to pull street cameras to see the journey between Dodge and the Miami Biscayne Blue Motel."

As they trade information, Kieron has walked away from the table and is on his smartphone.

"Daniel Creedon? It's Kieron at CSCI. Sorry to call you on a Saturday evening, but we need to be on your ship, Blue Sky, when it leaves here on Tuesday.

The suites if you have them available, and passenger and crew cabins. I need to take a team with interns on a training week over the holiday." He pauses to listen. Everyone is listening to him. "FBI? They are sitting right next to me, but they don't go to sea. Maybe we could meet for breakfast tomorrow."

Ted hears FBI and listens to the telephone conversation from then on.

"What's your plan?" Ted asks Kieron.

"Without causing panic on a ship," Ronni counters.

"By taking interns, they can be set training tasks like looking for terrorists, because we can't do it for real. But we can watch them, and direct them, while being there for Croc and Prisha's wedding."

"No," Croc says.

"I figure we may as well train a couple of kids while we're at your wedding."

"You use people," Croc reminds him.

"How about my mother. She will want to be there. And my brother, Bukka?" Prisha says.

"It's just an idea," Kieron says, and he excuses himself to go to the washroom. Ted follows him. They both walk past the toilet and into reception area.

"I figured you wanted to talk," Ted says.

"Yes. I could let this ship sail without us, but it feels wrong."

"I know what you mean, but I can't take a team away at Christmas just on a hunch, just as I can't arrest a bunch of kids for trying to be artists."

Kieron walks forward and touches the wall. "This is going to be our memorial wall. I can't believe Bedřiška is going to be on it. Hunter, Georgie, I guess I'll be there one day."

143

"Was that Ronni's idea?" Ted asks.

"No. I don't think so. Why?"

Ted nods, avoiding answering.

"She's only admitted to being a marine biologist who worked as a compliance officer on a ship, but I've seen her in action," Kieron says.

"Yeah. She was quite someone, so I'm told. I never made the grade for the agency, let alone a PooMoo."

"PooMoo?"

"Her husband died in service. She sat for days looking at the stars on the wall at Langley. Eventually they got her to leave, but she left the agency. Paramilitary Operations Officers, specialist CIA operatives, and she was special."

"I figured as much."

"I like it at the Bureau, and Florida is easy. She was bright, probably had a GPA of four. You need a three for basic service, and mine was a two. Look, I'm sorry your girl is dead, but there are no clues, and nothing for me to stop those kids going on their festive cruise."

"I get that. It's kinda why I need to go. The two girls I love the most are both on this wall, and one I almost fell for can't be on either."

Ted looks at the other walls, confused.

"Complicated story. I fell for a solo cruiser once and she was… strange."

"What's your plan?"

"I'm hoping Daniel Creedon allows us to put a team of interns on board for work experience. If I invite the whole group, but don't tell them where they're going, I think the three girls will stay with their planned holiday."

"It still doesn't mean they're terrorists, and how do you get a team on board?"

"A wedding. We are going to plan a wedding."

"I'll be waiting at the dock when you get back from your honeymoon."

"Do you have offices in the Dominican Republic or Jamaica?"

"No. Puerto Rico and Virgin Islands. That's it.."

"We're on our own then."

"Yeah," Ted says.

"With a wedding to plan."

"That's the bit you don't have to worry about."

8-37 THE LULL BEFORE

New Day. Sunday, Day 6 - 0900hrs Miami

Kieron and Daniel Creedon meet early for breakfast at the diner, and when the cruise CEO leaves he is charged with facilitating an evolving and dangerous plan. Kieron finishes his coffee, still thoughtful, but before he can escape to the ops room to think, Mary sits opposite him and he is nailed.

"Explain to me why a mother don't get invited to her son's wedding."

He has no answer.

"Or his sister's."

Kieron begins to realise that a real wedding has its own demands.

"Got it," he says. He rises and walks to an area of some safety.

"And that man Dwight; he been like a second father to that boy. Trained him up and straightened him out," she shouts.

"Got it." Kieron leaves before the problem gets bigger.

The rest of Sunday passed in a flash, unsure whether the excitement was Prisha shopping for a wedding dress with Macey and Izzy, or Mary tagging along because the mother of the bridegroom needs to look ultra-special.

Croc and Dwight took the children to see the Dolphins play the San Francisco 49ers at the square-shaped Hard Rock Stadium in Miami Gardens. The multi-purpose stadium has out-priced itself to many locals. As a boy Croc could not have dreamt of going there, but as a partner at CSCI he afforded seats in the 72 Club on the thirty-five yard line. Dwight had his legs back on, self-diagnosing and medicating because he was not going to a game in his chair. He was doing well, but the larger seats were perfect for him. Reyansh and Lakshmi will remember the included food and drinks as much as the football. Although the children did not fully understand the game, they enjoyed the atmosphere and entertainment. Both of them ended up with kit, although Lakshmi would have preferred the cheerleaders' white and marine blue uniform.

Ronni spent a quiet reflective day on her own, and Billy lurked around the diner doing a lot of what he never does much: thinking. He was missing Bedřiška. There were no workers at Palladium House. Stan was at the grill, but it was dormant. Vinnie had the run of the Palladium House, the new red hot spot in Little Tahiti and he carried a radio so he could listen to the game which he also had on many screens like a sports bar. He was in his element and was probably the only one who did not wish to be on the festive cruise. Vinnie was in a dream, examining the extensive changes to the building he had known and loved for many years. He enjoyed spying on the surrounding area and his yard by operating the movement feature of his new cameras, even though there was nothing but seagulls to focus on.

Monday, Day 7 - 0900hrs Miami

Monday the 21st December hangs as a day with confused purpose. If anyone was to count, there are only four days to Christmas and Croc and Prisha's wedding.

With the ops room and the security room both having the major fitting work finished, the carpenters are working in the yard, enjoying sunshine that blasts overhead at lunch time. Although still a classroom, morning training is a very light fun activity on self-defence techniques.

"These are simple but effective, so dangerous. Self-defence is never a game. Now I'm done for this year. But, before you go and have lunch, the boss is coming to see you," Billy shouts, calling a break.

While the cadets wait, they are drawn to the carpenter, who is making wooden stars.

"They for Christmas?" Nick, a student asks.

"No, they're for the memorial wall."

"For what? Dead people?"

Having heard the exchange, Wanda and Abi pay attention. "What's this?"

"Memorial Wall Stars, for those who died in service," the carpenter says.

147

Nick turns to try and catch Billy, but he has just gone into the diner. The door re-opens and Kieron enters the yard.

"Kieron. Are these for security people. Do security people die on ships?" Nick asks.

"It's a good question, and a fair one to ask," Kieron says, walking to the workbench, where the carpenter is polishing the first wooden star with a stain. "This one is for Hunter Witowski, the other founding partner of CSCI. He was killed in a diamond investigation off one of the islands in the Bahamas. The thief who took his life is now awaiting a death sentence in a Florida prison. The ship was sailing under an American flag, so he was brought here and handed over to the FBI."

"But there's a dozen stars."

"We need three on our CSCI wall. The other wall will be for ship's security workers, although we have not lost one of them yet."

"I'm pleased to hear that," Nick says.

"But there will be two stars up in there, for deputised crew or civilian agents."

"It's a dangerous job?"

"It's law enforcement at sea. Officers can die whichever service they are in, Nick, but crime is radically less at sea because there is a zero tolerance policy. Talking of which, I have a surprise change of plan for you. The course obviously includes practical hands-on units. At least one on a cruise ship. You will do shifts, you will get a credit, with the report written up by the ship's own head of security. It will help you find a job placement at the end."

"That's great."

"Kind of expected, no?" Wanda says, making little of it.

"We were always breaking up this week for the holidays. That's happening now. Schools out. Back next year on the third of January."

There is a cheer, which Kieron dampens down.

"Two more things: We are going to have a glass of spiced orange and a slightly alcoholic version is available for those not driving. When the engraver is done, we are going to toast my buddy Hunter, and put his star on the wall. Please join me; his wife and baby will be joining us."

They all agree. The carpenter hands the polished and stained wooden star to the engraver and that in itself has substance.

"Respect.'" Nick says.

"I can announce the first internship placement opportunity. Now, it is awkward timing, deliberately. It's not for everyone, and do not feel compelled to take this one up. There will be more next year."

"Next year. This year has only a couple of weeks left," Nick observes.

"Exactly. There is no pressure on anyone to do this. If you have plans for the holidays, continue with them and take up the next placement."

"When is this one?" Carol asks.

"Over the holidays. We think that the first one may start tomorrow."

"Where?" Wanda asks.

"Tomorrow?" Nick says, surprised.

"Could be anywhere. We deliberately don't tell you because this industry is about going away to the unknown. There will be other chances we fit into the course, and you will be able to catch up on what you miss."

"If it's over the holidays, we won't miss anything here," Nick says, computing.

"As Izzy negotiates all the chances next year, we will post the dates. Just dates, this industry doesn't care where it sends you. You are working on a ship that moves about the globe every day of the year. Destination is a lottery, that's the job you are in. That is why having a passport is conditional of joining this course. You have passports, so if you're ready to fly somewhere and genuinely have no plans for the holidays, please go and see Izzy in the ops room now."

"We're going on a ship for Christmas?" Nick asks, eagerly looking around.

All the others appear quite stunned, most of them muttering that they cannot go.

"It is not a holiday. It will be work. Maybe night shifts, because you will have to work shifts. Night shifts are the easiest," Kieron adds.

"But we don't have to go, right? Because I have plans," Wanda checks.

"Wanda, I will miss your challenging questions, but no. You don't. I respect your plans. You will definitely get practical experience early next year. You're a great candidate."

"Er, I don't think I can go," Craig, another of the students says. "My dad's in a home and I need to go see him. But, I'll be around most of the holidays if anyone is here and wants to meet up."

"Vinnie said he might cook up a big turkey roast. I think he would like some friends. Class is done for this year, back here next year on January the third. Well done, and merry Christmas."

8-38 WEDDING PLANNER
New Day. Tuesday, 22nd December, Day 8 - 0900hrs Miami

A steady flow of guests streams down the gangway, having completed their holiday, each carrying enough baggage to make boarding a challenge for those arriving. Although their larger cases have been taken to the collection area, the load in hand is still substantial.

At the foot of the gangway, Nick and Craig wait with small bags, looking overwhelmed by both the size of the ship and the throngs of people disembarking. Neither has cruised before, and they are stunned by the sight.

Kieron arrives, spinning his small suitcase to a stop and jolting the two young cadets out of their daze.

"Two of you."

"I cleared it with Izzy last night. My dad said go. He will be alone, but he says he hates Christmas and he has his TV. Which is all he has the rest of the year," Craig says.

"Glad to have you Craig. Now, let's get us on board."

"The officer said that we have to wait for all the guests to leave," Nick says.

Kieron nods, but leaves to approach the officer at the bottom of the gangway, who uses their radio back to the ship.

"He just gets stuff done, doesn't he?" Craig says.

151

"Yeah," Nick agrees, seeing the stream of leaving guests stop at the top of the gangway. "Wow."

When the gangway is clear, Kieron urges them to follow him up. "We wait at the top here. Our cruise cards are on their way."

When they settle by the desk just inside the open cargo door, the guests recommence their descent to land.

"This is going to be fun, only two of you."

"Is Billy, or any of the other instructors coming?" Nick asks.

"The whole of CSCI is here for a wedding. Not to look after you two. But, as there were only two of you, I got you on our ship so we can look after you," Kieron enthuses.

"Who is getting married?" Craig asks. "You?"

"No," Kieron laughs, but his attention is drawn by two approaching female officers in white uniforms.

"Commander Philips, sir. I'm Officer Dizzy Martel. Assistant Hotel Manager. Welcome aboard. This is Candice Wenger; she is our wedding planner."

"Pleased to meet both of you."

"Would you pass by reception and register a card?"

"I will, Dizzy and then I will introduce our two trainee interns here, Nick Gold, and Craig Anciano to security. But Candice, I dare not involve myself in any wedding arrangements. The bride and her two maids of honour will be here before midday."

"No worries sir. Their suites are ready."

A wedding planner is essentially an expert with extensive knowledge of the wedding industry, coordinating everything from caterers and florists to dressmakers, entertainers, and themed event designers. They can arrange the perfect transport to the venue, whether it's a horse and carriage or a vintage car, and manage the publicity around the wedding, which can be a top priority for some couples. Personal touches like hair and makeup require careful pre-planning, as does speechwriting - a commonly overlooked detail that can go disastrously wrong.

For most people, organising a major event is a once-in-a-lifetime experience. If weddings were a TV game show, one team would win, another would lose, and every misstep would be broadcast for laughs. In fact, a show featuring disastrous celebrations would likely make for both captivating and entertaining viewing. Failure is not a consideration on cruise weddings.

At sea, the team is there to make everything stress-free, with all the essentials close at hand: in-house florists, a range of dining options, a spa, beauty salon, and even a gym to ease pre-wedding nerves. With these resources at her fingertips, Candice's job becomes effortless. She can easily coordinate separate venues for the bride's party, the groom's gathering, and a reception for the parents - all within walking distance. Later, everyone comes together for a lively after-party, complete with a band playing into the night. By then, Candice can rest easy, knowing the cruise line's high standards and unique offerings have been captured by the ship's expert photographers.

Cruise ships are welcoming inclusive spaces that are generally non-denominational, so a blend of backgrounds and personalities among guests goes unquestioned. Many of the ship's venues, from restaurants to the grand atrium, feature elegant pianos. However, the one white upright piano is reserved for the ceremony room, available for guests to practice on when the room is free. There's almost always a tribute act on board, adding a touch of serendipity to each event - perhaps a 'star' will surprise the couple with a heartfelt rendition of a chart-topping hit.

A wedding at sea typically costs about ten percent of what a similar event on land would, representing a potential savings of up to ninety percent.

Of course, the cost of the cruise itself is additional, but this can easily be factored into the couple's honeymoon budget and the holiday budgets of their guests. It's a win-win situation - even for Prisha Nah, a pregnant Hindu mother of two, who is marrying the younger Winston Crocket, a lapsed Catholic, and whose ever-growing guest list is filling a ship with nearly no available bed space.

What could possibly go wrong? On this occasion, Candice has no idea.

8-39 SEE THIS FACE?
Tuesday, 22nd December, Day 8

Challenges can stifle even the best intentions, which is why every proposal should include a contingency plan that, ideally, will never need to be used. For Kieron, who once served in the military, preparing for "what if" scenarios would be second nature. When it comes to a wedding, having a simple backup for every possible hiccup is a smart strategy.

For instance, if the caterer didn't show, the contingency could involve a list of ten pizza delivery services, with cost estimates for ordering a dozen large pizzas from each and a clear plan for payment. Planning ahead reduces panic.

Yet, no such list exists here. The ship's Hotel Manager was likely called in within an hour of Kieron's breakfast meeting with Daniel C. Creedon yesterday morning. Although not Navy-trained like the Captain and Ship's Engineer, the Hotel Manager has a comprehensive background in hospitality, having managed one of the most complex "hotels" imaginable: a large cruise ship. Few land-based hotels match the scale or demands of a cruise liner. As part of the core leadership - alongside the Head of Security and Entertainment Manager - the Hotel Manager must somehow accommodate the ever-growing guest list. Most rooms need to be organised today, but fortunately, there is an additional day at sea to manage the remaining reservations before final guests fly into Puerto Plata airport in the Dominican Republic tomorrow to join the ship in Amber Cove on Christmas Eve. There is going to be a wedding on Christmas Day.

It may be a wedding, but for Kieron it is a mission and he should have a plan. A contingency list for a potential security threat. But he's missing critical details. It might be Christmas Day, and he may recognise a few members of his team, but he doesn't know the exact nature, motive, or target of any potential threat. His team could even become the focus of an attack, though that's not why he's pushing to act quickly.

He and his two cadets make their way down to the security office on the crew deck.

"Wow. It's so small," Craig remarks as they approach.

"On a ship, space is everything," Kieron replies. "You start to realise how little you actually need, and yet, how much is cleverly available."

Kieron knocks and steps inside.

"Jim Downing? I'm Kieron Philips. We have two trainees at CSCI whom your company has agreed to host this week. Specifically, we're focusing on a module about potential terrorist threats. If possible, I'd like them to scan every load being brought on board today."

"Wow! In that case, they're late. Better get them down to the loading dock right away."

Jim rises from his chair. "Drop your bags here. I'll have someone take them to your cabin." He steps out of the small office and leads Kieron to the crew stairwell. "You knew Witowski?"

"I did."

"Great guy. I served with him."

Kieron recognises that asking questions would only distract from his primary objective, so he follows Jim into the loading bay. As soon as his phone regains service, it rings.

"Kieron Philips, this is Anoataly Istov. Season's greetings. I've found the man whose picture you showed me."

"Who is he?"

"I don't know, and I can't ask. All I know is he's Russian, and you should be careful. Whatever he's up to, it can't be good. I can tell you he wasn't in America to find Bedřiška - she must have been a bonus for him. He's there for another purpose, but asking more could get me killed."

"Send me everything you have."

"That is all I know."

Kieron ends the call and catches up with Jim, who is explaining the goods being loaded to the two young men.

"We'll be back in a week, so it's not a huge load - about two hundred thousand eggs, twenty thousand pounds of chicken, and this week we got about ten thousand pounds of turkey. And all that's wine."

The two cadets are speechless.

"Jim, do you have a swab kit for nitro testing?" Kieron asks.

"Sure. I'll get two sent down and have one of the guys teach them how to use it. It's good practice for everyone," Jim replies, turning to lead the way back.

"Craig, Nick, I'll catch you later in the bar. Stay sharp and pay attention - don't miss a thing," Kieron says, flashing a smile. "Here's a tip: focus on anything out of the ordinary. Special attention on an unusual load like a new stage set or materials from the craft workshop instructor. You might find we've set something up for you to discover." He turns away and quickens his pace to catch up with Jim.

"So, what's the deal here?" Jim asks, as Kieron falls in step.

"Training."

"Training, my foot. You're way too senior to be babysitting a couple of newbies." Jim opens a door, giving him a sceptical look.

"I'm here for a wedding."

Jim arches a brow. "See this face? It's been around a while and there's a reason it has stayed this good-looking. You're too senior, too serious, and way too cautious. Why are they checking out the craft workshop instructor? What kind of trouble's my ship in?"

"Lets make sure it's in no trouble. Do you have any Russians in the crew or on the guest list?"

"Oh. That kind of trouble."

8-40 RECONNAISSANCE
Tuesday, 22nd December, Day 8

The Blue Sky boasts two Grand King Suites, both initially marked as vacant. Being Christmas, the suites had been reserved as a special treat for senior management: one for the hotel manager and his wife, and the other for the entertainment manager and her partner. However, their plans have been thwarted, and now the bride-to-be, Prisha, as well as Izzy, Macey, and Ronni, step into the first suite.

Izzy's eyes widen with admiration at the luxurious surroundings, though Prisha and Macey remain unfazed; they once shared an even more extravagant owner's suite during the art theft case that took them from New Orleans to Key West. That was the same case where the team first crossed paths with Istov in St. Petersburg, and where Macey met Richard, the love of her life. Meanwhile, Ronni, who has spent years aboard ships and is no stranger to the occasional night in a high-end suite, keeps her focus on the job.

The suite offers a spacious living area with two bedrooms, each with its own bathroom. The four women will have to make the setup work.

In the Grand King Suite on the opposite side of the ship, also with a forward-facing view, Croc is inspecting the mirrored layout of the rooms with Billy and Dwight who are more matter of fact. This suite, nearly identical to the one the women are occupying, will be their shared quarters. They've rolled in several cases filled with computer equipment which will establish an operations room, along with their suit bags containing evening wear.

Kieron arrives, glancing between the suites. "These paired suites keep us close together. Where are Dogg and Raul?"

"Down below," Dwight replies. "But don't worry, they're solid. They've got a cover story to blend in with the crew, and they're keeping tabs on Craig and Nick. It means we've got people stationed both above and below deck."

Kieron's phone rings, cutting Dwight off. Glancing at the screen, Kieron answers, "Kieron Philips."

"Kieron, it's Special Agent Edward Cronkite."

"Hello, Ted. Changed your mind about joining us on the cruise?" Kieron steps out onto the double balcony to get a clear signal. He knows full well that Ted's jurisdiction doesn't extend offshore, and as his immediate boss is in charge of four hundred FBI agents in Miami the file won't have been read yet. Ted won't be jumping on board at the last minute.

"Not today. But we've found a body - one of your people, I think. KooBaa? I might see you in Amber Cove."

The line goes dead, and Kieron returns to find Dwight picking up the thread of conversation. "Stan and Mary are set up in a family suite on Deck Eight with the kids. It keeps them out of our way."

"Stan and Mary? Or the kids?" Billy asks with a smirk.

"Both," Dwight replies, noticing Kieron's more somber expression. "What's up, boss?"

"KooBaa's dead," Kieron says, his tone flat but heavy. "I'll need to find Dogg and break the news to him. And Istov tells me the imposter is Russian. Croc, come with me. I'll introduce you to the head of security - you'll need to start running facial recognition on every passenger and crew member. If that Ghost has slipped on board, we need to know immediately."

Croc frowns. "This is my bachelor party. Wedding's in three days."

"Exactly. Which means you need to start now and move fast. Let's go," Kieron says, already heading toward the door.

Billy opens the mini-fridge in the living area, grabs two beers, pops the caps, and steps out onto the balcony, joining Dwight. Together, they gaze at the massive cruise ship docked in front of them.

"Why would the Russians be interested in a cruise ship, Dwight? What's their game here?"

"Maybe it's not the ship but someone on it," Dwight replies thoughtfully. "Could be an assassination. That would explain a small hit team - two women is ideal for that."

"Makes sense. The Ghost is their team leader, and he wouldn't need to be on board," Billy nods.

"No," Dwight agrees, "but he might make an appearance in Amber Cove on Christmas Eve."

"The day before the hit?"

Dwight turns to Billy, eyebrows raised. "No. The day after. Boxing Day, when we're docked in Jamaica. If the hit team fails, he'll be there to finish the job himself."

Billy smirks, catching on. "Croc needs to comb through the passenger list for a potential target, while we do a little reconnaissance of our own in the bar."

8-41 REPLICATION
Tuesday, 22nd December, Day 8

Tomorrow will be a full day at sea en route to Amber Cove. The day after is Christmas Day, and the ship will be at sea again, heading for Jamaica. Thereafter, two final days at sea bring the ship back to Miami. The mission will be over - whatever it turns out to be.

The seven-day route repeats every other week, with alternating weeks spent cruising up and down the Florida coast. The other leg of the ship's route would have provided the FBI with easier port access, which a terror cell may be avoiding. For regular guests, combining two weeks creates a fourteen-day holiday. Most cruise itineraries are repetitive, often rotating among three or four different routes from the same home port, allowing a mix and match choice.

Repetition means the company routinely schedules the same ports, such as St. John's in Antigua or, in this case, Amber Cove. This consistency fosters familiarity between the port staff and the ships. Daniel Creedon owns four ships that rotate these routes out of Miami, providing guests with a variety of departure dates.

The schedule changes only in the week leading up to Christmas, as holiday cruises must begin before the festivities. Christmas Day is typically spent at sea, as most ports are closed, and the cruise must conclude in time for ships to embark on their New Year's holiday itineraries.

Today is changeover day. As midday approaches, most guests have disembarked with their luggage, while new passengers and their bags wait to board. During this time, rooms are cleaned and prepared for the incoming guests. By late afternoon, the lifeboat drill signals that all tasks are complete, immigration formalities are wrapped up, and the ship is ready to depart. Departure is meticulously timed, and once the ship clears Miami Port, the local pilot disembarks the ship at sea, returning by boat to guide the next vessel out.

Zack is on the pilot boat, leaving no stone unturned. As the pilot steps off, Zack jumps onto the ship's platform, and the tug bounces away. He is the last of the team to join in Miami, and his unconventional entry confirms head of security Jim Downing's suspicions that something unusual is happening. Jim greets Zack with a firm handshake at the cargo door.

"Zack Stone. My name's Jim Downing, head of security. I've already met and been briefed by Kieron Philips."

Zack shakes his hand, sensing Jim knows less than he wants to know. He responds tersely.

"Maybe you'd be kind enough to take me to him."

Jim hands him a cruise card. "That's yours. But first, you'll need to come to my office so we can add your photo."

Zack is on high alert as he follows.

In the bar, Billy and Dwight are on their second beer and have chasers sitting ready when Jim finds them. He has Zack in tow.

"Is this a stowaway," Dwight says, before Jim can speak.

"Have you been arrested," Billy says, reading Jim's name badge which reveals his status.

"You can leave him with us, officer."

"Join us for a drink if you want. It could be quite a session," Billy says.

"My name's Dwight Ritter," the big man says, standing with a little wobble and shaking the officer's hand.

"Is that the alcohol already, or are you just getting your sea legs?"

Dwight pulls his trousers up at the knees to reveals his limbs.

"I'm happy with any legs I can find nowadays."

"Sorry. Welcome on board. Thank you for your service," Jim says, with a calculated guess.

Billy stands and shakes his hand. "Billy Granger, sir. How did you know where to find us?"

"I took your friend to the suite; his luggage seemed to have arrived by the usual method. This was my next guess."

"The bar," Dwight says.

"Your muster station."

Zack attracts a waiter with his cruise card to order himself a beer and a chaser, and another beer for each of his two colleagues. He then looks at Jim.

"Not me. I'm on duty and could be tested. Did you guys do your lifeboat drill?" Jim asks.

"That's how you knew we were here - everything has a logical answer," Dwight says.

"I hope so," Jim adds pointedly. "Did you two get the life jacket demonstration?"

They nod.

"Your friend here missed it. Pardon me while I explain. Zack, it goes over your head, Velcro at the front, and tie the straps around your waist. There's a whistle to attract attention. Got that?"

"I've done it a few times."

"It needs to be familiar so you can do it under stress."

"If you count being shot at and your plane about to ditch in the sea… I've done that drill."

"Yeah, I'm getting the vibe. Wear warm clothes if you hear the ship's alarm, and this is where you muster. You guys know each other, right? Are you working together?"

"Dwight was our platoon leader, but we're all retired now," Billy says. "I was left with… issues."

"But he's in therapy. We're about to start a session," Dwight adds, lifting his beer. "Join us anytime."

"I'm… I'm gonna look forward to that. I'm thinking this could be the most interesting Christmas I've had in a while."

The three exchange slight nods of agreement. They lift their glasses and toast him.

"Season's greetings, Jim."

Jim turns to Zack. "I don't expect the ship to be in any kind of trouble. But if it is, this is your muster station. I'll sign you off as having done the drill."

"Thanks, Jim."

Jim leaves, the waiter brings the drinks, and Zack sits and downs half his beer in a single gulp.

"If he's not the enemy, he could be useful," Zack says.

"We've been thinking."

"Billy, I've told you to leave that to the grown-ups," Zack replies with a smirk.

"Hear him out," Dwight interjects.

Before Billy can respond, Ronni and Kieron arrive at the table. Kieron signals to a waiter, who recognises the tables that have responded to his commission-driven enthusiasm since the start of the cruise.

"They started trying on wedding clothes, so I made my escape," Ronni says.

"Weddings not your thing?" Billy jokes.

Kieron shoots him a sharp look, cutting off any further remarks.

Billy quickly moves on. "The imposter said it was a terrorist attack. But why? Why tell us?"

"To draw us here," Kieron replies, following the theory they'd discussed earlier.

"Why would they want us on the ship?" Billy presses.

"Hear him out," Dwight says, placing a hand on Kieron's arm to stop him.

"It's not a terrorist attack; it's a hit."

"Then why invite us?" Kieron asks, almost without thinking.

"They needed us here," Billy concludes.

"Because we're the target," Kieron realises.

"With Bedřiška down, who's next?" Dwight asks.

"Not me; I'm not important. I don't know any Russians," Billy says.

"Me neither. But Kieron - you do. You made enemies there. Three of you: Hunter's gone, Bedi's gone. That makes three of a kind, and the Ghost is Russian," Dwight explains.

"Anatoly Istov," Kieron murmurs, his mind racing.

"And two or three women would make a perfect hit team."

Ronni shakes her head very slightly, drawing everyone's attention. They can tell a new thought has occurred to her.

"Who else would want to kill Hunter, Bedřiška, Kieron, and possibly me? In fact, all of us partners in CSCI."

She has everyone's full attention; no one speaks as a sense of dread settles over them.

"Elaine Witowski, Hunter's wife. She stands to gain the whole company and the millions," Ronni says.

The realisation chills them all.

8-42 THE VENUE
Tuesday, 22nd December, Day 8

Dressed to impress, Prisha strides joyously into the President's Room, moving straight across the elegant space with purpose before pushing open the double doors that lead to the West Wing. Both rooms are bright and welcoming, their bright white decor radiating a cheerful yet empowering atmosphere. There's nothing sombre or chapel-like about the setting - no hint of formality or religion. Rows of chairs are arranged, awaiting the next grand occasion. Macey and Izzy enter, also dressed for dinner, their eyes widening as they take in the grandeur of the room, imagining the event only days away. Candice waits quietly by the door.

Prisha picks up the smallest vase of flowers, though it's still huge, and cradles it like a wedding bouquet. The vibrant blossoms hide her as if she were lost in a tropical jungle of colour. Macey laughs, reaching over to part the lush arrangement, only to find that Prisha is crying.

"There's the bride! Already losing it," she teases.

"Backbone, girl!" Izzy chimes in with a smirk, but the laughter wanes when they realise that Prisha is upset.

"Wazzup?" Izzy asks softly.

Prisha shivers, voice barely above a whisper. "What if it's not his baby?" She clutches the vase tighter. "What am I doing to him? This… this whole thing feels like a lie."

Macey's expression softens. "But you love him, right?"

Prisha nods, blinking back tears. "So much."

"Then you get a free pass if it's the wrong baby," Izzy says gently. "You deserve a little grace."

Prisha's gaze drops to the floor. "But he doesn't deserve it. Look at your skin colour and look at mine. It will be obvious. He'll be heartbroken."

"He already loves your other two kids like they're his own," Macey says. "One more won't change that."

Prisha shakes her head, pulling herself together. "This isn't helping. I need to know. And if I've made a mistake, I have to tell him."

Izzy reaches for her hand. "Okay. When we get back, we'll get you tested."

Prisha pulls away, her resolve hardening. "No. I need to know before the wedding."

Macey steps to the huge window and looks out, her voice gentle but firm. "Look out there. We're in the middle of the ocean on a cruise ship, with dinner and wine waiting. No magical DNA lab in sight."

Prisha's face crumples. "Then... maybe we should call it off. I can't go through with this."

Candice, standing discreetly by the door, remains still, holding back any reaction to the emotional exchange she wasn't supposed to overhear. She inhales deeply, holding her breath, hoping to remain invisible in the tension-filled room.

"Can I just... get off this ship?" Prisha whispers, looking around like she's trapped.

Izzy shakes her head gently. "Nope. And your mom and brother are already en-route from India to the Dominican Republic. You don't have the superpowers to turn that plane around."

"This could just be wedding jitters," Macey says, offering a hopeful smile. "Maybe the dates are just... mixed up?"

Prisha's voice is heavy with resignation. "The scan shows I'm twenty-four weeks along, right on the edge of what they'll allow for cruising. Any further, and I'd never have been allowed on board. And any longer ago..." She trails off, closing her eyes. "It would have been impossible. I hadn't been with anyone for years - then, twenty-four weeks ago, on a ship for CSCI, I ran into an old friend, and it happened. Just once. I was undercover, staying below decks… and then, the very next day, I met Winston and fell in love."

The weight of her words fills the room, and her friends are silent for a moment.

"And you… slept with him right away?" Izzy raises an eyebrow.

Prisha nods, cheeks flushed.

Macey smirks. "Didn't think our brother had it in him."

Izzy shakes her head. "Prisha's agreeing with you."

Prisha sighs, exasperated. "No, that's not what I'm saying. He *did*. Winston's everything I want - loving, perfect."

"So… the wedding's still on?" Candice ventures from the doorway.

"Yeah, yeah, yeah," Izzy interjects, strolling towards her. "The wedding's happening, even if it's… not for real."

"That would make it worse," Prisha mutters.

"Look, is it on or off?" Candice asks, her voice tight.

"It's on, Candice. No worries," Izzy reassures her. "The wedding's paid for, even if… things change. Just assume it's all good."

"Right, it's definitely on," Candice replies, though the uncertainty in her voice lingers. "I'll be around if you need me - guest services, or just leave a clear message." With a hesitant smile, she slips out.

"Poor thing's so confused," Izzy says, turning back into the suite.

"She's confused?" Prisha replies, incredulous. "And you're worried about her?"

Macey clears her throat, easing the tension. "Shall we go to dinner?"

"Yes, let's eat," Izzy chimes, breezing toward the door. "You've got to eat. You're eating for two."

8-43 THE PUB
Tuesday, 22nd December, Day 8

Kieron and Zack, impeccably dressed in dinner suits with bow ties, sit across from their cadets, Nick Gold and Craig Anciano. Zack is scrolling through test results on an electronic pad, while the two younger men shift uncomfortably, feeling underdressed in their more casual attire amidst the formal atmosphere.

"Are you sure we're okay dressed like this?" Craig asks, glancing around nervously. "Feels... wrong."

"Yeah, I feel totally out of place," Nick adds, buttoning the collar of his shirt.

Kieron chuckles. "You're fine. There's no dress code in the pub or upstairs in the buffet. Relax and enjoy the evening. You've worked hard."

"No sign of explosives," Zack says, finishing with the screen.

"No. Have we failed? Was there something we were supposed to find?"

"We combed through everything, every inch of the place," Nick says, sounding worried. "Double-checked, triple-checked... drove the crew mad. But we couldn't find anything."

"Let's assume you're on a terror alert. Not the whole ship, just the two of you as part of your training. You can't find anything, and you know it's here. What do you do post search?"

The younger men shake their heads, uncertainty evident on their faces. Kieron turns to Zack for his input.

"Think like the terrorist. What would you need on board, how would you get it here?"

"It would take us this week to learn the ship," Nick suggests.

"That does not stop you trying. But, within all of your searching what must you never do?" Kieron asks.

They both remain silent, unable to answer.

"Let any of these people know and panic will spread faster than a virus."

"This is a serious learning curve," Craig says. "Just being here. Just feeling the problem... Thank you for the opportunity."

"I think it might be the ship that some of the women on the course have joined for their holiday. If it is, that is another brilliant learning experience. Because they will be like guests who are in panic. Why are you here? Why is the team here? Their thirst for fear won't let up."

"But we won't get to see them; we're below decks," Nick points out.

"Spend your leisure time above decks. Keep your eyes open. Be suspicious. Say nothing. Just wear that cruise ship smile."

"I'm really enjoying this week," Nick says.

"You don't have a week. The attack is in..." Kieron glances at Zack.

Zack shrugs. "Three days. Target day, Christmas Day. Solve it."

Kieron signals the waiter and orders another round of beers. "Get some rest tonight. Tomorrow's going to be a long day, and you'll need that cruise-ship smile ready at all times." With that, he and Zack stand up to leave.

"Sir?"

Kieron turns.

"The two guys in the cabin next to us - are they students?" Nick asks.

"They will be, on the next course. They got lucky with the trip that your colleagues didn't take up. You can talk to them, but ensure they know not to talk."

"Three days; that's it," Zack reminds them sternly.

8-44 THE BRIG
Tuesday Evening, 22nd December, Day 8

Larger ships like the Blue Sky have a brig - a reinforced cabin below deck used to confine offenders when necessary. However, like all spaces on a ship, it serves a dual purpose when not occupied by unruly guests. Both brig rooms double as storerooms for the entertainment department, housing costumes and stage props for shows not currently in rotation. With the CSCI staff needing rooms, these items have been pushed to the back and strapped safely, and the twin beds in each room have been prepared for occupancy.

Nick and Craig walk down the plain crew corridor toward their cabin, brig one. They're buzzing with excitement over the seemingly low-stakes challenge they've been given, eager to talk it through with someone - though they know they can't. At least, not with anyone except the two guys next to them, whom they'd glimpsed earlier. Craig lifts a hand to knock on their door, brig two.

Nick stops him. "What if they're asleep?"

Craig checks his watch. "Doubt it." He knocks.

Silence. He knocks again, a little louder. Just then, a young female crew member hurries into the corridor.

"They escaped," she jokes with a grin passing them. "They're at the bar."

Craig glances at Nick. "I didn't see them there."

"Me neither."

A door down the hall suddenly slams with the sharp metallic clang typical of all cruise cabin doors. Instinctively, they look, but the woman is gone. A moment later, her door swings open, and she's charging back down the corridor toward them as it closes behind her.

"Come, I'll show you."

Without a second thought, they fall in line behind her.

The crew bar is a whole different world from the demure pub three decks above. A live band pumps out rock music, and the small floor is packed with energetic dancers singing along. At the far end, the bar is bustling with crew members unwinding. That's where they spot the two men they're certain they'd seen earlier.

"This is more like it," Craig says, taking a step forward.

Nick grabs his arm and stops him. "Hold on. We're being tested, right? Maybe they're here to see exactly how much we'll spill."

Craig pauses, nodding thoughtfully. "OK. Let's grab a beer and feel it."

Two bottles are capped and the pair turn back and face the dancers.

"I think you guys are in the next brig to us," Nick starts.

"Yeah man. Brig two. What did they get you for?" Raul says.

Nick grins.

"This is a sweet camp," Raul says.

Dogg studies their faces, a serious look in his eyes. He's intimidating without even trying.

"You two want to work in security?" Craig asks.

"We already keep the block secure," Dogg says flatly, cutting off any further questions.

The woman from earlier slides up to Craig and takes his beer and drinks it. "What do you do?"

Craig is frozen with fear at his first test. He has no idea how to respond. She laughs and moves along to Dogg, who she can see is a more worthy opponent.

"And what do you do?"

Dogg offers her a big grin, which draws her closer.

"I drill for gold. I'm the ships new gigolo."

"A sugar baby, eh? But just for the guests?"

"Have to see if I can get me a day off."

The woman dances off with Craig's beer.

His bow tie loose from his neck, Kieron smiles at Ronni and opens the door to the Owners Suite in the private complex of the Blue Sky.

"I should have guessed," Ronni says, entering.

"I think I will have to give it over to Croc and Prisha if the wedding takes place."

"We better make the most of it then."

"There are two rooms," he says.

"So, which one shan't we use," she says, cheekily.

"Should we be complicating this mission?" he replies, raising his eyebrows.

"Certainly no more than we did the last one."

"I don't want you to feel under any pressure."

"I wouldn't, and I don't. And if you are referring to the moment I took at our proposed wall of honour back in Miami... it happens. I do that. But, it was a long time ago, and I'm pleased you now know. It helps."

"That I know you were a kick-ass CIA agent."

"You always knew that," she says, moving in to kiss him.

The embrace takes a while before they separate, comfortable being close together.

"Should we really be relaxing like this. The suggestion appears to be that you and I are the targets," he says.

"It's exactly why we should be. Life is too short not to."

"Were you serious about Elaine?"

"She has motive to kill us all. She gains, especially since you wrote in the partnership agreement that the trust that owns CSCI cannot be expanded by the addition of new members," she explains.

"If they are alive. That is what doubles down on her motive."

"But Elaine?"

"You don't know her. You rescued her, that's it."

"We rescued her," he says, playing the romance.

"Actually it was more me. I found the hide. I went in and took her out over the roof. Fact, I'm not sure as I saw you," she plays.

"You are the best."

"But she's not. I know her. I've known her for years and she joined the cruise industry to find a rich single man. Then, when she failed, she settled for a senior officer."

"Hunter was a great guy."

"A bit older than her. I'm sure she had her eye on a bigger prize. I wouldn't be surprised if we discovered that she was in on the money heist."

Macey is back in the Grand King Suite, laying on a double bed in a room she has all to herself. She is on the phone to her boyfriend, Richard.

"I can't stay on for long; the maritime rate is a killer," she says.

"Someone on the ship might be. Why did you agree to go?"

"I don't know. I guess it's my job."

"No. You're an artist, not an agent. You should be spending Christmas with me, and concentrating on your new gallery, not putting yourself in danger," Richard says. "The whole team doesn't debunk to a ship with no notice unless something dangerous is going on. What's happening?"

"Now you're being a journalist again," Macey says.

"No. I'm your boyfriend. I care. I love you."

"Well don't worry. The ship's not going down and I'm not the target. We will see the new year in together."

8-45 A RAY OF SUNLIGHT
New Day 23rd December, Day 9

The morning sun floods the Observation Lounge, casting a warm glow through the panoramic windows overlooking the vast sea. It's the perfect lighting for Heather Frost's art class, which she hosts with an inviting and day-one creative energy.

Kieron and Ronni sit at the bar on the upper level, and across on the opposite side of the lounge. They have seen three of their cadets; Wanda, Abi, and Carol, who are amongst the thirty three guests busy painting.

Jim creeps in and stands behind the pair.

"So, we didn't find any explosives," he says.

"Good morning," Kieron says, gesturing between the two. "Jim, this is Ronni, Ronni, Jim. Head of security."

Ronni meets his gaze and shakes his hand firmly, subtly ending his scrutiny.

"And you're not here for the jackpot bingo," he says.

"I love bingo," she says, with a hint of challenge in her smile.

"What should I be looking for, Philips?"

"You could start with a reason to collect all the names of those in the that art class."

Jim smiles as he walks off in the direction of the class. Kieron and Ronni watch him greet Heather as if she is a regular and take her list of names. He photographs it with his smartphone.

"You might need a bigger area, Heather," he says.

As he walks back towards the bar, Jim notices that his two friends have left. He steps outside, where he isn't surprised to find them waiting.

"You didn't want to be seen?" Jim asks.

"Your walk towards us would've drawn attention," Ronni replies. "We'd have lost any advantage."

"You know a few of them?" Jim asks, leading them down the corridor.

"Three," Kieron replies. "But if we get that list, we can run names."

"I'll pull their booking info when I'm back at the office," Jim offers.

"By then, I'll have full profiles on each," Kieron says, holding out his smartphone. "Send me the file?"

Jim taps his phone to Kieron's. "Where's it headed?"

"Already in motion - a deep dive on all of them," Kieron assures him, then stops suddenly. "I left my cruise card at the bar."

Jim frowns. "It'd help if I knew what's going on here."

"I've been saying the same thing for a week," Kieron sighs. "I have to update Mr. Creedon first. Then I'll brief you."

"Mr. Creedon? So that's how you're moving mountains," Jim muses. "I'll wait for you."

"I'll be down to your office shortly," Kieron says, heading back toward the lounge.

"Let's meet for lunch, twelve thirty. I'll book a table away from others."

Jim heads to the elevator, realising he won't get more from them yet. Kieron turns back to Ronni. She shakes her head, urging him on as the elevator doors have closed but it has not moved.

Kieron reaches the lounge and stops by the entrance, making small talk with a waiter while glancing back.

The elevator opens, and Jim steps out, approaching Ronni. "Just thought of something," he says, looking towards Kieron.

"What?" Ronni asks.

"Five minutes," Kieron calls out.

"It can wait. I'll see you at lunch," Jim says, taking the elevator with purpose this time.

Ronni watches him go, then turns to wave Kieron up.

"If someone's after us, is it the three women in the art class - or someone more like Jim?" she asks. "Elaine wouldn't have access to the watercolour painters. But she would know someone like Jim. They both worked on ships."

Kieron sighs, the mention of Elaine stirring something unsettling.

"Maybe we should have Macey walk through the art class, just to see if the three are genuine painters."

"What would that tell us? Their skill with a brush?" Ronni asks. "If we use that meeting, we need the interaction to reveal something useful."

As they step into the elevator, Kieron adds, "And plant seeds for what we might learn."

They ride down in silence until Kieron frowns. "Elaine's already set for life. Why risk prison for more wealth - an amount she can never spend?"

"Or a death sentence. It's Florida," Ronni replies.

"Exactly. Why?"

"Greed. It's one of the three modern triggers," Ronni says. "Algorithms thrive on it."

"What are the other two?" Kieron asks, as they approach the Atrium Cafe.

"Greed, hate, and sex. The top triggers for attention."

"That's… unsettling."

"It's the result of years of social media study - and now AI feeds on the same triggers."

"Which could be why Australia was first to restrict social media for anyone under sixteen."

"How will they enforce it?" he asks.

"They're fining the platforms. No other way, because you can't trust the people," she says, sitting down with Croc, Dwight, and Billy, who are having a late breakfast.

"Update," Croc starts. "Wanda's clean, but she was in London when Trump was elected the second time. Held briefly by police after a protest, then released with a caution."

"What charge?" Kieron asks.

"They don't say. I'm guessing if they'd detailed it, they'd have charged her - so there's nothing worth reading. I'm having press coverage on post-election demos scanned for more information."

"Why get involved in a protest if she's some kind of mercenary?" Ronni wonders aloud. "Maybe she was just an angry American on holiday."

"Ronni still suspects Elaine might be involved," Kieron explains.

"Elaine?" Croc asks.

"I don't get Elaine, and I don't get these cadets," Billy muses. "But I still think Creedon's ghost is behind this."

"He took out Bedi, then KooBaa," Dwight adds.

4 MURDERS, A WEDDING, AND A CRUISE

"I ran photo recognition - our ghost isn't on the crew or guest list. A few others flagged, but nothing concrete," Croc says.

"Check flights to the Dominican Republic," Kieron suggests. "If it were me, I'd board in Amber Cove tomorrow, where security will be light, and disembark on Boxing Day in Jamaica. Just in time to disappear."

"There's a link between him, Wanda, Abi, and Carol - our security cadets. They could be setting something up, ready for him," Billy says.

"Can we monitor all maritime communications from the ship?" Dwight asks Croc.

"You know, I'm supposed to be getting married in two days," Croc replies with a weary smile.

8-46 ART FOR ART'S SAKE
Late Morning, 23rd December, Day 9

Dizzy Martel, the Assistant Hotel Manager, guides Macey and Izzy into the lounge just as the art class is wrapping up. It's approaching midday, when the ship's bell will chime, and the officer of the watch will announce the vessel's position, progress, and weather - likely with a humorous anecdote to close. This ritual signals the start of lunch and the afternoon's programme.

Dizzy walks up to Heather Frost, who is a regular art instructor on many ships, and someone whose record Croc can only see as flawless. She is even a school governor and a chair of a charity. "Heather, I have the pleasure of introducing one of America's top young artists, May.I.See," she says, with a smile.

"Macey is fine, it's my real name," she says, with a modest yet radiant smile.

Izzy, sensing the surprise on the faces of the three cadets - Wanda, Abi, and Carol - launches into her well-rehearsed cover story. "No way, sisters! This is *your* ship?"

Wanda, caught off guard and stern-faced, asks, "What are you doing here?"

"A wedding. We're all here for a wedding," Izzy explains.

"All?"

"Wait, this isn't the cruise Kieron Philips offered to cadets?" Abi asks.

"It wasn't supposed to be, but as there were only two cadets available, that's how it turned out."

Carol's eyes widen. "So, we could've done this cruise for free?"

"You'd be working, not in this class," Izzy clarifies, nodding toward the other artists leaving as Heather closes lids on the pots of paint powder and stacks the unsold art kits onto a serving trolley.

Wanda raises an eyebrow. "Nick is here? And Craig?"

"Probably sleeping below deck after a night shift," Izzy says.

"Who's getting married?" Wanda asks.

"Winston - the guy from Mumbai setting up the tech. He's marrying Prisha, a girl from India."

Abi's eyebrows shoot up. "And you're here because?"

"We're his sisters," Izzy laughs.

"Wow, so random," Wanda remarks. "He just decided to get married? You never mentioned it."

"Actually, he returned to America for a hassle-free cruise wedding. You can invite as many as you like, but only close friends tend to show up," Izzy adds smiling.

"No awkward relatives that you never saw before and will never see again!" Carol says, chuckling.

"Exactly. And you three have to come," Izzy insists.

"Don't we fall into that 'never see again' category?" Wanda teases.

Carol laughs. "Will Nick and Craig be going? Nick's been a bit...clingy."

"He likes her," Abi chimes in.

Izzy grins. "Oh, I'll be sure to mention you're on board."

"Please don't," Carol murmurs. "Besides, if they're working..."

"They're not locked in the brig when they're off duty. They'll be up here exploring the ship," Izzy says.

"The brig?" Carol asks, curious.

"Yeah. The cells below decks, down by the engine room."

"They have prison cells on a ship?" Abi asks.

"Of course they do. Hasn't Billy mentioned what happens to criminals on a ship?"

"Not yet."

"Oh, he will."

"The cells are near the engine room?" Wanda asks.

"Yeah. Down in the nosiest and hottest part of the ship."

"But that's critical to the ship's operation. Why risk putting them down there?"

"They're locked up," Izzy says, keeping the tone light.

Macey joins them and beams with surprise. "What? No way!"

"Crazy, right? I invited them to the wedding," Izzy says, and the two launch into their double act.

"Why not? Perfect way to spend Christmas Day in the middle of the ocean," Macey adds.

"Christmas Day?" Wanda says, hesitating. "I might be busy."

"Busy, doing what? Art class is in the morning," Macey teases.

"We're planning to paint here in the afternoon," Wanda explains.

"Take a break! It's Christmas. Our brother's getting married," Macey urges.

Macey and Izzy are both wearing miniature microphone transmitters. Their team, hiding in the room behind the bar just forty strides away, listen in.

"The coincidence of you being here with us…it doesn't add up. Feels weird," Wanda says, narrowing her gaze with suspicion.

"We work on cruise ships - where else would he get married?" Izzy replies smoothly.

Macey sits in Wanda's chair, glancing at her work. She picks Wanda's cloth brush roll, slips a tiny microphone into the compartment, and replaces the brush casually.

"Don't study that too closely. I'm just an enthusiast," Wanda says.

"I like your brush roll. And your work is good; you've been at this a while," Macey comments.

"Not that long."

"We have to go, sis - spa date. Formal night tonight and we're dressing up. I'll message you," Izzy says, turning to go.

"How will you know where we are?" Wanda asks, cautious. "Our phones are in flight mode at sea."

Izzy laughs. "Kieron and Billy work in ship security. They'll track you down." She leaves before anyone can press for details, making a smooth exit.

Outside the lounge, the two siblings duck through a crew door into the stockroom behind the bar. There, Croc, Dwight, Kieron and Zack listen in on the receiver. The girls each take an earbud from a wired set and share.

"Her painting isn't very good and her brush roll looks new. She's not been doing it long," Macey reports.

They all listen to the muffled conversation from the lounge.

"That's messed up our Christmas Day plans," Abi says.

"Maybe we make the wedding our afternoon plan," Wanda suggests.

Macey pulls her earpiece out. "That's backfired on us."

"Why?" Kieron asks.

"They're now planning to target the wedding?"

"No, she was asking about the brig being near the engine room," Zack says. "She sounded like she wants down there to cause maximum damage."

"Exactly," Izzy agrees. "She disrupts Croc's wedding, gets herself thrown into the brig, and ends up near the engine room."

"We've turned the wedding into a ticking time bomb," Macey adds.

"How would they get out of the brig?" Izzy wonders. "They'll definitely aim for the wedding."

"If they are capable of taking down a ship, they won't worry about getting out of the brig. And whatever they're planning, its probably below decks. They're not here to crash a wedding they had no knowledge of. Changing plans at the last minute is often fatal to a mission," Zack explains.

"We make sure they succeed in getting out of the brig," Kieron says. "Find out what they are up to. Control it. Film it. This is perfect training material."

"We need Croc and Prisha's okay to turn their wedding into a training exercise," Macey says, eyeing Kieron sharply. "And let's run it by Daniel Creedon to see if he's cool having his engine room put at risk mid ocean".

"I have to go, I've got lunch. Dwight has a plan for your next meeting," Kieron says, grabbing a wedge of printed A4 sheets from Croc and leaving.

Macey turns to Dwight. "I told them we have a spa appointment."

"Your appointment got pushed back, they're busy," Dwight says

8-47 LUNCH

Lunch time, 23rd December, Day 9

The grand dining room looks entirely different in the bright midday sun compared to its dark evening allure. Sections of the restaurant are bustling with activity, while other areas are set for the evening with no staff assigned. At one such table by the window,

Jim Downing, Head of Security, sits across from Billy, both gazing out at the view. An open bottle of wine rests in a cooler next to the table, though no food has been served.

"He's late. Not like a military man," Jim says, attempting to break the silence.

"He's checking people and names."

"Mine?" Jim asks.

"Everybody's, if he's doing his job right. What's he likely to find on you?"

"Depends on where he's looking."

"Oh, he'll be looking everywhere."

Kieron hurries up to the table, still reading the top sheet.

"I was starting to think you wouldn't show. Billy said you were a 'dry white' man," Jim says with a grin, pouring wine into Kieron's glass.

Kieron takes a sip, looking up with a slight smile. "You're quite an intriguing character, Jim."

"Am I?" Jim raises an eyebrow fishing for more information.

"You know, I don't usually get called 'intriguing.' Especially by the people I'm supposed to be overseeing," Jim says, leaning back, casual, but with a sharp gaze.

"I guess you're not used to someone digging into your past," Kieron replies, his tone calm but probing.

Jim swirls the wine in his glass, finishes the last, then leans forward. Before he can refill, Kieron reaches for the bottle and beats him to it.

"Does everyone on board have a file now?"

"Everyone who matters," Kieron answers. "And you stand out. Military police, international security firms, a stint with UN peacekeeping. Not the typical background for a ship's head of security."

Jim's posture shifts, his demeanour a bit more guarded. "Maybe I just wanted a change of scenery. Can't all be career men."

Kieron raises his glass, eyeing Jim over the rim. "Fair enough. But tell me, Jim, are you here for the scenery, or is there something more? You've not been in the role that long."

Jim pauses, the faintest hint of a smirk on his lips. "Let's just say I have a particular interest in keeping things… orderly. On land or, as this opportunity came along, at sea. It's all the same to me."

Kieron nods thoughtfully. "Orderly. That's good to hear. Because things could get interesting on this cruise, and I need people I can rely on."

Jim raises his glass in a silent toast. "Here's to interesting."

Kieron tops his glass up. "Nice choice. I thought you couldn't drink while on duty."

"My cumulative hours are up for the week. I'm done for the day. In fact I'm done for three days now."

"Convenient timing," Billy chimes in, stepping into the conversation with a grin. Ever a team player, he has a knack for saying what his partner might rather avoid. "Guess you know how to manipulate the hours."

"Hope you weren't planning on needing me," Jim replies with a smirk.

Kieron collects the sheets from the table. "I'll give you these when you're back, and the dust has settled. If it does. Then you might be in need of a new job."

Jim chuckles. "Is that an offer."

"Could be a change of scenery," Kieron says, leaning back. "Though Florida's not to everyone's taste."

"If we're horse trading, I'll need to see more cards on the table before I pull any of next week's hours forward." Jim says, his tone steady. "Because, whatever's going on, I'm not your suspect. But I can see you've got cadets below, searching for explosives, and three of the names in the art class have been posting on social media about how much they've been looking forward to the cruise - now they're in training to move into cruise security. Don't treat me as an idiot."

Kieron puts two sheets in the centre of the table. "Two crew members, not in your department, who have a few minor blemishes in their past that can't be ignored. Maybe you have some input."

Jim turns over the first, then looks at the second. "No, none."

The sheets on the three girls are then placed in the centre. Jim looks at them, his expression unreadable.

"I have the feeling I'm still hungry. Like I've not had the main course," Jim says, waving a server over. "Let's see if this guy's more use than you've been."

The three of them order food, and they all know it is Kieron's turn to talk.

"I work for, and report to, Daniel Creedon. I've been calling him, but he hasn't returned my call, yet."

Jim shrugs. "Well, it's the holidays."

"Not for us. I need permission to share more information than what you already know. Do you have a line to Creedon?"

"What? The CEO of this company? No."

"So, if you can get through and loop yourself in, I'll share. Straight away. If he comes back to me, I'll be down to you like a shot."

"I won't be in my office."

"Bet you will be by the time we get down there," Billy chimes in, his words carrying weight due to his silence up until then."

"I feel confident that nothing is going to happen today, or tomorrow, in Amber Cove. But my people will be checking everything that comes on board there," Kieron adds, as the tension at the table eases slightly.

"Very convenient, this training of yours," Jim remarks. "Although I'm amazed how easily everybody believes what they're fed."

Kieron nods, and the food is served. As the servers leave, the three begin to eat in silence.

"So, we suspect some form of publicity-orientated terrorist attack on Christmas Day. Shall I order another bottle of wine?" Jim asks, now speaking very casually, as if the weight of the conversation has lifted.

8-48 UNDERCOVER
Lunch Time, 23rd December, Day 9

Wanda, Abi, and Carol sit in a small area, cordoned off by nothing more than a decorative, semi-permanent partition that gives the space an air of exclusivity. By night, it transforms into The Bamboo Grove, the ship's Asian Fusion Restaurant, where a small premium is required. However, at lunchtime, it serves as a quiet, private retreat for any guest enjoying the adjacent complimentary buffet. The three girls relax, savouring the calm away from the hustle of the larger, more crowded dining area.

"Why do they have to be on this cruise? And why invite us to this damn wedding?" Wanda mutters, leaning back in her seat.

"Have you started to like them, Wanda?" Abi asks, sarcastically.

"We don't have to like them. We met them at college; we'll never see them again."

"What's your problem?" Carol asks.

Wanda sighs, nervous and annoyed. "It feels like we're being set up. What's really going on here?"

Carol glances between her two friends, a creeping unease beginning to spoil their day at sea. "Maybe we're overthinking it. Let's try and have a nice day and enjoy the cruise, right?"

A voice interrupts their conversation. "Knock, knock."

They turn to see Nick at the entrance, balancing a tray of food. Craig is behind him, hesitating. But Big Dogg and Raul, push in past them with practiced ease, taking seats like they own the place. Dogg slides closer to Abi.

Wanda's gaze hardens. "Did Macey tell you we were here?"

Nick shakes his head as he places the tray on the table next to them, connected only by the long bench seat against the back wall. "No, the crew use this area. It's away from the guests."

Carol raises an eyebrow, smirking slightly. "Oh. So, you're crew now?"

"They're only here to run with us for a few days. But if you staying longer, we here. We always here," Raul adds, offering his hand to Carol. She reaches out to shake it, but Raul lifts her hand and kisses it with exaggerated flourish.

Dogg, meanwhile, is eyeing Abi with an intense, appraising look. "Look at you, glowing. Must be all that vitamin D you've been soaking up. Your skin, it's... radiant."

Wanda rolls her eyes. "Is anyone else feeling trapped here?" she asks, shifting in her seat.

Raul glances at Dogg and raises an eyebrow. "No."

"No," Dogg echoes, his gaze still fixed on Abi.

Wanda scoffs. "You thought Nick was clingy?" she says, her voice dripping with sarcasm. "These two are adhesive."

"I'm what?" Nick's brows knit in confusion. "Clingy?"

Dogg grins, completely unbothered. "I see a beautiful woman, I speak my mind. No disrespect. I just blinded by your aura."

Abi's expression twitches, showing a slight discomfort as she smirks.

Wanda mutters under her breath. "This food feels unstable in my stomach."

Raul, catching Wanda's discomfort, leans forward, a knowing look. "You gotta wear a wristband, my friend. Me gotta spare pair - helps with seasickness."

Wanda shakes her head. "It's not the sea," she says, pointedly.

"¿Qué bolá?" Dogg asks, brow raised.

Abi leans to her and explains. "It means, 'Wazzup'."

"I know." Wanda replies, flatly.

Ignoring the wall that Wanda is trying to erect to keep him at bay, Dogg inches closer. "You wanna go pata sucia? We can take you below, down to the crew disco. Flash that chonga vibe."

"Sorry?" Wanda asks, raising an eyebrow.

"Sister," he says, leaning in even closer, his voice dropping to a smooth, confident tone. "Let that fierce, unapologetic, wild energy out. Slide below deck, rock those big hoops, go bold with the paint, and share what you got with those who know how to appreciate it."

"Yeah," Nick adds, trying to be included.

Wanda looks at Nick, then back at Dogg. "Below decks?"

"Risky is always best," Raul adds with a huge wide white teeth smile, as Dogg holds her gaze, not flinching.

"Won't I get locked in the brig?" Wanda asks, her interest piqued by a guy with street smarts well-honed before his time with CSCI, but now sharpened to military grade.

"Not this week. Beavis and Butthead are living there - ain't a spare cabin on the ship."

"No way," Wanda beams, showing some genuine excitement for the first time. "You're down near the engine room?"

"Oh yeah! Come down anytime," Nick says.

"Thanks," Abi says, her tone sincere, her previous concerns fading.

"What are you ladies up to tomorrow?" Dogg asks.

"Were busy tomorrow, got plans, but tomorrow night could be perfect. Tonight could be a party too," Wanda says, getting up.

Dogg takes Wanda's hand and writes his phone number in her palm.

"Don't get it tattooed," he says with a wink. "They can change my cabin."

She nods, then leads the others out. Dogg settles back in his seat and starts eating, his demeanour returning to its usual self. After his first bite, he glances at Nick.

"You know what that girl needs?"

"No," Nick replies.

"That's your trouble, bro," Raul says, shaking his head.

"You in training this week," Dogg continues, with a smirk. "Watch and learn. You might even get laid."

8-49 TEA LEAVES
Afternoon, 23rd December, Day 9

The entire CSCI team is gathered in the men's suite for a debrief. It's late afternoon, and many on the ship are already dressed for the formal evening. Here, however, the only nods to formality so far are plates of canapés, delivered by the butler they share with the other suites - and Ronni popping open a bottle of champagne.

"This might be our last if the ship's going down," she quips, pouring the first glasses.

Dwight raises his glass high, cutting through the chatter with a shout. "So, the wedding is saved." He toasts Prisha and Croc, then dives into the meeting. "Our perps don't need to get themselves arrested by crashing the ceremony just to get interned near the engine room."

"Thank you," Prisha says, gesturing her gratitude dramatically. "Now we have to stop them sinking the ship."

"Not that they would have bothered with a wedding," Dwight mutters. "They're on a mission."

"Nice play, everyone," Billy says, raising his glass and then downing it like it's a session beer.

"Seriously good undercover work - both of you," Ronni says, nodding to Dogg and including Raul in her praise.

"Er. Excuse me," Macey interrupts, raising a hand and arching a brow.

"Yeah. What?" Ronni replies flatly, her tone pointedly dismissive.

Kieron steps in, ending the banter. "Well played, Macey. Well played, Izzy. Well played Dogg, and Raul."

Prisha lets out a little cough. The team turns her way briefly but then looks away, feigning indifference. She knows better than to dig into military humour - she's been down that road before.

"Yeah, Dogg, you're smooth," Croc chimes in with a grin. "I might keep that recording for the CSCI blooper reel."

"I didn't do anything wrong!" Dogg protests.

"It's all in the editing, my friend. 'Rock those big hoops'," he mimics, "and you might get laid."

Dwight jumps in, redirecting the discussion. "Since Heather isn't with the group, we can assume she's not part of this three-girl unit."

"Yeah, her record's spotless. She's been working on these ships for years. Most likely, the cell is just using her," Croc reports.

"Agree," Ronni says. "But how did they connect with her? Trace that fishing line, find out how see how she got reeled in. It could lead us to their motive."

"And why have they used Heather's group?" Billy asks.

"Good question," Kieron says, thoughtfully. "I feel like CSCI has finally come of age, just when my interest might've been waning. Now, we get to the bottom of the cup, and read the tea leaves."

"So, we get the girls down below deck tonight, and finally young Nick gets laid. Right?" Dogg jokes.

"Well, he's not actually one of the team," Dwight says.

"That mean I'm on deck for this?" Raul asks, with his trademark wry grin.

"Sometimes, we all have to take one for the team," Kieron says.

That remark hits Prisha, who, remembers her tense undercover night on their last mission. The night before her and Croc got together. She bows her head, as Dogg pulls focus with a huge sigh. He glances to Raul. "One of us is going to have to take two for the team; there's three of them, and only two of us. Unless, Croc wants a bachelor night out."

"Nope. I'm good," Croc says, catching Prisha's uneasy look.

"That thing you want us to do with their phone. You could do that yourself," Raul says.

"You've got this," Croc says.

Dogg shrugs and turns to Raul.

"Straws. Or rock-paper-scissors," Raul suggests with a huge smirk.

"Tonight, while you're keeping them occupied, we'll be searching their cabins," Dwight explains.

"That search better be real fast as you only have minutes," Ronni adds, ribbing them.

"That long? You two that good," Billy jokes.

Dogg raises a brow, feigning offence. "You take your time with that search. We're good for it. We both do the job thoroughly."

"You better be good, because unless they fall asleep afterwards, a girl does not part with her phone," Izzy says.

"What exactly are we looking for?" Zack asks.

"Anything on that 'ghost', whose name we don't know," Billy throws in.

"Who could be Russian," Kieron adds. "Or any clue about an arranged meet for tomorrow in Amber Cove."

"We should tail them in Amber Cove. It could be easy as there is a bar high up with a three-sixty view," Ronni explains.

"I will be collecting my mother and brother from the airport," Prisha announces.

"Maybe we can suggest spending the day, see what that shakes loose," Raul suggests.

"Yeah. Take them to the amber museum," Ronni says.

"Is it any good?" Dogg asks.

"Not really," Ronni chuckles. "But it could be better than the disappointing night they had. There's a town square, a beach, and a fort. Every Caribbean island has a fort."

"Alright. Meeting's over. Get dressed up and enjoy the formal night," Dwight says. "Tomorrow's tail plans will be in your inbox before bedtime."

8-50 THEORY OF RELATIVITY
Afternoon, 23rd December, Day 9

The ship's aft resembles a layered wedding cake, each deck a distinct tier presenting itself to the sugary, white, meringue-like wake trailing the vessel. The balconies curve like crescent moons, the smallest perched at the top, tapering down to the lowest deck with its small children's pool. This pool, unique on the ship, has shallow steps for easy access, unlike the adult pools that require more effort and agility to navigate their ladders.

Behind the pool lies a bustling youth area filled with play zones and a toddler's splash pool of minimal depth. Here, water features and toys - designed for filling, pouring, and splashing - create endless amusement and demand the constant attention of tiny hands.

Lakshmi and Reyansh, have discovered this floating playground. Although new to such luxuries, they need no manual or encouragement to dive in. The pool sparkles with children's laughter.

"Nanny, come in the pool!" Lakshmi calls out, her voice ringing with excitement.

"That pool is for children only!" Mary retorts from her spot on a sun lounger. She watches the children play with a mix of amusement and her trademark air of authority. Mary and Stan, new grandparents to this

198

extended family, are still finding their footing in these roles.

Stan, reclining beside her, wears a wide grin, clearly enjoying the children. Mary, however, has the same expression she wears when weighing whether a customer will simply order her breakfast or require a lesson in table manners.

"You know, Stan," she begins, then pauses, lost in thought.

Eventually, he turns to her, patient as ever. "Not sure I do, Mary. Not sure I do."

"You wouldn't," she replies curtly.

He lets her words sit for a moment. Then, with a sage nod, he says, "Is it one of them things I never learned? So, I wouldn't know."

Mary purses her lips, her tone sharpening. "If I'd had one of those abortions, the world wouldn't have been blessed with those two wonderful children."

Stan, his gaze still fixed on the children, starts to nod in agreement, but the logic catches him off guard. He turns to her, puzzled.

Mary doesn't need to look. "Why do I feel you're looking at me?"

"What don't I understand?" Stan says, genuinely trying to keep up.

"Why a woman doesn't get rid of the children inside her! You're a man; you wouldn't understand that. It's a woman's nature."

Stan gives a slow, deliberate nod. "Woman's nature?"

"Yeah."

"Like woman's logic?"

"Exactly. You don't have it. You don't understand it."

He glances back at the children, then at Mary. "You're doing it again. Looking."

"I'm not looking; I'm trying to understand."

"Not gonna happen," she snaps.

"Will you help me understand?"

"What?"

"How, if an African woman living in Miami had an abortion, then an Indian girl living in Mumbai wouldn't have these two children."

Mary glares, incredulous. "I told you - you wouldn't understand!"

Stan's face twists into an expression of confusion he hasn't worn in hours.

"It's the circle of life!" Mary declares with finality.

Stan looks skyward, exasperated. "Circle of life? Elton, you know not what you started."

Mary glances up. "Who are you looking at?"

Stan sighs. "I get it. If you hadn't had Croc, he wouldn't have met Prisha, and we wouldn't be grandparents."

"Like I said - the circle of life."

"That's more the theory of relativity," Stan mutters.

Mary's eyes narrow, her look sharp enough to cut glass. Mary is never wrong. "You suggesting I'm wrong?"

"I saw it in one of those science documentaries," Stan muses. "Not sure I understood it. But sometimes it works on you."

"What?" she barks.

"It was science."

"Science. Where did that ever get us?"

"Just a theory." Stan says.

"What theory?"

"Science. If you look at something, it's there. If you don't look, and you can't see it, it's not."

Mary shuts her eyes.

"Have the kids gone?" Stan asks.

"No!" Mary exclaims. "I can still hear them." She opens her eyes. "Look - they're still there."

"No, they came back when you opened your eyes."

Mary stares at him. "I told you, I did the right thing. We've got three great kids and two great-grandchildren."

Stan nods slowly. "You kept your eyes open."

"I did." Mary gives him a pat on the shoulder. "And soon, our son will have another grandchild. When they look a little more like us, you'll understand."

"But… "

"There ain't no buts. The Lord works in mysterious ways. Reyansh, Lakshmi, that's enough playing for today. We're going shopping."

"Shopping?" Reyansh echoes, puzzled.

"They don't want to shop," Stan mutters.

Mary rises, collecting her things. She points upwards. "And his name ain't Elton."

8-51 THE SEARCH
Evening, 23rd December, Day 9

Every cruise ship corridor feels the same: a long, narrow passageway lined with identical doors. On the outer side of the ship, these doors lead to passenger cabins equipped with picture windows or private balconies. On the inner side, they conceal storage rooms or windowless budget cabins. The corridors are punctuated by stairwells and elevators, clearly marked as emergency exits. These are the only guest-accessible pathways in and out. Hidden within the unmarked interior doors are additional staircases and lifts used exclusively by the crew. In stark contrast to the polished guest areas, these spaces are utilitarian, brightly lit with bare steel walls, stripped of any warmth or decor.

Wanda, Carol, and Abi each have their own cabin within the same section of the corridor, making it easier to coordinate the search for their rooms. Macey holds her position at one end of the passage, near the stairwell, while Izzy stands guard at the other. Both women are dressed in elegant evening attire for the ship's formal night, an ironic backdrop to their covert roles. Their mission is clear: if any of the girls return, they must discreetly trigger an alarm and stall them long enough for the team to escape through the opposite stairwell. Jim, in his crisp officer's uniform, lingers nearby, having unlocked the cabins for the search.

Below deck, the three girls are with Dogg and Raul, who are plying them with drinks and charm, while Zack, Ronni, and Kieron meticulously search their cabins above. The operation is a delicate balance of misdirection and stealth, with each move reported back to Dwight. From his luxurious suite, Dwight monitors the mission, dressed for the evening in a sharp dinner jacket and bow tie. Beside him, Croc sits at a workstation, keeping an eye on live feeds across three screens, ready to step into the formal event if necessary.

Prisha, however, remains isolated, left in the suite the girls share. With her wedding just two days away, she wrestles with a storm of emotions. What should be a time of joy is overshadowed by a gnawing fear: is Winston Crocket, her soon-to-be husband, the father of her unborn child? Or could it be an old flame from a past undercover mission? How can she find the courage to tell him?

Years of sacrifice have left Prisha's life deeply fractured. She had given up time with her children to work abroad, providing for them as an estranged, single mother. After years of celibacy, her guarded heart had stumbled into an unexpected dalliance. Now, standing on the fault line of chance, she fears that the truth - or the lie - might lead to disaster.

Elsewhere, Billy patrols the lowest passenger deck, the central atrium; his presence a watchful waiting game, his mind still drifting back to his own lost love. Bedřiška is dead. The three women below could theoretically slip away through any of the hidden crew doors, a scattered labyrinth connecting the ship's guest and crew areas. One possible exit even lies within the corridor currently being searched, but it is unlikely they would stay in crew quarters and climb that many floors; the guest reception offers the most direct escape route, positioned just above the warren of crew-only zones. Like Macey and Izzy, Billy's role is to remain on standby, ready to report back to Dwight. Ideally, though, the first alarm will come from Dogg or Raul, this mission's embedded agents. For now, the two cadets, Nick and Craig, remain unaware of the full scope of the operation - or that the girls are actually under surveillance.

In the crew's private lounge - a vibrant hub below decks - the tension of the mission is replaced by camaraderie. The space buzzes with life: a bar, dance floor, small stage for live performances, and a quiet lounge with a large screen. Here, Dogg and Abi move in sync on the dance floor, Raul chats with Carol at the bar, and Wanda sits at a table with Nick and Craig, casually observing.

"Where's the brig, then?" Wanda asks, her tone light but curious.

"It's just a cabin," Nick replies.

"Half full of rubbish," Craig adds.

"I asked where it was, not what it looks like."

"Down further," Nick says. "Why? Do you really want to go there?"

"Yeah."

"We'd better wait for Dogg," Nick suggests. "No one seems to question him."

"Or he just doesn't care," Craig interjects.

"I'll ask him," Wanda says, glancing toward the dance floor.

"He looks pretty busy right now," Nick points out.

"I can wait," Wanda replies, unfazed.

Craig leans forward. "Do you want to dance while you wait?"

"No," Wanda says flatly.

Having finished her search of Abi's cabin, Ronni steps into the corridor and moves to the next-door cabin. She knocks gently. The door opens slightly, revealing Kieron.

"Abi's room is clean," she reports.

"Come in," he says, stepping back just enough to let her through.

Ronni enters cautiously, but Kieron doesn't move far. The tight space between the door and the cabin's compact washroom forces them close as he shuts the door behind her.

"Look at this," Kieron says, gesturing toward the back of the door. A series of deck plans are affixed with tiny round magnets.

"These are from a brochure," Ronni observes, leaning in.

"Exactly. Why would they have these?"

"Amateurs. Or," she adds, her eyes narrowing, "as I've been saying, Elaine's hired Jim."

"You're persistent," Kieron remarks, their faces close.

Ronni smirks and pecks his lips. He leans in for a deeper kiss, but it's interrupted by a knock at the door.

"We could take the rest of the night off," Kieron murmurs, his voice low. "I've got champagne in my fridge."

"Of course you do - you're in the owner's suite," she teases.

The knock comes again, louder this time. Ignoring it, Kieron kisses her softly.

Ronni pulls back slightly, her expression suddenly serious. "Before we spend any more time together, I should probably tell you - I'm not on any form of contraception."

Kieron pauses, their faces still close. "Is there a second part to that statement?"

Ronni closes her eyes briefly, exhaling. "I don't think so. Did you want to add anything?"

He considers her for a moment. "No."

The knock repeats, insistent this time.

"Time to move," Jim's voice calls from outside.

Kieron opens the door. "Jim, come in. Look at this."

Jim and Zack enter, though the cramped space makes movement awkward. Kieron points to the deck plans on the door.

"These have been ripped from a brochure," Jim notes. "You can grab one from Future Bookings on Deck 7. They're available to everyone - there might have even been one in the room originally. They don't show crew areas or engineering sections."

"But it's strange, isn't it?" Kieron presses.

"Wanda seems to be the one in charge," Zack offers.

"In charge of what? She might just be the group's holiday planner," Jim counters. "What's going on?"

"Check the room for the rest of the brochure," Zack suggests. "She might've doodled on a facing page before tearing these out."

Jim walks to the magazine rack and flips through its contents. He pulls out a brochure and examines it. "Yep. Pages are torn out. No scribbles, though."

"Can we grab a fresh copy to leave here and take this one for analysis? Look for indentations?" Kieron asks.

Jim shrugs and exits, crossing the narrow corridor to the room opposite. He knocks and announces, "Security," before stepping inside.

Ronni watches as Jim retrieves a new brochure. He returns, swapping it for the torn one.

"I need the safe opened," Kieron says.

"Wrong department. That's hotel management," Jim replies. "You'll need Creedon for that. But seriously, I need to know what's going on."

"I agree," Kieron says. "But, you'll need Creedon for that. We're done here."

8-52 FORMAL NIGHT
Evening, 23rd December, Day 9

At the formal night dinner, Billy, Dwight, and Zack sit together, reminiscing as old platoon mates often do. Their laughter carries a tone of shared history and inside jokes. Croc sits next to them, flanked by Prisha, Izzy, and Macey. Two seats at the far end remain conspicuously empty; no one expects Kieron or Ronni to appear, their well-known romance a subject no one feels the need to broach. Mary and Stan's seats are also vacant for now - they're upstairs trying to get the children to sleep.

The table is set for eleven, but everyone knows they'll be lucky to fill nine.

Prisha scans the room nervously. The formal dining hall is alive with the shimmer of gowns and the crisp elegance of dinner suits. Men exchange pleasantries over glasses of wine; women, in an array of luxurious dresses, sparkle under the soft chandeliers. Despite the glamour, Prisha feels like an outsider. She's seated at the table marked for the CSCI team but remains the only one whose identity isn't openly tied to the mission - except as the bride-to-be of one of the team's key players.

"I hope those security cadets don't make it here tonight," Prisha mutters. "If they see me, I'm sure they'll recognise me."

"They won't," Croc assures her. "Dogg and Raul are covering that duty."

"And they're rocking disco threads tonight," Izzy adds with a smirk. "They're not stepping foot in here dressed like that."

"They wouldn't care about the dress code," Billy says dryly. "They don't care about anything other than themselves."

"What are we going to do with you, Prisha?" Zack teases. "If you're worried about being recognised, maybe we should disguise you for the wedding."

"Disguise me? Make me look like someone completely different for my own wedding?"

"There's a certain logic to it," Zack says with a shrug.

"Maybe Winston would prefer to marry someone else," Prisha snaps, sarcasm masking her unease. "I could wear a Cher wig. I'm sure the stage crew has a costume or two I could borrow."

Before anyone can respond, Prisha's attention shifts sharply across the room. Her expression hardens into one of outright shock.

Lakshmi and Reyansh approach the table. The young boy looks dapper in a small dinner suit, complete with a white shirt and black bow tie. Lakshmi is radiant in a dress Prisha doesn't recognise

- one she would never have bought for her daughter. Both children wear expressions that shout *'Look at me!'* mixed with the sleepy excitement of staying up far too late.

Prisha's face twists into outrage. She turns to Croc, her voice a low hiss. "Winston, why are they awake at this hour? And dressed like that?"

"Do you have any other questions I can't answer?" Croc replies with quiet exasperation.

"That makes talking shop difficult," Dwight observes, his tone neutral but firm.

"Take the evening off," Mary says sharply, as she pulls chairs back for the children. Her tone leaves no room for argument.

"For clarification," Dwight begins, "this might be a cruise ship, but we're not here on holiday."

"I'll take them up after they've eaten," Mary snaps, glaring at Dwight. "Then you can talk shop to your heart's content."

Prisha turns to Croc, whispering harshly. "Winston, this is not how they dress."

"They look great," Croc replies, his voice light but steady.

"They're children. They should be in bed. Their real grandmother arrives tomorrow."

"Two grandmothers," Croc corrects with a faint smile.

"Oh my God," Prisha mutters, her voice cracking under the strain. "I can't see this working."

The waiter hands menus to Lakshmi and Reyansh.

"What are you having, kids?" Croc asks brightly.

"They are *my* children, not yours," Prisha snaps, her voice trembling.

"Not mine?" Croc echoes, his tone pointed but calm.

"I didn't mean that," Prisha says quickly, stumbling over her words. "I meant -"

"I know what you meant," Croc interrupts, his voice lower now. "And I want you to know something: our new child - will be no more or less mine than these two already are."

"I'm sorry," Prisha whispers, her composure faltering. Her eyes glisten, but she blinks back the tears. "I'm just... seeing a problem."

"A problem?" Croc says, leaning closer. "It's a tsunami warning."

Prisha looks away, the weight of his words sinking in. Across the table, the children chatter happily over their menus, oblivious to the storm brewing in the adults' world.

8-53 WAKE UP

Early Morning, 24th December, Day 10

"Kieron, wake up," Ronni says, leaning over him in her bathrobe.

"What?" he mumbles, his eyes snapping open, instantly alert.

"Jim gave you the swab testing kits for the cadets, right?"

"Yeah."

"Could he have recalibrated them so they don't work properly?"

"No idea. That's a Croc question. But I doubt it," he replies, sitting up.

"Check on it. If they can't be tampered with, I'll drop my objection to bringing Jim into the loop. But there's someone else involved - those girls don't convince me."

"Sure. Call Croc."

"I already did," she says. "He wants us upstairs. There's a new development."

Ronni moves to leave, but Kieron grabs the edge of her robe, spinning her back around. It slips open slightly as he pulls her close. Their eyes lock.

"What?" she asks softly.

"You're not a practicing Catholic, are you?"

"No."

"And you're not worried that we…"

"I don't think so," she says, her voice uncertain. "Strange, huh?"

He kisses her, and their moment is interrupted by the faint voice of the officer of the watch over the address system:

"Formalities have been concluded and guests are now free to go ashore using the forward gangway and enjoy their Christmas Eve. Merry Christmas!"

"Merry Christmas," Kieron murmurs, smiling against her lips.

Croc is alone in the men's suite, seated at his workstation with additional screens when Kieron and Ronni finally arrive.

"Where is everyone?" Kieron asks.

"Billy, Dwight, and Zack left the ship before the announcement. Dwight's setting up at the rooftop bar by the zip line. I'll join him once he's good to go."

"So, what's new?" Ronni asks.

Croc leans back, his fingers tapping the desk. "I've been digging into their bank accounts."

"And?" Kieron prompts.

"All three girls are drowning in debt - student loans, credit cards, you name it. No steady jobs, no real prospects."

Ronni crosses her arms. "That doesn't make them terrorists."

"No, but how are they affording separate rooms instead of sharing to save money?" Kieron asks, throwing Ronni a smug glance. "Keep going, Croc."

"No payments for this trip have come from their accounts. Someone else footed the bill."

Ronni raises an eyebrow. "Okay, that's suspicious. Who's paying?"

Croc swivels in his chair. "Here's the kicker: Wanda made one payment - just one - to join an online art class called Frosty Art by Heather. That's it. Nothing else, no other links. No monthly payments."

"Which means someone else is paying for Heather's setup too," Ronni guesses.

"Exactly. Heather's account is flooded with incoming payments, mostly from online class subscriptions. It's a lucrative cover. I'm still untangling her web."

"Any leads on the flights into Puerto Plata?" Kieron asks.

"Prisha's at the airport, watching," Croc replies.

"She's alone?" Kieron frowns.

Croc smirks. "Do I look stupid? Raul's with her."

"Good," Kieron mutters. "Most of those scenarios don't fit. For example, why would they need to be on board to plant limpet mines? And if they've left an explosive device, they would skip re-boarding."

"That may be the plan," Croc counters.

"We can't afford to dismiss any theory," Ronni says.

"But I think they're integral to the operation. They're too involved for a simple handoff."

"They're no hit team, that's for sure. If those three take me out, I don't deserve to be on this planet," Ronni quips.

"And we were just talking about starting a family," Kieron adds, with a sarcastic grin.

"This port isn't for supplies," Ronni points out. "Seven day cruise: in and out of Miami. Nothing comes on board here; it's not a smuggling hotspot."

"Unless today's about them picking something up to bring back on board," Kieron suggests.

"Possible," Ronni says. "The question is, *what?*"

"Contamination, explosives, even a homing device for a drone strike at sea," Croc says.

"That would imply a suicide mission," Kieron says.

Croc chuckles darkly. "They come back and leave again before we sail. What's the collective noun for drones? A confetti of drones?"

"They're too flaky for traditional weapons," Ronni says dismissively. "Contamination is more likely."

"How much bottled water did they have stockpiled in their cabins?" Croc asks.

"Nothing noteworthy," Kieron says.

"Everyone's searched coming back on board," Ronni reminds them.

"Should I loop Jim in, or is he still on probation?" Croc asks.

Kieron looks at Ronni.

"Your call," she says. "You know how I feel."

4 MURDERS, A WEDDING, AND A CRUISE

"I'll see Jim," Kieron decides. "I'll set up training drills and get Nick and Craig on full alert."

"Phones ready for data extraction?" Croc asks.

"Always," Kieron replies. "But if they've stored anything in their room safes, I'll have to push Creedon to let us in."

"The x-ray scanners aren't enough time to rinse their phones?" Ronni asks.

"No," Croc says firmly. "And they'd see us try anything suspicious."

Ronni has an idea. "A flare gun. That will trigger a swab tester. We can use them to control test the swab equipment."

"That's why you're paid more than me," Croc grins. "Now, field agents, go find whoever's meeting them. I'll test the ETD kit and then brief Nick and Craig to use it again."

As Kieron and Ronni reach the door, Croc stops them with a smirk. "So… starting a family, huh?"

8-54 PUERTO PLATA AIRPORT
Morning, 24th December, Day 10

Raul and Prisha walk briskly from the car park into the Puerto Plata airport terminal. The usual chaos is subdued today; many hawkers have already broken early for the holidays.

Prisha glances briefly at the departures and arrivals board. "It's landed," she says, hurrying toward the arrivals area, where a cluster of taxi drivers hold up signs with their passengers' names.

214

Raul lags behind, absorbed in his phone, chuckling at a funny reel now that his service is back. From the corner of his eye, he notices Prisha suddenly stopping and turning toward a man striding past her, empty-handed. Raul fumbles to switch his phone to record mode but is too late.

The man walks with a sharp, deliberate pace. Raul spins, letting out an awkward cheer. "Woo! My son just got into college!" he yells, eventually swiping his phone to record while pretending to dance. He twists his hips theatrically, his rear accidentally grazing the man as he passes.

The man halts, glaring, his eyes icy.

"Sorry, bro!" Raul blurts, throwing his hands up in mock apology. "No offence. No war. Just good vibes!" He awkwardly raises a hand for a high five.

The man stares for a tense moment before turning abruptly and heading for the exit.

Raul mutters to himself, "Yup, devil in his eyes." He presses send on his phone and jogs to catch up with Prisha.

"Was that the Ghost?" she asks, her tone low but sharp.

Raul nods, adrenaline kicking in. "For real. I'll follow him. You're on your own."

"Raul, don't! Your cover's blown!" Prisha calls after him, her voice rising. "He's killed two others who tried that!" But Raul is already weaving through the sparse crowd, vanishing from the terminal.

Prisha sighs, pulling out her phone and dialling. Her eyes remain fixed on the arrivals board. "Winston, we just saw the Ghost."

"Yes," Croc replies tersely. "Confirmed. Stay away. Don't blow the mission. We need this to play out."

"Raul's already on his tail," she says, frustrated.

Her attention snaps back as her mother - Mummy-Gee - and her brother Bukka emerge from the arrivals gate, each struggling with over packed suitcases.

"Mummy! What on earth do you have with you? The cruise is only a few days!" Prisha exclaims.

"I have come to live here in America," Mummy-Gee declares, unbothered.

Prisha freezes. "No, Mummy. You're joking."

"I don't think she is," Bukka quips, shaking his head.

Prisha groans, hugging her brother before muttering under her breath. "Please. No."

Outside, Raul slides into a waiting taxi, slamming the door behind him. "Follow that cab!" he orders, tossing two twenties onto the front seat. "I only have US dollars."

The driver hesitates but nods. "He's heading out of town."

"Which way?"

"Maybe to the cruise ships."

"Amber Cove," Raul mutters, his mind racing. "That's where I'm going."

The driver hands back a business card. "Pepe. Call if you need a tour."

"Not now, man. Just drive," Raul snaps, his focus glued to his phone. He's just received confirmation: the man in the other taxi is indeed the Ghost.

"How long to Amber Cove?" Raul asks, his voice tight.

"Fifteen minutes."

Raul dials Croc. "Did you hear that?"

"I did. Don't engage," Croc warns. "Let the game play out."

"Roger that," Raul replies.

Suddenly, the taxi ahead slams its brakes. Raul's driver curses, swerving around the obstruction.

"He's following us now," Pepe says, glancing nervously in the mirror.

Raul ducks low. "Keep driving. Straight to Amber Cove. Fast."

The Ghost's cab revs aggressively, tailing them. Raul updates Croc: "He's chasing me now, Croc. This guy doesn't mess around."

"Drive past the resort. Don't stop. I'll call when it's safe," Croc says, before abruptly ending the call.

On the cruise ship, Croc sits in his suite, surrounded by monitors. His fingers fly across the keyboard as he types a report for the team:

The Ghost is en-route to Amber Cove, ETA 11:55. Suspected ID: Viktor Mikhailov. Possible alias for Russian operative Grigory Dolinsky. Details to follow.

Croc uploads a frame grab from Raul's shaky video into the facial recognition software and initiates a search. As potential matches start populating, his attention locks on one name: *Grigory Dolinsky.*

He clicks 'Contacts' and selects a familiar name from the dropdown.

"Cronkite," a clipped voice answers.

"Ted, this is Winston Crocket on the ship," Croc begins. "Our Russian has landed in the Dominican Republic. I'm tracking a Viktor Mikhailov, possibly an alias for Grigory Dolinsky. I've sent you the details."

"I'll handle it," Ted replies curtly.

Croc doesn't pause. He's already calling Dwight Ritter.

"Dwight," the big man answers.

"I'm on the move," Croc says, snapping his laptop shut and disconnecting his monitors in one fluid motion. Within seconds, he's out the door, striding toward the next phase.

8-55 STAR-SHAPPED
Afternoon, 24th December, Day 10

The big hollow letters spelling "Amber Cove" are visible from the star-shaped bar perched two stories high at the resort's centre. They sit at the bay's edge, clearly intended for guest photo ops rather than a warm welcome viewed from an incoming ship, to which the letters appear backward. Dwight lets the oddity hold his attention longer than it deserves before he turns back to the binoculars on the table he has commandeered.

The circular balcony surrounds the shaped bar with two rows of tables offering a 360-degree view of the resort. Caribbean Christmas music echoes through the air. Dwight grabs his binoculars, rests his elbows on the safety rail, and focuses on the car and coach park beyond the resort gate. The excursion coaches have left, and only a few taxis linger. He checks his watch.

On the ground, Billy surveys the shore, where a canoeist paddles into view, towing five other boats. The man hops out, plants a javelin-like stake into the sand, and ties the boats to it.

"You interested, man? Thirty-five dollars an hour."

"If I miss boarding time, I'll be needing one to catch the ship," Billy replies.

"You'd be spending Christmas with my family," the man says with a laugh.

Billy strolls onto an ornate wooden bridge spanning a canal that connects the children's pool - with its small slides - to the catching pool beneath the towering blue flumes that start near Dwight's perch. Ahead, a giant chess set draws a few curious players, while crew members shoot hoops on the open basketball court. Around the pool, sun loungers begin to fill with guests.

Screams of delight come from above as two young guests zip down the overhead line. Billy smiles at their joy, but his expression falters on seeing a female staff member in a bikini top made with halved coconut shells. He turns back and drops onto a double hammock strung between two palm trees. His posture deceptively relaxed, but the weight of his mission still presses down - he is waiting to meet the man who killed Bedřiška, the woman he'd fallen in love with.

From the hammock, he monitors the bar with its massive upturned umbrella. His phone buzzes and he reads the message: "Three girls leaving ship." His head turns from the bar to the ship.

At the end of the L-shaped jetty, he spots the three girls on a blue bicycle chariot, from the line up by the ship's gangway. The driver pedals leisurely, while Ronni follows close behind on foot, matching the trike's pace.

Billy loses sight of them as they pass behind a mock fort, but he stays put. They are off the trike and walking through the shop and will reappear on the other side. Moments later, the girls stroll by, seemingly carefree. Billy tilts his hat over his face, feigning sleep.

The girls cross the bridge. By the pool, Abi lies on a white plastic lounger, while Wanda and Carol continue toward the excursion hut near the amber store.

"They took Abi's cruise card," Ronni reports to Dwight over the phone. "The Ghost will be using it to gain entry with them."

Dwight circles the bar, watching the exit. Right on cue, a taxi pulls up, and a man - the Ghost - steps out. Through his binoculars, Dwight captures the meeting, then, clips his phone to the lenses to snap a clear photo.

As Kieron joins Dwight, the image is posted.

"Why come inside the resort unless he wants to board the ship?" Kieron asks.

"He's carrying a bag - not them. If he gets stopped, they're clean," Dwight replies.

The two girls re-enter the resort, now part of the ship's "safe-area," where cruise cards suffice as identification. Beyond the gates lies the Dominican Republic, requiring passports for entry. Ghost follows them in.

They reunite with Abi by the pool, and the Ghost places the bag beside her sun lounger, then walks away. Free of it, he wanders over to the giant chess set and waits for Wanda.

"The two killers," Billy says.

"We need to know what's in that bag," Dwight mutters.

"Can we hear what they're saying? A gun microphone?" Kieron asks.

"Not with this music blaring."

Kieron frowns. "A pass by. Do we have anyone they won't recognise?"

"Prisha, maybe," Dwight suggests.

Kieron shakes his head. "The Ghost will clock her."We need to tap into their phones."

Ronni joins them, her tone wary. "What if they're just keeping us busy while something bigger's happening?"

Kieron raises his phone. "Zack, what's happening on the ship?"

"Nothing," Zack replies, patrolling the promenade deck. "Dark side of the moon, no ships, no activity."

Kieron sighs.

"What's Jim up to?" Ronni asks, then follows with, "Can we call Raul back in?"

Kieron nods at Dwight. "Have him turn right at the gate, head into the shop, and straight to the ship."

Dwight stands. "We can't let the Ghost on board."

"He's not going on board," Kieron says. "The contaminant is already in play. There must be a sleeper on board. The person deploying it is below deck, with full access."

"Or it's just flowers and a lottery ticket in that bag," Dwight mutters. "And we're watching paint dry."

8-56 FESTIVE SECURITY
Christmas Eve - Late afternoon, 24th December, Day 10

An easy-up awning has been set up at the base of the gangway. Beneath it, a long table is laden with Christmas cheer. At each end, urns of hot mulled wine, and between them, stacks of mince pies are generously dusted with icing sugar. Dogg is among the staff, who are festively adorned with tinsel and baubles, giving away the Christmas spirit.

A merry queue of guests stretches up the gangway, singing carols. Not necessarily the same carol, nor to the same tune, or in unison, but the sentiment is high.

Inside the sea door, security is tight. As usual, everything is passing through the x-ray machine, but for those unlucky enough to be singled out they are sent to a separate table where bags and pockets are being searched and swabbed by Nick and Craig,

A male guest, clearly overindulged in festive cheer, hurls harsh words at them as they finish with his belongings. They let him take his things back, and feeling scalded, they glance to Kieron for reassurance. He stands with Croc, Jim, and Ronni, ship-side of the entrance operation.

"It happens, but you need to stay calm and polite. This is a tough test for you," Kieron tells his trainees. "Festive merriment at the base of the gangway, security at the top for everyone's safety. You are tasked with searching everyone thoroughly, even if they hate it. Take the verbal abuse, step back from any physical threats, and defuse the situation. But you must check everything. Ask, 'What is this? What's it for?'"

"No friends, no favouritism, no allowances," Jim adds from behind, as Kieron steps back to join him. Then he addresses Kieron as he shakes his head. "Do you have any idea what you're looking for?"

"It's training," Kieron replies.

"Training my arthritic knee?" Jim retorts. Kieron tries to ease him away from the guests potentially overhearing as Jim continues. "You're no closer to solving anything, and you're putting my guests in discomfort."

"Maybe," Kieron says, as they meet up with Croc and Ronni. "But, there's a Russian agent on board."

Kieron looks at Croc to continue.

"Grigory Dolinsky. He's suspected to have led the Salisbury poisonings," Croc says before pausing. He wasn't supposed to reveal more.

"The woman he's playing chess with is Wanda Everett, an American with no criminal record. However, she's a cadet with CSCI and a guest on your ship. Her two friends are similar. He's smuggled a bag into the resort area. If he hands it to them to bring on board, I want to know exactly what's in it."

"So do I," Jim insists.

"Then you stay and watch. Because I can't be here, I can't be seen, but I need to know everything," Kieron says. "And as for being closer to knowing what's going on, we're deep in the weeds here. Croc's been in contact with the FBI all day."

Kieron gives Croc the nod.

"Special Agent Edward Cronkite is in charge at the Miami office. The whole network will be prosecuted under U.S. law."

"We want to take everyone down, not just the three girls," Ronni adds. "We're deep diving everything - bank accounts, school records, church affiliations - whoever they are, we'll find them."

It's as though she's been waiting to say that to Jim. Raul approaches with an update.

"The girls are at the bottom of the gangway," Raul reports before heading off.

"We have to leave you to it," Kieron says, turning to Jim.

"Watch for any contaminants they might try to smuggle on board," Ronni says.

"We'll be just above on the promenade deck," Kieron adds, leading Ronni and Croc away.

As they go to join Zack at the back of the promenade deck, he's not at the rail. "They're on the gangway. They'll see you at the front. Looks like the Russian's heading up to the bar."

"Is Dwight still there?" Kieron asks.

"Yes. And Billy's watching from below. Within striking distance."

Ronni creeps forward and looks down. "They're on board now, and they've made sure they're the last ones. The refreshment table is folded, and the crew's bringing the kit back on board. Nice touch - they left the mince pies for the staff. The gangway's being untied. You need to make a decision on Billy and Dwight, or they won't be opening their presents here in the morning."

Kieron is on the phone. "Dwight, hold your position. I need to know what he's up to. You can come out with the tug that collects the pilot."

"I don't like leaving them with him," Zack says. "We know he's a killer."

"Should we go ashore?" Ronni asks, then leans over to see the gangway being pulled up. "It can go back down. We only have to ask."

"No. It would attract attention and could escalate things unnecessarily," Kieron says.

Ronni watches as the local shore staff loosen the ropes, and the Amber Cove team in Christmas trimmings wave goodbye, enjoying their mince pies.

At the security table, just the three young women remain - Wanda, Carol, and Abi. The bag is carefully opened. Nick pulls out three large one-kilogram bags of plain flour, two boxes of icing sugar, small bottles of food colouring, and a few other boxes of art materials.

"What is this for?" Nick asks, holding up a bag of flour, puzzled. Jim is watching him.

"I'm going to make a cake," Wanda replies cheekily. "Come on, Nick, you're not getting into my knickers."

"Officer, do your job properly," Jim insists from behind, still perplexed by the contents.

"It's flour," Carol says.

"Don't you like the food on board?" Jim asks, a touch of sarcasm in his voice. "Swab it. Is it flour? Why would they have flour?"

"It's good this security training," Carol says.

"Tomorrow morning's Christmas art class. We're making a Christmas scene," Abi explains, hanging on the word scene just a little more than she should.

"We have flour in the ship's kitchen," Jim responds.

"Sure, we asked for some, but it might not come," Carol adds.

"Swab it," Jim says.

Craig uses the swab, places it in the EDT, and waits for the results. "It's negative."

Carol looks up at Jim. "Flour!"

"For the art class tomorrow?" Jim presses.

"Yes," Abi answers.

"Not to dust Santa's footprints down every corridor at midnight?" Jim asks, still sceptical.

"No," Abi replies, firmly.

"I suggest we hold these items for you," Jim says, and points to Nick's receipt book.

"You know how to fill this in?"

"Yes, sir," he turns to the girls. "We'll issue a receipt and deliver them to your class in the morning," Nick says confidently.

Jim nods, impressed with the young cadets.

"No. Come on, grow up, Nick," Wanda says.

"It will be there."

"Good job," Jim says.

8-57 SIDE THRUSTER
Christmas Eve - Late afternoon, 24th December, Day 10

Grigory Dolinsky walks into the Star Bar just as the ship's side thrusters begin to hum.

"A bottle of beer," he demands, his Russian accent thick.

"Closed, sir," the barman replies politely.

"Then open it. Get me a beer."

"Sir, we are closed. My terminal's off now."

Grigory eyes Dwight, who is seated at the bar, absorbed in his laptop with a beer beside him.

"He has beer," Grigory says, pointing.

"Give the man a drink," Dwight says, his voice low but firm, trying to defuse the situation. "It'll be on the house."

The waiter hesitates, about to question who Dwight is, potentially blowing his cover, but Dwight cuts him off.

"I said, give the man a drink." Dwight stands, sliding a fake shield across the bar, keeping it hidden from Grigory's view. The barman notices and, with a nod, tops a bottle of beer for the Russian.

"Thank you," Grigory mutters, grabbing the bottle.

"Enjoy. It's Christmas," Dwight says, folding up his laptop and dropping it into its bag. Outside, the staff on the shore cheer as they wave at the crowd on the top deck. A Mexican wave begins, rolling from ship to shore and back again.

On the promenade deck, Kieron, Ronni, Croc, and Raul stand at the rail, watching the scene unfold.

"I don't like the look of this," Ronni mutters, eyes fixed on Grigory.

Kieron pulls out binoculars and scans the Russian. "What's he up to?" he asks, his voice tight.

Ronni grabs the binoculars and looks down to the water's edge where Billy is keeping a watchful eye on the dock.

Below, the canoe man returns, preparing to collect the boats. He unties them from the spike, glancing up at Billy before looking out toward the ship.

"You weren't joking," he shouts to Billy. "You do need a canoe to get out to the ship."

Billy grins, standing up. "No. I'm spending Christmas with you and yours," he replies, heading toward the man.

"Yeah, yeah. You're welcome," the man says, paddling off with the canoes in tow.

The ship's horn begins blasting, a sound that cuts through the air like a thunderclap. On the pool deck, a band kicks into a lively Christmas tune, and the sail-away party begins. A cacophony of sounds fills the air.

Back at the bar, Grigory walks to the front rail, staring out at the ship. Dwight watches him carefully, his posture stiffening as he senses danger. Grigory's hand slips into his pocket, and Dwight's expression sharpens, a surge of urgency flooding his mind. He glances at the barman, silently mouthing, *"Get out of here."*

Ronni watches Grigory through the glass. "Bomb," she whispers.

Kieron's eyes snap to the screen of his phone as he zooms in. "Shit. We missed it."

The ship's horn blares again, drowning out everything else, deep blasts vibrating the air.

Dwight reacts instinctively. He sees the remote in Grigory's hand and, without hesitation, grabs a nearby chair. Swinging it in a wide arc, he brings it crashing down onto Grigory's arm. The remote slips from Grigory's fingers.

Ronni watches, frozen, as the small device falls two floors. Time seems to stretch as she watches it tumble. "Brace," she mutters under her breath. It hits the floor with a dull thud. No explosion. She shifts her gaze back up, her heart racing, as Grigory strikes Dwight.

On the raised deck, Grigory's attacks are sharp and fast, each blow landing with deadly precision. Dwight blocks them all with the skill of a seasoned hand-to-hand fighter, but the Russian is quicker, more agile. Dwight is forced back, his movements less fluid, hampered by his artificial legs. The fight moves out of view from the crowd, the two men exchanging brutal blows and vicious neck grips, tumbling down to a lower platform.

Dwight is Grigory's equal in strength, but not when standing. On the floor, he continues to fight - head butts, punches, fingers to throats, jabs to the eyes - but he's slowing. Each time they break apart, Dwight pulls Grigory back, refusing to give him space.

Grigory grabs a nearby glass, smashing it on the edge of the bar before wielding the jagged shards like a weapon. Dwight blocks each deadly swipe, but Grigory shifts tactics, slamming the sharp edges into Dwight's thigh where major arteries should be - except Dwight has no legs. Instead, the glass embeds into the artificial limb with a sickening *crunch*.

Grigory's momentary surprise gives Dwight the opening he needs. With a snarl, Dwight wrenches the glass free and drives it into Grigory's face, his neck, his side - again and again. The Russian backs away, stumbles down a step into the an equipment hut, disoriented. Dwight uses the safety rail to pull himself upright; he isn't done. He uses it to stumble down the short set of steps.

Grigory makes a desperate move, cornering himself in the zip-line hut. With a frantic snatch, he grabs the pulley system and hurls himself into the open air, sliding down the wire, blood streaming from his wounds.

Dwight watches helplessly as the Russian escapes. The ship's horn blasts once more, a thunderous warning.

As Grigory plummets down, Billy appears from nowhere, the stake from the canoe in hand. With Herculean strength, he hurls it at the falling Russian, the point driving into Grigory's side. The pole rips through him and out his back, and Grigory's body crumples to the ground, lifeless.

Billy watches him fall, and quickly follows, leaping feet-first onto the Russian's wound, ensuring a painful death.

"Die. And die hard for Bedřiška," Billy mutters coldly, as Grigory's last breath comes out in a bloody cough.

"Did the girl help you?"

Grigory laughs.

Billy leans on the spear, churning his inside organs. But Grigory dies laughing. Billy searches the body, pulling out the Russian's phone and papers, then yanking the broken pole free. He kicks Grigory's lifeless body into a nearby hedge and sprints toward the bar. He climbs the stairs two and three at a time.

"Ritter! Where are you?" Billy shouts.

"Down here!" Dwight's voice calls back, and Billy turns to see his former commander searching ground level. "We need that remote switch."

Billy swings over the rail, slides down a roof and drops to the floor to join the search. Their eyes scan the area, Billy finally spotting the remote where they hadn't expected it.

Dwight pulls out his phone. "Can that pilot boat collect us from the jetty?"

8-58 DRESS REHEARSAL
Christmas Eve - Late afternoon, 24th December, Day 10

The wedding dress billows as petite Prisha twirls, drawing excited applause from her mother. For the single mother of two, it's a day neither of them thought they'd see. Izzy and Macey, her maids of honour, bustle about with matching energy.

"Macey, you better get that boy Richard of yours to put a ring on it," Mary teases, watching the scene unfold.

"You deserve this, my sister," says Bukka, Prisha's brother. His tone carries warmth, though perhaps not as much visible excitement as Lakshmi and Reyansh show.

Mary steps forward to adjust Prisha's headdress.

"No," Mama Gee interjects, stepping in to restore it to its original state.

Lakshmi, holding her doll, offers it to Prisha with a wide grin. "Pretend flowers, Mummy."

Mary chuckles and says, "You'll look real pretty next to your mamma in that dress I got you yesterday."

"She has a dress for the wedding," Prisha replies, her voice firm but calm. "My mother made it for her."

Lakshmi opens her mouth to respond, but Prisha silences her with a gentle yet decisive finger.

Mama Gee turns her attention to Mary, inspecting her outfit. "What are you wearing?"

"This," Mary replies.

"Oh," Mamma-Gee says, but behaving under the watchful eye of her daughter.

"My daughters took me shopping at The Webster. I got myself this Celine," Mary says with a hint of pride.

"Celines? Is that previously loved? Something old?"

"No. Celine is a label."

"I'm an excellent seamstress if it needs altering," Mama Gee offers, her tone a masterful blend of courtesy and veiled critique.

Prisha decides it's time to diffuse the building tension. "Shall we eat?" she suggests, lightly brushing her mother's shoulder as she moves toward the bedroom.

Her mother follows, catching up to whisper, "You need to stop this ship."

"Mamma, trust me. You're not the first person to suggest that this week. We all feared an explosion - just didn't expect it to be between the old grandmas."

Mama-Gee smirks. "Less of the 'old,' please. And I won't explode. But I do need to shop."

"We have a shop," Prisha says, her tone softening. "But you'll look stunning in your traditional clothes. They have character. Americans don't have a heritage of their own, so let her wear her labels. It boosts their economy, and collects taxes."

Meanwhile, the vessel cruises at low speed, and its wake fans out from both sides. A pilot boat draws alongside a platform lowered on Deck 5, ready for the local pilot to disembark. But before he can, two unexpected passengers leap onto the ship.

Billy is the first, then steadying himself he turns to help Dwight, who follows awkwardly.

"Who are you two?" the pilot demands, shocked.

"We missed the ship," Billy explains nonchalantly.

"You can't just board here. Immigration - "

"We were never in your country. The resort's a safe zone," Dwight interrupts.

"But this boat departed Puerto Plata. You'll need to return with me."

"It picked us up at the jetty. You have no immigration jurisdiction here - it's not the pilot's problem," Dwight says firmly. "Merry Christmas."

"Happy holidays," Billy adds with a grin.

The baffled pilot watches as his boat retreats and the ship's platform retracts as the duo disappears.

Inside the ship they are greeted like heroes by Zack and Kieron.

"He needs to see the doc," Billy says, motioning toward Dwight.

"I'm fine," Dwight protests.

But Zack and Kieron gently guide him to the medical centre just off Deck 4.

Inside, the medical team moves swiftly.

"Dwight had issues with his leg before the trip. He also fell ashore," Billy explains.

What Dwight hadn't noticed - but Billy had - is the blood seeping through his pants about a foot below the waistband. As a trained soldier, Billy had immediately checked his partner for injuries.

"Pants down," the doctor instructs.

In a seamless, practiced move, the team seats Dwight, removes his trainers, and pulls off his pants.

Dwight glances down and chuckles. "Well, I never." He raises a hand and Billy high-fives him.

"I learned from the best," Billy replies, grinning. He hands Grigory's belongings - a phone, passport, notebook, and flight ticket - to Kieron.

"I left a bit of a mess," Billy admits.

"Yeah. We saw your Greek God impression," Kieron remarks.

Billy shrugs. "That was my PB for the javelin."

"You're lucky their attention was elsewhere," Zack notes, taking the items from Kieron.

The doctor examines the wound. "The cut's at the end of the stump - very clean. But there's an infection. That can't be new."

Dwight winces. "It's been painful lately. That's the antibiotic I've been on."

Dwight has all his medical information, which he hands to the doctor.

"We don't have that medication, but we'll find an alternative. Any allergies?" the doctor asks.

"Just my ex-wife," Dwight quips.

The team laughs, and the doctor orders a blood test. "Run a full panel, compare results in two hours."

As Dwight is tended to, Zack turns to Billy. "Impressive work back there."

"He didn't say much."

"Did you give him a chance?"

"He wasn't going to talk," Billy says.

Zack takes the Russian's belongings and heads off, "I'll get these bagged and logged."

Kieron dials out as the watertight sea door closes. "Ted, it's Kieron. Do you have a clean-up team in the Dominican Republic?"

"You know we don't operate there."

"Well, Grigory's body is under a bush at Amber Cove, near the end of the zip line. Maybe approach by sea after hours. I'll send a pin."

Ted sighs. "This is going to make good reading. Send it over with the report, and leave it with me."

"He had a remote. Looked like he was about to trigger something when the boat was near shore. Didn't want another Vasa."

"Vasa?"

"Old Swedish galleon. Sank just after leaving the harbour. Great museum in Stockholm."

Ted chuckles. "What was the remote for?"

"Still figuring that out. I'll need to open some safes on board - the three girls and Jim Downing's. Got anything on him?"

"Mercenary type. Works for whoever pays him."

"Typical. Call me later if you find anything."

"It's Christmas."

"If you see us on the news, you'll know I didn't solve it," Kieron jokes.

Ted laughs. "Don't mess with Father Christmas. My daughter's waiting for him."

8-59 CHRISTMAS EVE
Christmas Eve - Evening, 24th December, Day 10

Officer Jim Downing is hosting a table of sixteen, for tonight's Grand Gala Christmas Eve Dinner. Prisha and Croc sit with their two children, Reyansh and Lakshmi, between them. Surrounding them are Izzy, Macey, Stan, Mary, Prisha's mother and brother, and the CSCI group of ex-military personnel -

Dwight, Zack, Billy, Ronni, and Kieron. The evening's directive: dress festively.

The atmosphere hums with cheer and camaraderie. Laughter echoes as Kieron's phone is passed between them to re-watching the video of Billy's dramatic manoeuvre.

"Amazing," Dwight says, handing the phone to Jim. "Straight out of *Troy*. You could've been Brad Pitt."

"I hear that a lot," Billy replies, smirking.

Jim winces as he watches the clip. "Was that necessary?"

Kieron catches his expression. "Why? Was he a friend of yours?"

Jim shakes his head. "No, it's just... an odd way to handle a guest."

Billy chuckles darkly. "Jim, look again. Does that man really look like a guest? He looks like the man who ended my friendship with a wonderful lady."

Jim replays the video, wincing again.

"Can we see, please?" Reyansh asks, eagerly.

"No," Prisha says firmly. "It's not for children."

"Were they fighting?" Lakshmi chimes in.

"No," Croc interjects. "Just being silly. And they won't be getting presents tonight."

The children's meals arrive, and the adults encourage them to eat, knowing the little ones won't last the whole evening.

Billy leans toward Jim, speaking low. "That man was marked from the moment he killed her. but that's just the kind of guy I am."

Reyansh, ever curious, notices the exchange. "Were you naughty, Uncle Billy?"

"No," Billy says, smiling.

"Yes, he was," Jim counters with a wink.

Dwight grins. "Is there a video of me somewhere, doing my best *Gladiator* impression?"

"Nope," Zack quips. "Nothing worth filming. What did you do, anyway?"

Kieron's phone buzzes. Glancing at the caller ID, he excuses himself, rising from the table and stepping outside the restaurant. He answers as he moves into the quieter space.

"Istov. Merry Christmas."

"Merry Christmas. And thank you for the photos," Istov replies, his tone even. "I can confirm you killed KGB agent Grigory Dolinsky. But I'm not sure that's something you want widely known."

"That's life, Istov."

"You understand, your problems may not be over."

"They never are. I was born that kind of guy."

Istov chuckles dryly. "Do you know the old Russian saying about problems?"

"Enlighten me."

"A man inherits the problems of his father, wrestles with his own, and dies solving his children's."

"What's the new problem I'm destined to solve?"

"We all have problems. We all die. Call your daughter in New York."

Kieron's demeanour shifts, growing serious. "Istov, do you know the English version of that saying?"

"I'm sure you'll tell me."

"If two men have a problem, only the survivor lives to worry about it. Rest easy - I'm not your problem."

Istov sighs. "Dolinsky was running a disruption programme. Many cells, many leaders, many operatives across America. His work will continue without him. Whatever he has set up is already in motion."

"Happy holidays," Kieron says curtly, before hanging up.

He pulls out his phone and snaps a photo of Jim Downing from a distance. Attaching the image to a message, he sends it to Agent Edward Cronkite. Then, dialling again, he steps further into the night.

"Ted."

"Kieron, it's Christmas Eve."

"I just sent you a picture of Jim Downing. He winced at the video of Grigory's killing. That worried me. First time I've doubted him," Kieron says.

"I'd like to see that footage."

"It's never going to be evidence, so don't expect it under your Christmas tree."

"Okay, send me the report on your conversation with Istov."

"Before Santa arrives," Kieron promises, hanging up. Scrolling through his contacts, he selects 'Auli'i – Daughter' and presses the call button.

By the time Kieron returns to the table, food has been served, and Croc has taken the children to bed.

"Oh, I missed saying goodnight," Kieron mutters, sitting down. He sends Croc a text: Set facial recognition on Jim Downing's photo.

Picking up his spoon to start his soup, he pauses, tossing a small remote onto the table in front of Jim.

"What do you use these for on the ship?" Kieron asks.

Jim picks it up, examining it. "Nothing. Never seen one of these before."

"Maybe it's for a bomb," Kieron says, casually.

Jim drops it instantly. "What? No B-word."

Zack inspects it, turning it over. "Battery's removed."

"Still wouldn't press it," Ronni jokes, her voice carrying an edge. "Just in case it sinks the ship. We've been speculating about this for days."

Jim looks uneasy. "No… Not here. Not on board. Could we not say the B-word out load?"

"Well, I have been informed that whatever the Russian had set up, the wheels are in motion.

Jim glances nervously around the room.

8-60 MERRY CHRISTMAS
Late Christmas Eve, 24th December, Day 10

The largest Christmas tree on the ship dominates the atrium, a grand hall spanning three decks. At twenty feet tall, the tree is still dwarfed by the atrium's soaring height. On the dance floor of Deck 5, the poorly named "silent disco" entertains Billy, Zack, Kieron, and Ronni for a few minutes before they decide to move on. They take the forward elevator to the Crow's Nest Lounge, a cosy space filled with holiday cheer and the lively tunes of a jazz band that has likely been gifted more drinks tonight than all week. Hopefully none will be subject to a random breath test.

The team find a table by the front port-side window, though there's little to see outside beyond a few distant ship lights moving along the same channel.

The bandleader speaks as the music fades. "We're going to take a short break. After the Captain rings in Christmas Day, we'll be back to take you all the way to present-opening time!"

Kieron suddenly narrows his eyes at the bandleader, his brow furrowing as a memory surfaces.

"What's up?" Ronni asks, noticing his expression.

Kieron winces. "I've seen that bandleader before - on another ship. It was during that serial killer case. He was talking with a guest about Burt Bacharach. She got up to sing with him - a real treat. But…"

"But?" Billy prompts.

Kieron sighs. "The woman I was with in the bar left just before me. When I took the crew stairs, she was hiding behind the door. Tossed me right over the rail."

"Ouch," Zack offers sympathetically.

"It took me a while to recover from that head injury," Kieron admits.

"I was referring to your poor choice in women," Zack quips.

Billy grins. "Yeah, you do pick 'em."

"Enough from you, soldier," Ronni interjects, smirking.

Kieron shrugs. "I just hope it's not a bad omen."

The ship's bell rings out. The horns blast, and the crowd erupts into cheers, the atmosphere as jubilant as New Year's Eve. Kieron leans over and kisses Ronni.

"I hope you're not planning to kill me," he jokes.

"There's no sex like Christmas sex," she replies, arching a brow. "It's up to you to survive."

"Merry Christmas, everyone!" booms a voice over the speakers. "From me, Captain Paul, and all on the bridge. We're about to put the ship into autopilot and join you - just kidding. Merry Christmas!"

As the band kicks back in, Zack flags down a waiter to order drinks. "So," he muses, "today is the target day. Whatever it is."

Kieron and Ronni are already slipping into work mode.

"Art class," Ronni says, glancing around. "In here in ten hours. Do they get their shopping back?"

"Who wants to do an art class on Christmas Day?" Billy asks, incredulous.

"Solo cruisers. People without families. Those who want to forget," Kieron explains.

"And those who want to blow up the ship," Zack adds darkly.

Ronni nods. "We'll X-ray their shopping, look for a second remote. If it's clear, we'll return it - but we'll need to check for anything small, like the remote we found earlier."

"If it's clean, you can deliver it to the class," Kieron suggests.

"Not me. They know me," Billy says.

"Same," Zack agrees, glancing at Ronni.

"They might have seen me at CSCI," Ronni admits. "But I would be better sitting in here watching them."

"Dizzy, the assistant hotel manager, can handle it," Kieron suggests. "Ronni, you're right. Grab a book and stay here."

"A perfect Christmas," Ronni mutters.

"What if we're not the target?" Billy interjects.

Kieron turns to him. "Explain."

Billy leans forward. "The cell - those three girls on board. They're angry, but they wouldn't go down with the ship."

"Go on," Ronni encourages.

"What if the real target is another ship? The *Blue Ocean*. We rendezvous with it tomorrow evening mid ocean for Christmas fireworks."

"Leave it to Billy to come up with a theory no one else thought of," Zack says.

"But should have," Kieron adds.

"A drone attack," Billy continues. "Short-range drones with a heavy payload. They could launch from this ship to strike the other during the fireworks."

"It's plausible," Kieron agrees. "But why the remote?"

"To open a door," Zack suggests. "The cell gets their equipment and instructions when it opens."

"Or," Ronni counters, "the remote could trigger a sleeper agent. If it's not pressed, the sleeper stays dormant. But if it's activated…"

"They're armed," Zack finishes, grimly.

"Jim Downing," Ronni says, quietly.

"But we're still guessing," Zack warns. "Why not just press the remote?"

"Because we might blow-up the ship," Kieron replies, pulling out his phone. He dials a number as Ronni wakes Croc on hers.

"Ted," Kieron says when his call connects.

"You know it's Christmas Eve, right?" Ted's voice crackles through.

"No, it's Christmas Day now," Kieron replies. "I'm here with Billy, Zack, and your old friend Ronni. Merry Christmas."

"That's... thoughtful," Ted replies, clearly sceptical. "But my wife and I were about to get..."

"Sorry to interrupt your fun," Kieron cuts him off, "but we think this ship might be part of a plan to hit the *Blue Ocean* tomorrow during the rendezvous. Fireworks and all."

"I'm listening," Ted says, his tone shifting to business.

"Croc has the passenger list up," Ronni interjects.

"We need to know if there's an important asset on that ship," Kieron says.

Ronni glances at her phone. Her eyes narrow. "There is. Daniel Creedon. And his family."

8-61 SECRET SANTA
Early Christmas Day Morning, 25th December, Day 11

Wanda's breathless climax - deeper and more intense than anything she's experienced before - stirs Abi in the next bed.

Half-awake, Abi opens her eyes and smirks sleepily. "Go, girl," she mumbles, before rolling onto her side.

Wanda collapses onto her back, staring at the ceiling, overwhelmed and confused. She turns to face the wall, seeking refuge in the cool distance of the sheets. Dogg, lying beside her, catches Abi's gaze. His look is a silent invitation. Without hesitation, Abi slips out of bed, careful not to wake Raul, who is wrapped around Carol. Sliding into Dogg's bed, Abi fits perfectly into his waiting embrace.

Wanda sits up abruptly, throwing the sheets off in frustration.

"What? You had your fun," Abi teases, grinning as Dogg's hands begin to work their magic. She shifts to make room, setting off a ripple effect. Carol stirs, and an unexpected arousal wakes her fully.

"Oh, for the love of - please!" Wanda groans, clearly disgusted.

"Wanda, it's Christmas!" Carol replies, her voice husky. She grips the mattress, locking eyes with Abi. "Merry Christmas, Abi."

"Merry Christmas, Carol. How's it treating you so far?" Abi fires back with a mischievous smirk.

Wanda, now almost fully dressed, glares at them. "Come on, you two."

"What's the rush?" Dogg asks lazily, not bothering to cover himself.

"Enough from you. And honestly, I don't know why they call you Big Dogg," Wanda snaps.

"Oh, I do," Abi purrs, smirking.

Raul, still half-asleep, chuckles. "What could be so important that it beats staying in bed? Come on, Wanda. Get back in here."

Wanda shakes her head, exasperated. "Thank you, but I've had *quite* the start to my Christmas Day. Now it's time to open presents." She looks pointedly at Abi and Carol. "You two. Get up."

Neither makes a move.

"What present you got?" Dogg asks, clearly intrigued as he props himself up.

"I don't know," Wanda replies curtly. "It's a present. You don't know what's in it until you open the box."

"Oh, you know," Raul says, smirking. "Girls always know. You probably picked it out yourself."

"She's right. What's in your box?" Dogg presses.

Wanda rolls her eyes. "I *don't* know. It's Secret Santa."

"You only got one box?" Dogg asks, still probing.

"Just one," Wanda replies.

Dogg turns to Abi. "What about you?"

"One," Abi says with a shrug. "It can wait until lunch time."

"And you don't know what's inside?"

"Nope."

Dogg looks over at Carol, who is too preoccupied with her crescendo to answer. When she finally collapses into a satisfied heap, she weakly nods in agreement. "Lunchtime."

"Well, that settles it," Wanda declares, pulling the duvets off Abi and Carol. "Up you get. It's Christmas morning, and we've got things to do."

"I can't move yet," Carol groans, limp but grinning.

Dogg sits up, undeterred. "You all just got one box? Who's it from?"

"That's the point of Secret Santa," Abi replies. "You don't know."

"Secret Santa?" Dogg's eyes light up. "I wanna come with you. Watch you open them. I didn't get a present."

Carol's eyes widen as she glances at Dogg's naked form. Mouth agape, she silently mouths *wow* to Abi, who bites her lip and nods.

"We open them at lunch, after art class," Wanda says firmly.

"How can you wait?" Raul asks, baffled. "If I had a present, I'd have opened it already."

"We've had them since the start of the cruise," Wanda replies. "A few more hours won't hurt."

"You've been staring at them for days? No way. I'd have ripped mine open," Dogg says, shaking his head.

"We hid them," Abi says softly.

"Where?" Raul asks, scanning the cramped room. "There's nowhere to hide anything in a cabin."

"Behind the life jackets, up on the shelf," Abi whispers.

"Exactly," Wanda says, her patience wearing thin. "Now, up you get!"

No one moves and Wanda leaves, alone.

Dogg watches her leave before turning back to the two naked women lounging in bed. "You wanna swap before you go?" he asks with a sly grin.

8-62 CHRISTMAS MORNING

Christmas Day - Early Morning, 25th December, Day 11

A knock on the door wakes Kieron and Ronni. He grabs a bathrobe and walks through the living area and opens it to find Izzy. "Good morning."

"Can I come in?" she says. "Sorry, Prisha had us up early."

"Whereas I was up late…" Kieron starts.

"Typing the report I read. Am I missing something or is this the easiest disaster to stop?"

"How?" Kieron asks.

"If the ships never meet, then they can't attack each other," Izzy explains.

Kieron has started to boil the kettle and he turns and looks at her.

"If that is the plan, and as yet we don't know for sure," Izzy continues. "It is one crazy plot you came up with after more than a few bottles of wine."

"You don't like it then?" Ronni says, walking out of the bedroom in her bathrobe. She goes to the boiling kettle and makes a coffee. She looks to Izzy who shakes her head, not wanting a drink. Kieron opens a tea bag and makes his drink.

"It is a bit moviesque; three girls firing drones at a ship which they hit exactly in the right place. Nine times," Izzy says.

"It is possible, and therefore a scenario we can't ignore," Kieron says, sitting on the sofa that the living area suite has.

"Then stop the ships from meeting."

"That is too easy," Ronni says. "What would you do if plan A was scuppered?"

"Evoke plan B," Kieron says.

"Which is?" Izzy asks.

"Us," Kieron says. "We could still be the hit. What else is there?"

"And there is a report in from Dogg. They interrogated the three girls all night, and each has a Secret Santa box hidden on the top shelf behind their life jacket."

Both Kieron and Ronni frown, they don't miss things in a search.

"I pulled the life jacket forward, waved my hand backwards and forwards across that shelf," Kieron says.

"Me too."

"Pulled the jacket forward or took it out?" Izzy asks.

"Pulled it," Ronni says.

"So it could have been attached to the life jacket, and moved with it."

"It is nearly eight o'clock now, so the meeting of ships is exactly twelve hours away," Ronni starts.

"If something is happening today, and we don't know that for sure. Eight o'clock tonight is likely to be the last chance. Looking for what's going to happen, whatever, whenever, starts now," Kieron suggests. He does not like missing things.

"We search their rooms again while they're in the art class."

"Well, one of us is up and dressed," Izzy says.

There is another knock at the door, and it is opened to reveal Croc.

"Nice," he says, walking in. After looking around, he sees they both have a drink so makes himself one.

"Make yourself at home," Kieron starts. "This is for you and Prisha after the wedding. Honeymoon suite.'

"We were just enjoying a last morning here," Ronni says.

"Wow." Croc says, inspecting the area with more enthusiasm. "I hope they change the sheets."

There is another knock at the door.

"At this rate they won't need to," Ronni says, going to open it. Dwight stands there. "Come in, we're just about to order for everyone."

Dwight walks in and sees the others.

"How your leg?" Croc asks Dwight.

"The infection's back. Doc is arranging stronger antibiotics from a hospital in Jamaica tomorrow. He thinks I should stay there."

Ronni is on the room phone. "Hi, could we get a breakfast trolley, to the owner's suite please. Thanks." She puts the phone down and looks at the others. "Carry on without me while I shower and get dressed."

"So, your midnight scenario," Croc starts.

"How far-fetched is it? A remote opening a box on the ship," Kieron says.

"And another box opening for the sleeper agent, if the remote is not activated. A reserve," Dwight adds.

"It sounds like James Bond stuff, but actually every smartphone can do it for every house in America," Croc says, holding up his phone. "Household systems. Phone, switch the light on. Phone, turn my heating up one degree. Phone, put milk on the shopping list. Phone, set an alarm for eight hours. Any of a dozen household apps could control an 'IFTTT'."

"Ift?" Kieron asks.

"If this, then that. Rhythms with gift. If I press this button; start a countdown of what? The ship left at eighteen hundred hours, so if the cell expects their orders at same time tomorrow - the countdown is for twenty-four hours. When that is complete, the app says 'open this switch', and that opens the box with the orders in."

"And if the app does not get a command, then the sleeper, maybe Jim gets his box opened…"

"At a prescheduled time. But if executed, it cancels his need to become involved."

"I might be a bit woozy on these drugs, but that's the point I don't get," Dwight says. "If that is how it all works, then that is daft. Ift, right? Why not just have a box that opens. Assume everything is somewhere on the ship and has been for weeks. Why does Grigory need to be at Amber Cove? Why did he have to trigger a remote to open something already on the ship? Already fitted with commands?"

"That is the advantage of being sober," Kieron says. "Last night it sounded good."

"Exactly. If you can do all that fancy triggering, then why not do it without Grigory?" Dwight says.

"If the target is not Creedon, it could still be you, or us," Izzy suggest.

"We might be back to it being a hit on the ship," Dwight agrees.

"Elaine has set us all up to die so she owns CSCI," Ronni says.

"If we die, there is no CSCI," Kieron says.

"With that much money, she won't need the active agency," Izzy concludes.

"That brings me to why I popped up to see you rather than write a report. Prisha and I were thinking that we could fly to Bequia and use one of the company houses for our honeymoon," Croc suggests.

"Sure," Kieron says.

"But we can't."

"Why not?"

"I rang Sylvie, the realtor who looks after them, and she told me that Elaine had given her orders to start renting them. Both properties have tenants," Croc explains.

"Elaine's done what? Technically, they don't belong to CSCI. They belonged to me and Georgie.

Georgie died and left everything she had to Bedřiška, so she and I were joint owners," Kieron reveals while thinking.

"Bedřiška is dead. And with you dead, who owns them?" Ronni asks.

"The agency."

"Elaine," Dwight says. "I wonder if she knows my first wife?"

There is a knock at the door. They all turn, a little suspicious until they hear. "Room service."

"Croc, when you get this room, we will all be in for tea and coffee first thing," Kieron says.

8-63 D-DAY
Christmas Day - Mid Morning, 25th December, Day 11

Ronni sits in a plush armchair, the kind meant for basking in the glow of a crackling fire at Christmas - not to broil under the scorching morning sun streaming through the Crow's Nest Lounge's expansive windows. It's ten o'clock, and the team braces for what they've ominously dubbed *D-Day - Disaster Day*. Her eyes stay locked on Heather Frost, who is busy arranging her setup for the Christmas art class. Box after box is hauled from trolleys to the desks reserved for aspiring artists.

Nearby, Wanda is already laying out her art supplies, retrieving items from a square backpack that seems comically overfull. The other two girls haven't arrived yet, but Ronni notes their identical backpacks.

Assistant Hotel Manager Dizzy Martel approaches Heather, holding a shopping bag confiscated from Wanda earlier. Wanda tilts her head, a flicker of irritation crossing her face as she recalls the incident.

"I believe you needed this today," Dizzy says, with a warm smile. "What are you making for us, Heather?"

Heather pauses mid-arrangement. "Let's see if anyone actually shows up today. My plans could be scuppered."

"I'm here," Wanda chimes in, reclaiming her bag.

"One person doesn't make a class," Heather mutters, her tone flat.

"Oh, I do."

"You'll be fine," Dizzy reassures her before strolling away. As she passes more people entering the lounge, she calls back over her shoulder. "See? You're filling up now!"

True enough, Abi and Carol enter with a group of eleven, and the participants spread their work across the tables. But the numbers aren't what Ronni focuses on - it's the backpacks. Of the fourteen attendees, only the three girls under investigation carry matching, oversized square packs.

"All three are here," Ronni murmurs into her comms. "It's a go for the cabin search. And for the record, they're the only ones with matching, empty square backpacks."

At the other end of the ship, at the breakfast buffet, Dogg and Raul arrive just before closing time. Staff are already in the change-over, setting up for Christmas lunch. The two undercover agents, who had a hard night, have plates piled high with food as they weave through the dining area and head into the quieter section used by the crew.

Prisha and Croc sit nursing their coffees, having already finished eating.

"My God," Prisha says, eyeing the mountains of food on their plates.

"We need energy, sister," Raul says, with a grin.

"We earned this," Dogg adds. "Found out there's a secret Secret Santa going on."

"You managed without me?" Croc teases.

"Barely," Dogg retorts. "But we kept the three suspects happy."

Raul smirks. "We make a good team. And if one of those sweeties ends up pregnant, they'll have to guess which of us it was."

The comment hits like a slap. Prisha freezes, her face going pale, and she abruptly stands. Without a word, she leaves the table.

"Hey! Sorry, sister!" Raul calls after her, his voice laden with guilt. Turning to Croc, he adds, "Man, I didn't mean..."

Croc shakes his head. "Guess she didn't find that funny. Wedding-day nerves."

"You seeing her before the wedding? That bad luck," Dogg says, leaning back in his chair.

Below, in the girls' corridor, the team works with precision. Ronni stays in the Crow's Nest, monitoring the operation. Jim has been excluded this time because he has become a growing concern. If there's a sleeper agent or team leader on board, Jim now tops the list of suspects.

Unfortunately, deeper dives into his background and face-recognition matches have hit a frustrating wall - a troubling echo of their earlier work on Grigory Dolinsky, the Ghost.

Assistant Manager Dizzy Martel proves an asset. With authorisation to unlock cabins and safes, she was seconded in after a supposed call from cruise line CEO Daniel Creedon. Flattered by the rare direct contact, Dizzy doesn't realise it was Zack impersonating Creedon.

The first cabin is unlocked, and the team moves quickly. From the top shelf of the closet, a life jacket is pulled down and flipped inside out. Its attached whistle dangles uselessly, swaying with the movement. Then, a small, folded envelope slips out and flutters to the floor. Stamped across it in neat lettering are the words: *Wanda's Secret Santa.*

Billy immediately moves to search Abi's cabin while Kieron examines the envelope in detail.

Dizzy lingers nearby, looking at the prize.

"Can this be opened and resealed?" Kieron asks, handing her the envelope. He turns his attention to the cabin safe. With Dizzy's master key and override code, the safe opens to reveal a passport, driver's license, and Temporary Navigation Certificate. Kieron photographs the documents but finds no clues.

Billy returns, holding another envelope. "*Abi's Secret Santa.* Same exact style."

"This doesn't feel like a gift exchange," Kieron mutters under his breath.

Zack appears with a third envelope. "*Carol's Secret Santa.*"

Billy doesn't wait - he tears one open. "You're either about to be shot, or we're about to be bombed," he says flatly.

"What?" Dizzy gasps, as her eyes widen.

"Figure of speech," Billy replies, pulling out the contents: three tickets to a Billy Joel concert at Madison Square Garden.

"Nice Christmas gift," Dizzy says, exhaling slightly.

But Zack frowns, his instincts flaring. "Kieron, this doesn't sit right."

Kieron nods grimly. "Exactly. Zack, get Croc to review the Amber Cove footage. Did Grigory hand these envelopes to the girls, or did they pull them from the shopping before it was confiscated?"

Zack hesitates. "It's Prisha's wedding day."

"It's hours away," Kieron snaps. "If Grigory handed them over, that's why he came in person."

"These aren't gifts," Zack adds, "these are assignments."

8-64 WINTER SCENES

Christmas Day - 11am, 25th December, Day 11

Heather Frost stands at the front of the class, effortlessly guiding her students on how to transform their snowy base paintings into enchanting winter landscapes. Her movements are confident and almost theatrical as she wields a plastic grouting tool with practiced ease. With precise, vertical strokes, she creates the illusion of wooden logs forming the rustic walls of a cosy cabin, each scrape of dark paint adding texture and depth.

"Don't overthink it," Heather encourages. "The logs don't have to be perfect. Just scrape, scrape,

scrape!" She layers dark brown paint with deliberate abandon, her strokes adding texture to the scene.

Next, she moves to the trees. With the same tool, she drags vertical lines to create the trunks of tall firs surrounding the lake nestled at the foot of a jagged mountain. "The branches are weighed down by snow, so we'll add that last," she explains, switching to a thinner edge of the tool for branches. Cleaning it meticulously, she transitions to green paint, sliding it across the canvas to shape diagonal branches.

Heather's artistry is mesmerising, and her casual approach makes even the most hesitant participants feel confident. After wiping the green clean, she loads her spatula with thick white paint and begins forming snowy roofs and frost-laden tree boughs with quick, fluid motions.

"This is the finishing touch," she says, demonstrating how to drag the white into soft, sweeping shapes. The result is a cosy winter scene that seems almost effortless to replicate.

While most of the class focuses on painting, a few participants are busy creating festive decorations at nearby tables. One group works on an elaborate centrepiece of twigs, pinecones, and dried leaves, painting them in shimmering silver and white. Another table is more traditional. Wanda, Carol, and Abi are constructing a nativity scene on a large serving trolley. The mountain centrepiece of their display is wrapped in fabric, concealing whatever they've hidden beneath it. Ronni, keeping an eye on them from a distance, knows it's not just a harmless holiday project.

She's already surreptitiously filmed their work and sent clips to her team. The trio started by mixing orange powder paint with flour to create a thick base for their autumnal "mountain," which they then dusted with white flour for a snowy effect. The scene includes a small box acting as a barn, though its significance remains unclear. Their focus, however, isn't on crafting a nativity. It's on the flour. A massive mixing bowl - clearly borrowed from the kitchen - is filled with flour, red and yellow powder paint, mustard, and other unidentified substances. They've covered the bowl with a towel to contain the dust and are using long gloves and face masks to handle the mixture. It's clear they've planned this meticulously, and Ronni can't ignore the possibility of something more sinister.

Curious, Ronni rises from her observation point and approaches Heather, who is putting the final touches on her demo painting.

"This is incredible," Ronni says, feigning excitement. "I wish I'd joined this class."

"You're welcome to join us for the sea day after Jamaica," Heather offers, handing her a glossy leaflet.

"Oh, I'd never be able to pull this off. I'm hopeless at painting."

"You'd be surprised," Heather replies warmly. "My classes are beginner-friendly, and if you're interested, I also teach online. The dates for my cruise sessions are listed on my website."

"I've never painted before and look at what I've done in three days!" a man nearby chimes in, proudly holding up his work. While clearly that of a novice, it's impressive for someone just starting. "All our work will be displayed at the Christmas Fair this afternoon," he adds.

Ronni's ears perk up. The fair must be a public event, likely in the atrium. As she moves away, she makes a mental note of the timing - it will be after lunch, she suspects. Glancing back at the girls, she sees them, filling small bags with the coloured flour mixture and slipping them into their identical square backpacks. The concoction isn't white anymore; it's brightly coloured, and their meticulous handling confirms her suspicions.

Reaching the bar, she addresses the staff preparing for the noon opening. "Do you have a copy of today's programme?"

"Sorry, ma'am, no," a waiter replies. "You can check the app or the screens near the elevators."

Ronni nods but doesn't bother. Instead, she pulls out her phone to make a call. "Dwight," she says sharply, "they're making coloured flour bombs. The art class will be part of today's Christmas Fair."

8-65 THE PLAN
Christmas Day - 11am, 25th December, Day 11

In the suite, Billy and Zack work furiously to repair the three Secret Santas, while Kieron places a call to Agent Edward Cronkite. Dwight and Croc monitor the screens, ready to act.

"Ted, Merry Christmas," Kieron says.

"I wondered when you'd call," Cronkite replies, his voice dripping with sarcasm. "I've missed you."

"We believe the ship is their immediate target," Kieron explains, "but we suspect they've received orders for future attacks."

"I'm listening."

"A concert at Madison Square Garden, a lecture at the New York Library, and an art exhibition near Central Park - all scheduled for January."

"How do you know this?"

"We intercepted the tickets."

Dwight appears, urgency written all over his face. Kieron raises a questioning hand, silently asking if it's urgent enough to interrupt. Dwight nods. Switching to speakerphone, Kieron continues.

"Ted, you're on speaker. Dwight has an update."

"Merry Christmas, Ted," Dwight begins. "There's a Christmas Fair scheduled in the ship's atrium at 1500 hours. It includes carols by the Guest Choir, an address by the captain, and an art class showcase. The atrium spans three tiers, and hundreds of guests are expected. We believe the plan involves a flour and powder paint attack."

"That's it?" Ted asks, sceptical. "Seems low-level."

"Not if every ship in the fleet is targeted," Kieron counters. "This could cause major disruptions, dominate social media, and make headlines over Christmas. If each ship has an active cell and orders for follow-up attacks, this could escalate into a massive January campaign. Imagine seventy ships, each with three to four attackers. That's a major operation."

"Russians?" Ted probes. "They don't have that kind of manpower here in America."

"They're inspiring Americans," Kieron explains. "This kind of chaos breeds copycats. It's designed to escalate."

"I see the theory. But who's behind it, and how are they pulling it off?"

"We're closing in on answers. Right now, we need to act. If this plays out, thousands of guests will be doused in paint. It's simple, but effective chaos."

"Alright," Ted says, his tone sharp. "I'm calling people in. You'd better have this right."

As the call ends, Billy and Zack present the repaired Secret Santas to Dwight.

"They're good," Dwight confirms, and then speaks into the comms. "Ronni, are the girls still in their rooms?"

"Confirmed. Still making snowballs and filling backpacks," Ronni replies.

"We're revisiting their cabins. Report any status changes," Dwight orders.

"Snowballs?" Billy asks, confused.

"It's part of the attack - flour and powder paint in the atrium at three," Kieron explains. "Get those envelopes back into the correct cabins and return ASAP."

"I'll handle it," Billy volunteers, grabbing the envelopes and rushing out.

Kieron's phone buzzes. He glances at the screen before answering, "Mr. Creedon, sir." The call is brief.

"That was Daniel Creedon," Kieron informs the group. "He's relieved we've uncovered the plot but wants background checks on every art group member across the fleet - any affiliations, clubs, anything suspicious."

Croc folds his laptop and begins packing his equipment.

"I'll coordinate with security and connect with the other ships."

"Treat everyone as a suspect," Kieron warns. "Even Jim. This could be a Russian operation months in the making. They won't hesitate to escalate."

"I'll go with him," Zack offers, and the two head out.

Dwight issues instructions over the network: "Izzy, Macey, travel with Billy. Clear the cabins and report back ASAP." His voice-to-text system logs the updates in the mission report.

As names from art classes across the fleet scroll across Dwight's screen, an alert pops up.

"Lunch break called for the art group," Dwight announces. "Billy, get out of there. They might be heading down."

Reports flood in. Dwight scans them quickly.

"Three ships report art classes taking fire extinguishers," he notes. "Why would they need fire extinguishers?"

Kieron frowns. "Water-based? They could spray it to make the flour and paint rain down. It'll soak in and increase the damage. Coloured rain."

"Potentially toxic rain," Dwight adds grimly. "We don't know what else they've mixed in."

Kieron relays new orders. "Billy, a fire officer is checking for water-based extinguishers. Stay alert."

Dwight leans back, his expression tense. "This isn't just chaos - it's coordinated. But if we're right, how do they plan to escape?"

"Under cover of the flour cloud," Kieron theorises. "They blend in with the victims. Take the disguise off, fake injuries, and disappear into the crowd."

"Possible, but risky for first-timers," Dwight counters.

"Not if they're fanatics," Kieron argues. "They've been groomed for this. We need to stop them before it happens."

Dwight nods grimly. "If you're right, we'll know soon enough."

8-66 REHEARSAL
Christmas Day - 12 noon, 25th December, Day 11

Candice observes the florist putting the finishing touches on the decorations in the President's Room and the Board Room, preparing for the wedding later that afternoon. Without being obvious, she also keeps an eye on the family, who are inspecting the room and rehearsing their roles. They're discussing where everyone needs to stand and what to expect. Candice steps up to the white lectern, glances at her watch, and clears her throat.

"I have a lot to do today. Is the bridegroom coming?" she asks.

"He should be," Prisha replies, her tone uncertain. "But he has a lot going on today too."

"I know - his wedding." Candice's voice carries a subtle edge.

"He's busy."

"This rehearsal should have been done before today."

"He's been overwhelmed with work problems," Prisha defends.

Mama-Gee steps up to Prisha and places a protective hand on the slight bump of her stomach, a visible sign of her pregnancy beginning to show. "He had better be coming. My daughter was left at the altar once before," she says sharply.

Mary stiffens, taking the comment as a pointed jab. "My son will be here," she retorts.

Izzy and Macey quickly move to Prisha's side, sensing the tension. The looming presence of two interfering mothers is too much for the already frail bride.

"Last time, she was left a single mother, raising two children on her own," Mama-Gee presses. "You can't imagine how that feels."

"Mummy, please stop," Prisha pleads softly.

"You see how upset she is? And now she's pregnant again," Mama-Gee adds.

Mary fires back, her voice cold and sharp. "I raised three children as a single mother after I was raped. I didn't even know who the father was." Her words land like a gauntlet thrown in a twisted game of one-upmanship.

"Can we please stop this!" Prisha interjects, her voice shaking as tears threaten. "If this wedding is called off, it won't be because of Winston!" Her declaration cuts through the tension like a blade, leaving Candice and the two mothers momentarily speechless.

Candice regains her composure. "The Captain has a very tight schedule for this wedding. If the rehearsal is delayed again, the wedding will have to be cancelled."

"Fine! Call it off!" Prisha snaps, storming out of the room.

Macey hurries after her. "Prisha, wait!"

Out in the corridor, Macey pulls Prisha into a calming embrace. "Breathe, okay? Deep breaths," she soothes, dialling her brother's number as Prisha tries to steady herself.

"Croc, where are you?" Macey demands when he picks up.

"Have you been reading the reports?" Croc's voice comes through on speaker, calm but tense.

"No. We're at the wedding rehearsal."

"You need to catch up on what we're dealing with."

"No, Winston. I'm dealing with *our* mother, *your* mother, and a bride on the verge of a breakdown. You're supposed to be here for this rehearsal."

"I can't," Croc says firmly. "For this wedding to happen, we have to stop an attack on the Christmas Fair."

"Let Dwight handle it!" Macey snaps.

"We're all stretched thin. If I can't make it, one of my sisters will have to step in. Fill me in later."

Macey ends the call, frustration etched on her face. "Something's definitely going on," she mutters, pulling Prisha back toward the room. "If he's not here, I'll play groom for this rehearsal."

Back inside, Macey takes her position opposite Prisha at the lectern while Candice observes from the captain's side.

"I don't like this," Mama-Gee mutters loudly. "It looks like one of those same-sex marriages. That's bad luck."

"Mummy, it's a rehearsal!" Prisha snaps.

"And I don't like all these Christmas decorations," Mama-Gee adds.

"They're for Diwali, Mum," Prisha sighs.

Izzy ushers the children into position behind Prisha and Macey. Once the bride is in place, the children are directed to the side, and the family steps back so everyone can visualise the setup.

"Is that it? Rehearsal over?" Mary asks impatiently.

"Remember your positions and the timing," Candice says firmly. "And explain this to the groom when he shows up."

As the group disperses, Mary and Mama-Gee both reach for the children, only for the kids to resist.

"Can we go back to our club?" one of them whines.

Prisha and Macey re-join Izzy, who is deep in reports.

"I doubt those three girls will show up as guests," Izzy remarks grimly, glancing up. "It's confirmed - a coloured paint attack."

"Like Holi," Prisha says. "We do that."

"Not like this," Izzy replies. "Our agency has found cells on thirty ships so far. That's what Croc's tied up with."

Prisha hesitates, guilt flickering across her face. "Honestly, I hope he can't make the wedding. I don't know how to tell him... but I don't want this to go ahead."

"You'll go through with it," Macey insists. "No nonsense."

Prisha shakes her head, her resolve breaking. "No. I've made up my mind."

8-67 TIME TO MOVE
Christmas Day - 1210hrs, 25th December, Day 11

Heather Frost's art class winds down for lunch, leaving her tidying around the tables. Most of the students leave, except for a focused painter dissatisfied with his work and two women delicately adding silver touches to a festive centrepiece. Wanda, Abi, and Carol have already left for lunch.

A man Heather doesn't recognise enters the room, accompanied by a uniformed ship's fire officer.

"Can I help you gentlemen?" Heather asks, her tone polite but curious.

"Just looking," the man - Billy - replies smoothly, stepping forward. He smiles disarmingly, diverting her attention from the fire officer, who moves toward a trolley covered with a protective sheet.

"Do you mind if I take some photos? This is great work," Billy adds, gesturing to the artwork.

Heather nods, distracted as the fire officer uncovers the trolley and inspects its contents. To her surprise, he pulls out two red fire extinguishers.

"What are you doing?" she asks, concern creeping into her voice. "That trolley is one of our exhibits."

"Not the extinguishers," the officer replies. "These are mine. I left them unattended on a trolley, and they vanished." He seals the cover back over the trolley.

"We were given it for our artwork," Heather explains defensively.

"It's fine. My mistake," the officer says, lifting the extinguishers. "I didn't realise it had been repurposed. I'll put these back where they belong and finish my shift."

"Good thing you found them," Billy chimes in, recording the exchange on his phone.

Heather smiles politely. "Have a great Christmas Day."

As the officer exits past Ronni, seated near the bar, she discreetly reports through her comms: "Two water fire extinguishers removed."

Billy turns back to Heather. "Do you need help moving this stuff to the atrium? I've got about ten minutes."

Heather hesitates. "Not right now. We can't move anything until after lunch. If you could come back at 2:15 - "

"I can't make it then," Billy interrupts. "And surely that's too late. The atrium will get crowded long before the event starts. Moving things will be impossible by then."

"That's a good point," the painter agrees, looking up from his canvas.

Heather frowns. "We have to get to deck seven of the atrium."

"It'll take time to get elevators when it's busy."

"We should take the centrepiece down as soon as it's ready," one of the women suggests.

"Yes, we do need to start moving things," Heather agrees.

Billy nods enthusiastically. "I'll move what I can to the door for now," he offers, pointing to the bar's exit near Ronni. Without waiting for a reply, he lifts three backpacks and carries them to the side of the bar.

He returns quickly. "What about this?" Billy asks, indicating a stock table Heather is sorting through.

"No, not that," Heather replies.

Billy shifts his focus, pulling three Santa Claus suits from a box. Holding one up for his camera, he grins. "Who's playing Santa?"

"Our young ladies," Heather says, amused.

"Really? Which ones?"

"Several of them. They decided it was time for a female Santa Claus," she chuckles.

"I'm with them," Billy says, still recording. "Which is their art?"

"The snow mountain and nativity scene over there."

"How did they make that convincing snow?"

"It's just flour," Heather says proudly.

"Clever."

Billy picks up a box of supplies Heather hands him. "I'll take this to the elevator now. Then I'll come back to help with the centrepiece. After that, I have to meet my wife."

Meanwhile, Ronni discreetly moves the backpacks into a corridor and turns into a "crew only" door. She positions her phone to record the process and empties the bags, revealing dozens of compact flour balls, perfect for throwing.

"These are packed with flour," she reports to Dwight. "If tossed, they'd create chaos."

"Empty them safely and seal the contents in a waste bag," Dwight instructs.

Ronni complies, carefully transferring the flour balls into large waste bags. One breaks apart during the process, spilling a fine orange-and-white powder. She quickly seals the rest and discards them in a wheeled bin.

"We have a problem," she says. "To replace the weight convincingly, I'd need something heavy, like bottles of sparkling water or juice. But if these bags are dropped from Deck Seven, they could seriously injure someone below."

"Remove the flour completely," Dwight orders. "We'll handle the rest."

"If the switch is discovered before the atrium, they'll know," Ronni warns.

"Then arrest them," Dwight says, firmly.

Back near the elevator, Billy sets down the box and reports in. "Santa suits, beards, and hats, for the three girls. But there's another group of Santas, likely another cell. They've got smaller bags, too. I'm heading back for a closer look."

"Billy, clear out now," Dwight commands. "If they suspect you, they'll change the plan, and we'll lose control."

"Not yet. We need them in the atrium," Billy replies, stepping back into the lounge. He dodges Heather's offer of paintings to carry, saying, "I'll let the staff know you need help. My wife's waiting on Deck Five."

He continues his sweep, scanning the area for signs of the second group of Santas.

In the bar's stockroom, Billy finds Ronni cleaning up the last of the spilled flour.

"Careful," she warns. "This stuff's everywhere."

Billy glances at the bags. "Can these go?"

"Two of them, yes. But this one's a mess."

Billy grabs the clean bags. "The art class leader needs help moving supplies. Easy cover to get involved, but they know me."

"Who is the other group with smaller bags," Ronni says.

"Don't know, but there are two more Santa Suits."

269

"Even a couple of these snowballs could cause major damage," she says.

Billy lifts the two bags, exits, and carries them toward the elevator.

Ronni is trying to clean the contaminated third bag. "Dwight, I need a vacuum, or housekeeping in the Crow's Nest stockroom - fast," Ronni reports.

8-68 WHAT POWDER?
Christmas Day - 1230hrs, 25th December, Day 11

"Roger that, will delay if we can," Dogg mutters into his earbud, balancing five mugs of coffee as he approaches the corner of the restaurant where Raul sits with Wanda and the girls. "But they might decide their coffee is to-go."

"Offer to help," Dwight's voice replies in his ear. "Travel upstairs with them where the instructor needs extra hands. She'll rope you in even if they insist they don't need help."

Dogg places the cups on the table and grabs Abi's Secret Santa envelope.

"Do we open our presents now?" Abi asks eagerly.

"Open and go," Carol says, checking the time. "The Fair starts soon."

Wanda glances at phone. "Relax, we've got time."

Dogg chuckles as he holds Abi's envelope. "Let me open one. I don't have anything to open."

"Billy no-mates," Wanda teases, smirking.

Dogg tears into the first envelope and pulls out three tickets. "Three tickets. So, where are you going?" he asks, raising an eyebrow.

"That's what we'd like to know," Abi chimes in.

Meanwhile, in the suite, the CSCI team listens in on Dogg's undercover work.

"Sing-sing," Dwight murmurs. "That's where the tickets are for."

"We need actual evidence of a crime," Kieron says firmly. "Let this play out as far as we safely can."

"Dogg's really leaning into this whole agent thing," Dwight remarks to Kieron. "Kid's got a future."

"Good," Kieron replies, dialling Agent Cronkite.

Ronni's voice crackles through the line. "I need more time. The powder is everywhere - it's orange, and I'm itching all over. There could be something in it. I need a vacuum."

"Negative on the vacuum," Dwight responds. "No time to find you one."

"I broke a ball, and it doesn't brush off, and I can't risk making it wet. If they're down one backpack, they might panic."

"Roger that. We'll make do with two," Kieron says grimly.

"Without a vacuum, I'm out. I'm part orange," Ronni quips.

Kieron updates Cronkite. "We might need to act early. Ronni's neutralised two backpacks, and the third's compromised. Covered in coloured paint."

"What colour?" Cronkite asks.

"Orange. And it's causing itching."

Cronkite pauses. "Orange - the colour used by the international oil protesters."

"Right," Kieron says. "Orange paint was sprayed on the American Embassy in London after Trump's election. Media said it was anti-Trump, but it was oil protestors. Wanda was there - arrested in London, released without charge. Can anyone confirm she was spraying orange?"

Ted chimes in from Miami. "Fourteen ship's art class attendees are known climate or oil activists. But oil protesters aren't usually this organised - they're annoying amateurs."

"But the Russians have groomed them," Croc suggests, walking in with Zack.

"If they're Russian puppets, why did the imposter almost blow their own mission? That doesn't add up."

"Good question," Kieron says. "We need to stay sharp. Who do we trust?"

Croc answers first. "The assistant head of security in charge today - Marisol Navarro. She's solid. Communication between ships has been quick and efficient."

Zack nods. "I trust her too."

"What's her name?" Dwight asks. "I'll run a check on her."

"Marisol Navarro. One of three assistant heads of security."

"We will too," Ted says.

"She needs to warn the other ships," Kieron says. "Tell all ships the attackers might be disguised as Santas. Shut down guest and crew Wi-Fi immediately - no leaks to social media. That's what they want. Any attackers must be stopped before this powder becomes airborne. It could be toxic - anthrax-level dangerous."

"Got it," Croc says, plugging back into his extra monitors on the desk and relaying the orders to Marisol.

"And here," Zack adds, "she needs a team in the Crow's Nest to assist the art-class carry-down."

"Another team on deck seven," Kieron says, "ready to take down anyone in a Santa suit."

"She doesn't have that kind of manpower," Croc says.

Kieron looks directly at Zack. "Zack, you're in charge of that Santa takedown. If we pull this off…"

"… maybe Prisha and I will have our wedding," Croc adds with a grim smile.

8-69 FANATICISM
Christmas Day - 1330hrs, 25th December, Day 11

Billy steps into the stockroom behind the bar, vacuum in hand, and hands Ronni the plug. She glances into the lounge, unplugs a drink mixer and plugs in the vacuum cord.

Billy starts vacuuming, going over the bag repeatedly. "This stuff is ridiculously hard to suck up," he grumbles.

Ronni watches, her expression tense. "And it's making my skin crawl."

"Go in a shower," Billy says without looking up. "Is this bag clean enough?"

"Yes. Just be careful with it."

"Shower. That's an order."

Ronni doesn't need to be told twice. She rushes down the internal crew stairs while Billy finishes the clean-up. He lifts the last bag and heads out into the public area and along to the elevator.

In the command centre set up in the men's Grand King Suite, Zack, Dwight, Croc, and Kieron monitor the situation.

"Fear is the key," Kieron says, his voice steady but grim. "Those who can be made to feel fear can be groomed into terrorists. The more fanatical they are about their cause, the easier they are to manipulate."

"Sitrep," Dwight interjects, making his speech an auto-dictated report. "Billy's taken the last bag to the elevator. Local crew are on their way to assist Heather - they've got cuffs and are ready to make arrests if needed. Ronni's in the shower. Should Billy shower too?"

"He should, but he won't go," Zack says. "Not unless his skin starts reacting badly." Zack leaves.

"Dogg and Raul are still with the girls. They'll be in the lounge any minute now," Dwight updates his machine.

"Keep them away from the bags," Kieron warns. "Croc, have them carry something else - like the centrepiece. Anything but the bags."

"Got it," Croc replies, typing quickly.

"Meanwhile, Izzy and Macey are turning the brig into a functional prison with Craig and Nick," Dwight says. "The three of us should move to deck seven."

"Dwight, no," Kieron cautions. "Just me and Zack. You don't want to risk catching something else. Your system's still recovering."

"I'll stay on the far side of the deck and assist with crowd control," Dwight suggests. "Croc, let's have Craig and Nick join me on deck seven."

"What happens if the powder goes airborne?" Croc asks.

"That's not happening," Dwight says, confidence unwavering.

"Not a chance," Kieron agrees, leaving, but Dwight lingers a moment longer.

"Let's keep the families - and Prisha - away from the Fair," he tells Croc. "We still don't know the full story: the remote, Dolinsky, or Jim Downing's real intentions for this ship."

Meanwhile, in the brig, Marisol Navarro supervises the relocation, opening both doors to the brig cabins. Izzy and Macey work with Nick and Craig quickly clearing the prison cells. The two young men have no idea why they've been roped into moving all their belongings out of the brig cabins, or why they and Dogg and Raul are being relocated. If they had military or detective training, they might question why Dogg and Raul's cabin is so sparse for men who supposedly had been on board for a long time.

As the doors shut with a heavy metallic click, Marisol turns to Izzy. "These bags will be locked in security until your new cabins are ready," she says.

Nick and Craig are oblivious to the tension. For them, the move feels like an upgrade - a chance to escape the spartan accommodations of the brig. Neither shows that they suspect the danger hanging over the ship.

Marisol, however, seems to sense it. "This will go down in my diary as a very special day," she remarks, almost casually.

"Why?" Nick asks, curious.

Izzy steps in. "When people drink too much, things happen. You two need to be on deck seven now. Billy, Zack, and Dwight will be there. Report only to them. Don't speak to any guests. Understood?"

"Yes, ma'am," Nick replies.

Craig hesitates. "What is going on? Why are we here?"

"Don't get 'uniform mist,'" Macey warns, cutting him off.

"What's that?" Nick asks.

"It's when you start feeling self-important just because you're wearing a uniform."

"But we don't have uniforms," Nick points out.

"Exactly," Macey says sharply. "Now, move. Deck seven. Now."

Nick and Craig leave, and Marisol moves to follow, but Izzy stops her. "We need these doors open again."

Marisol complies, and Izzy and Macey re-enter the first brig cabin. They inspect every inch of the space. Macey lifts the mattress while Izzy pulls the bedframe forward, revealing an old toolbox underneath.

"What's in this?" Izzy asks.

Marisol checks. "Tools."

"They could escape as fast as we put them in," Izzy mutters, displeased.

Macey rifles through the cupboards, finding nothing. Once satisfied, they move to the second cabin, where Marisol finds yet more tools and parts under the bed.

"These rooms double as storage for extra staff," Marisol explains.

Izzy and Macey exchange a look but say nothing.

"Thanks, Marisol," Izzy says as they head upstairs. They exit the crew-only area and enter the guest section, where the atmosphere is decidedly lighter.

"On our way to meet Prisha and the kids at the play area," Macey says. "But keep an eye on Marisol. She left escape tools in both cells? That's not an error we'd ever get away with."

8-70 TRUST NO-ONE
Christmas Day - 1355hrs, 25th December, Day 11

Ignoring the Christmas presents they have unwrapped earlier that morning, children are running wild in the Kids Zone. Their party outfits are adorned with glitter and tinsel, but their spontaneous joy eclipses the festive story.

Lakshmi and Reyansh slide down the slide, bounce on the soft play area, dive into the ball pit, then run back to repeat it all over again. Their laughter fills the air.

"Makes me exhausted just watching them," Mary says.

"I run after them all day, every day. It keeps me slim," Mama-Gee replies with a laugh.

Mary stiffens, her smile faltering. Was it an innocent remark? She weighs her words carefully, damping down her usual quick temper. "I should get you a mirror," she mutters, letting her irritation melt into a wry grin.

On the side lines, Stan stands with his arm around Izzy, his quasi-daughter. They smile as they watch the children play. In contrast, Macey is visibly agitated. Without a word, she storms out of the room.

The spiralling steps of the atrium create a striking stage for the choir. Fifty performers, dressed in red, green, and gold with festive trimmings stand together with officers in formal day-time whites. Glasses of champagne circulate through the crowd as guests, still entering, realise they're too late for any hope of reaching the front. Spirits are high as everyone gathers on all three levels of the atrium, anticipation buzzing in the air.

At the base of the stairs, a spotlight highlights the centrepiece, the art class's elaborate table decoration playing support act to the chef's towering Christmas cake.

Two decks above, on Deck 7 of the atrium, Kieron surveys the scene with Bukka and several security staff. Smartphones and jacket cameras are ready to record every moment.

"Santas entering from the Diamond Room, port side," Kieron says, pointing towards three in one direction and two in another. "Keep filming them. No matter what happens, keep filming." He moves off to check the local deputies before heading towards the Santas who split up near the art exhibit and move to take different positions.

Zack shadows the first Santa, who wears a huge white beard and a backpack strapped to their front. Santa One weaves through the crowd, their red suit granting them a peculiar status. Billy trails the second Santa, while Ronni, freshly cleaned up, follows the third.

The choir finishes their final Christmas song, and attention shifts to the bottom of the staircase, where the captain is expected to appear.

278

Meanwhile, Croc buries himself in reports detailing fanatical climate and oil protesters on board ships across the Caribbean and various fleets. Many have already been detained and all ships are on full alert.

Macey bursts into the room, pulling his attention. "You should lock your door, bro."

"No one's coming in here. The action's in the atrium," Croc replies, not looking up.

"Trust no one," Macey snaps. "It could be Marisol coming to mess you up - or Nick or Craig. Actually, no, they're not smart enough."

"Easy, sis. I'm busy."

"There were tools in both brig cabins," she blurts out.

Croc finally looks up. "Tools? Like guns?"

"No, actual old-school tools - workshop tools. We left that out of our brief. Big mistake. Report everything, right?"

"Yeah, but it was a storage room. We've got it covered."

"No, listen. When we cleared the brig to use them as prison cells again, Izzy and I found tools hidden under the beds in both cabins. Tools for escaping. Marisol left them there."

Croc stiffens. "Not Marisol."

"She did. Her name literally means 'sea' and 'sun.' It's a fake name, genius."

"No, she fessed that to me."

"Stop. Think. Someone was planning an escape. You think Nick or Craig planted tools under the beds? Or Dogg or Raul? Or it was 'just a mistake'?" Macey's voice drips with sarcasm.

Croc rubs his temple. "I'll put it in the report."

"You'd better. Because if you don't, and something goes sideways, that's on you. 'Peril,' bro. Spanish for 'get your act together.'" She storms out, leaving Croc muttering to himself.

Back in the atrium, Santa One pulls something from their bag: snowballs. They start tossing them into the crowd. A moment of confusion hangs in the air as Santa realises they are too light. They are children's soft play balls.

Zack has the evidence and reacts. Grabbing Santa One's wrist, he twists her arm behind her back, forcing her down. She struggles wildly, but Zack's precision movements leave her powerless. A swift kick behind her knees sees her collapse against the safety rail.

On the other side of the atrium, Kieron commands, "Take them all!"

Billy and Ronni have already efficiently subdued Santa Two and Santa Three. Security staff swarm the remaining Santas. Nick and Craig rush to assist, pushing through the parting crowd but by the time they arrive it is all over and the bags of balls made safe. Cameras are rolling as the Santas' protest, lost in the crowd's laughter and loud music.

The captain descends the staircase. "My apologies to anyone hit by children's play balls from the Kids Zone. Please don't handle them; the elf police will collect them to fingerprint. Charges will be brought against the very naughty Santas," he says with a grin, drawing laughter. "No naughty Santas on my ship. Enjoy the Christmas Fair. I'll see you all at dinner - and after I have a Christmas wedding to officiate."

At the crowded bar, Dwight finds a seat, wincing with pain. "Do you mind? I don't like to play the needy card, but my stumps are killing me," he says, tapping his prosthetic legs.

A woman notices his trousers, darkened with blood. "You're bleeding! Someone get a medic!"

"We need a chair," her husband shouts.

"If you knew what it took to get out of a chair, you'd understand why I won't go back. I'd rather die," Dwight replies flatly. He has stopped hearing or seeing whatever is happening around him. He slumps sideways. Unconscious, he topples off the chair.

8-71 THANK YOU FOR YOU SERVICE
Christmas Day - 1515hrs, 25th December, Day 11

Croc leans back in his chair with a sigh of relief so profound he overbalances, crashing to the floor. The chair spins sideways, and he bounces back to his feet in a flurry of embarrassment, regaining his dignity despite being alone. Checking his watch, a grin spreads across his face. "I can get married!" he shouts, dialling Prisha.

In the children's room, Prisha glances at her phone as it rings. Seeing Croc's name, her face tightens, and she hands it to Izzy without a word.

Izzy answers. "Hi, Croc."

"We're getting married! Green light! The wedding is on!" Croc's voice brims with excitement.

"Okay," Izzy replies, her tone measured, almost flat. "I'll let everyone know."

"Can I talk to Prisha?"

Izzy looks at Prisha, who shakes her head vehemently.

"It's your wedding, bro. You've already had too much contact," Izzy says, ending the call before Croc can respond. She turns to the children playing in the zone. "Chop, chop, kids. Mummy and Daddy's wedding is happening in less than half an hour. Get ready!"

"What?" Mary shouts, grabbing Lakshmi's hand and pulling her away from the play area. "That's not enough time!"

Mama-Gee, already panicking, scoops up Reyansh. "It is time!"

As the family rushes out in a whirlwind, Prisha remains rooted in place, her face pale. She stares at Izzy, her expression full of dread.

"No. I can't do it," Prisha whispers. "I'm a fraud. Please, call it off."

Izzy pulls her aside, away from the noise of the play zone. They settle near the elevators, but Prisha's anxiety only deepens.

"The threat's been handled. It's safe. Get yourself together," Izzy says, her voice firm but encouraging.

"To marry a man and not knowing if I am carrying another man's child - it's a sin," Prisha says, trembling.

"Then tell him," Izzy says. "What you've done isn't a sin. It was bad timing."

"It will end the wedding. Winston Crocket deserves better than this."

Izzy's expression softens. "Listen. He's not perfect. I know. I loved Croc before he was my brother."

Prisha stares confused. "What are you saying?"

Izzy exhales slowly. "Before we knew we were siblings, I loved Winston - as more than a brother."

Prisha's face contorts with shock. "You *slept* with your brother?"

"We didn't know!" Izzy says quickly. "We were in love. It was complicated."

"Oh my God," Prisha mutters, horrified.

"And Macey - my sister - had been with him before me. Briefly."

"He slept with *both* of his sisters?"

"Yes. But, again, none of us knew we were related. So you see, no one's perfect. If I have to accept that, you can tell him the truth."

Prisha rises abruptly, shaking her head. "The wedding is off! I can't do this." She storms away, leaving Izzy frozen in place.

Izzy starts after her, but Prisha waves her off. Izzy stands there, guilt tightening her chest. She'd meant to help but only made things worse.

In the depths of the ship, Wanda, Abi, and Carol are unceremoniously shoved into the first brig cell, stripped of their Santa disguises.

"I want my phone! I want to call my lawyer!" Wanda demands, venom in her voice.

"You've got no rights," Ronni says coolly. "You're in the middle of the ocean."

"I'm an American!"

"You'll be in a Jamaican prison tomorrow. Arrested prisoners get offloaded at the first port. Your lawyer can request repatriation," Ronni replies, walking off.

Inside the cell, Wanda's fury simmers. "That's what she thinks," she hisses, turning to Abi and Carol.

She flips the first bed over, expecting an escape kit. Nothing.

She moves to the second bed, her frustration mounting. Again, nothing.

Carol lowers the bed back down and sits, her expression resigned. "Looks like this didn't go according to plan."

Wanda spins to face the locked door, pounding on it with clenched fists. "I want my phone call! I want my lawyer!"

The door opens abruptly, and Kieron stands there, holding his phone. He thrusts it toward her, displaying an image - a photo of Dolinsky's lifeless body. Ronni is behind him.

"Is this your lawyer?" he asks coldly. Before Wanda can snatch the phone, he pulls it back.

"He died at Amber Cove," Kieron continues. "You're in international waters now. Not America. The man you worked for is a Russian spy."

"I didn't work for him."

"Working for him makes you a Russian spy, acting against your nation. That's no longer a domestic crime," Ronni says, slamming the door shut, her voice echoing. "You're gonna need a very good lawyer."

Two security guards, Dogg, Raul, Nick, and Craig escort two more women - both stripped of Santa hats and beards - toward the second cell. The prisoners resist, but their protests are silenced as they're shoved inside.

"Make yourselves comfortable, and get used to a cell," Kieron says dryly. "You're all going to be interned for quite some time."

8-72 GET DRESSED
Christmas Day - 1535hrs, 25th December, Day 11

Croc adjusts his suit in front of the mirror. He is the only one in the men's suite preparing for the wedding. Across the room, Zack scrolls through reports at Croc's station, while Billy hovers, fidgeting.

"Not one successful attack so far," Zack reports as Ronni enters the room.

"The day's not over," Ronni replies. "I'm still worried about the ships meeting and the fireworks. The two extra Santas weren't carrying snowballs and claimed they just used the two spare costumes to join in the fun."

"One of us should check on Dwight in the medical centre," Billy suggests.

"Agreed," Ronni says. "We're close to Jamaica now. If the doctor's uncertain, call for a medivac."

"Roger that." Billy heads out.

Zack swivels in Croc's chair. "Dwight will be airlifted and in a hospital within hours," he assures Ronni.

Ronni frowns. "We still need to figure out why Grigory went to Amber Cove. Something doesn't add up." She dials Ted and switches to speakerphone as the line connects.

"Ronni!" Ted answers warmly. "I'm so glad you and the team joined my family for Christmas. It's been a blast having you around."

Croc steps into the room, fully suited-up, grinning broadly. His exaggerated gesture begs for acknowledgment, but everyone ignores him.

"And look how it's turned out for you, Ted," Ronni says. "How many arrests?"

285

"Still counting," Ted replies. "But I can confirm - it's Christmas!"

"What do you have on the two extra detainees?" Zack asks.

"Not much on them yet. But we have a few statements from arrests on other ships. The on board teams aren't trained for proper interrogations, but being in international waters and accused of treason and terrorism with no rights is causing some concern. I trust your team can handle interrogation a little better."

"Make sure all ships check the brig for hidden escape kits - especially the rectal kind," Ronni says dryly.

Ted chuckles. "Will do. Did *you* check?"

"I was going to," Ronni says, "but they claimed they didn't identify as women. Kieron's handling it now."

"Gotta love this generation."

"What about the possibility of a second wave or a different target? Why did Grigory make the trip to Amber Cove?" Ronni presses.

"In agreement with Creedon and the captains, we've moved up the ship rendezvous as you suggested," Ted says.

"I'm getting married!" Croc interrupts.

"You're not," Ted quips, without missing a beat.

"What's the new ETA?" Zack cuts in.

"Ships will be alongside each other by 1800 hours," Ted confirms.

"Good," Ronni says. "That disrupts their timing, but we've only got two hours to figure out their endgame."

"There's still time for a wedding," Croc tries again.

"No, there's not," Ted counters. "Anyway, all checks on Jim Downing came back clean. He's no climate activist. His facial injuries came from an explosion, not glue. That's why the facial recognition failed. He's legit, with long-term shipping employment."

"Marisol Navarro?" Zack asks.

"Completely fake name," Ted says. "She's Filipina, not Spanish descent. Many take slightly altered names for easier pronunciation. Low risk there."

"What's the real target?" Ronni asks.

"Our team agrees on one thing: It's you guys. It's CSCI."

"What?" Croc blurts.

Ted continues. "Grigory's main hotel room had a laptop with cell lists matching the ship arrests. Incredible work on your part. He also had a go-bag - passports, escape gear, and a ticket home. But we're sure he was ready to blow his cover to get on *your* ship."

"Why?" Croc asks.

"To ruin your wedding, obviously," Ted jokes.

"He sure did that," Croc mutters, glancing at his watch. "Four o'clock. It should be starting now."

Ted ignores him. "We think Grigory discovered CSCI and wanted to test how powerful you really are."

"Then why invite us in?" Ronni asks.

"Bedřiška Kossof. Once he found her name, he had to act. Big game fishing."

"But he killed her. Wasn't the job done?"

"You'd think," Ted explains. "From communications on his computer, there is a trail of exchanges. After confirming Bedřiška Kossoff's kill, an art dealer alerted him to a bounty on two others."

"Anoataly Istov," Kieron interjects, stepping in.

"Correct. The kill list was for three: Bedřiška Kossof, Hunter Witowski - already dead - and you, Kieron Philips. Grigory wanted to finish the job personally. You are a big win."

"Thanks for that," Kieron says dryly. "Nice to know I'm on a Russian hit list."

"You are," Ted says. "His original mission was to disrupt and turn Americans against their own country. His greed for stardom allowed us to dismantle his operation."

"I deserve a medal," Kieron quips.

"So do I," Ted retorts. "Miami Bureau address. Send bottles of cheer."

"What about the Santas?" Ronni asks. "The girls in the art class only had to bring costumes aboard - one for each of them, one for Grigory, and one for…"

"Father Christmas?" Ted finishes. "Let me know when you find out."

The call ends abruptly, leaving Ronni staring at the screen.

"Wedding's at 1830," Croc announces, grinning ear to ear. "On deck ceremony and fireworks just for us!"

"Creedon is planning to board?" Ronni asks as her mind churns. Something still doesn't feel right. "The girls carried Santa suits for a reason. The last one was for…" Her voice trails off, tension thick in the room.

8-73 Wedding Plans
Christmas Day - 1700hrs, 25th December, Day 11

Candice knocks on the door of the Grand King Suite aboard the Blue Sky cruise ship. Inside, the women are abuzz with last-minute wedding preparations.

"Hello?" she calls out hesitantly.

Mary opens the door, her new gown shimmering under the suite's lights. A matching hat perches perfectly on her styled hair, and her makeup is immaculate. She waves Candice inside.

Mama-Gee stands regal in a vibrant, jewel-toned sari, her bangles clinking softly as she adjusts her dupatta. Across the room, Izzy and Macey are meticulously applying their makeup in chic cocktail dresses. Prisha, still partially dressed, flits nervously into the bedroom.

"I need to go over the updated wedding plans," Candice says, clutching her clipboard. "Things are... a bit more complicated now."

Mary snorts, adjusting her hat. "You can say that again."

Mama-Gee steps forward, curiosity flashing in her eyes. "Complicated how?"

Candice clears her throat. "The timing now hinges on Mr. Daniel Creedon's transfer from the Blue Ocean ship to the Blue Sky via open top tender boat to tumultuous applause. That will be filmed."

Mary arches a sceptical eyebrow. "Filming the ships now?"

"It's... the tender boat," Candice corrects, fumbling with her notes.

Mary smirks. "How about this? We send our tender to pick him up," Mary suggests.

"The Blue Ocean have their own tenders," Candice stammers.

"Yes, but in our tender, the bride stays hidden as it crosses to him, then she comes back as the star of mister Creedon's ride. To tumultuous applause."

"Very funny," Candice says, realising too late that Mary isn't joking. She lifts her clipboard and continues reading, quickly.

"We have the wedding. Then the captain's speech will be broadcast across the public address systems on both ships, and… "

"Wait, the captain gets to broadcast on all the speakers?" Mary interrupts.

"Yes, both ships. Then, after Mr. Dwight Ritter will be airlifted off by helicopter to 'tumultuous applause,'" Candice reads from her notes.

"Let's circle back to the wedding vows," Mary says. "Add that they'll be broadcast on the PA systems on both ships, and *those* finish to tumultuous applause."

"But these orders came from Miami," Candice protests weakly.

Mary plucks a pen from her bag. "So's this pen. Write it down."

Candice obeys, as Mama-Gee speaks firmly. "And write this: the bride arrives on the tender with her mother."

"And mother-in-law," Mary adds briskly.

"To tumultuous applause," Mama-Gee insists.

Candice scribbles furiously as Prisha bursts from the bedroom, tears streaming down her face. "No! I

290

can't do this! It's not Winston's baby, and I can't go through with this!"

Prisha bolts from the suite, leaving stunned silence in her wake.

Candice stares, slack-jawed. "Is the wedding still on?"

Mary folds her arms, unfazed. "Of course it is."

Izzy moves to follow Prisha, but Macey stops her. "No, you've done enough by telling her we both slept with him." She rushes out after Prisha.

Candice blinks. "Wait... aren't you his sisters?"

Mama-Gee sighs, resignation heavy in her voice. "Looks like I'll be raising another child for a daughter without a father."

"Oh no," Mary interjects. "That baby's coming to Miami."

Candice looks utterly lost. "Should I... tell Miami?"

Mary waves her off. "You tell Miami to push the sunset by twenty minutes. We'll handle the rest."

Meanwhile, in the men's suite, tension runs high. Evidence bags containing Santa suits are strewn across the table.

"There's an extra suit," Ronni says, holding two of the bags. "Grigory wanted Kieron dead. We can't ignore the possibility of another sleeper agent."

"I get it," Croc replies, leaning against a chair. "But now we've got a wedding with fireworks and a helicopter. As long as Kieron stays out of sight, we're good."

Kieron scoffs. "Thanks. I'll just hang out in a spotlight at the other end of the ship, shall I?"

Ronni examines the suits carefully. "Wanda, Abi, Carol," she mutters, sorting three aside. She holds up the remaining two. "Grigory and... who's this?"

"It's not Elaine Witowski," Kieron says flatly.

Ronni's gaze sharpens. "Never discount a theory."

Kieron shakes his head. "Elaine? Really? She's no fanatic, and she's definitely not stupid."

Ronni presses on. "Dolinsky could've exploited her grief over losing Hunter. If we're all dead, she inherits CSCI."

"You think Elaine wants me dead?" Kieron asks.

Ronni hesitates, then offers a faint smile. "No. You're safe now."

Kieron softens. "You fixed it?"

She nods. "I wasn't losing another man I love."

Before he can respond, Macey bursts in. "Prisha's crying on the stairs. Croc, you need to talk to her."

On the stairwell, Prisha sobs as Croc approaches.

"Fireworks, a helicopter... what a wedding day," he says gently, sitting beside her.

"I can't do this," she whispers.

"Why not? You don't love me?"

"I do. But I've been dishonest."

Croc chuckles. "Me too. Once a rogue - "

"No, listen!" she interrupts. "I'm pregnant. And the baby might not be yours."

Croc jolts upright. "What?!"

Prisha grabs his arm, pleading. "I'm sorry! The night before we met, I was undercover, and... I slept with someone else."

Croc exhales, sitting back down. "I knew that."

"You did?"

"Of course I read the mission reports."

"And you're okay if... if the baby isn't yours?"

His face hardens. "Wait. What?"

Before she can clarify, he blurts out, "I hacked into the medical records and changed your pregnancy dates."

"What?!"

"I didn't want my visa to India denied because of my criminal record. I hacked into the medical data on your scan and made it look like we conceived earlier. So, there was no way they could claim we might abort the baby. The date on the visa application is wrong."

Her mouth drops open. "So the baby is yours?"

"Yes!" Croc admits, relief washing over him.

"But the date of conception?"

"I made it less than 24 weeks so we could cruise and get married. I chose the date that ours eyes met and we both knew. The date the child's future was conceived."

Tears of relief spill down Prisha's face. "Oh, Winston, I thought... I almost..."

"What?"

"I was in such distress I considered abortion."

"What?"

"I couldn't bear the thought of burdening you with another man's child. But, I was turned away. Abortion is not allowed after just eight weeks in Miami."

"What?" Croc says. "It changed?"

"We needn't have gone through all this pain. Why didn't you tell me?"

"Because immigration and visa officials can be terrifying. I didn't want you to have to lie." Croc pulls her into a fierce hug.

"How pregnant am I?

"Fourteen weeks. Please. Let's get married. Now."

She nods, her joy radiating. Then she hesitates. "But you slept with Izzy. And Macey."

8-74 HOLI WEDDING
Christmas Day - 1830hrs, 25th December, Day 11

Mary feels like a queen, her hand tracing lazy circles in the air as she glides across the twilight waves aboard Daniel Creedon's tender. Positioned at the back of the wedding party with Mama-Gee, she feels no less significant. At the front, Prisha - the radiant bride - is the centrepiece of the open-top lifeboat, carried toward her waiting groom with regal grace.

Behind her, Daniel Creedon and the captain stand tall and proud, while her 'maids of dishonour,' Macey and Izzy, sit on either side, trying to look innocent. Prisha's two children clutch baskets of grain and petals, their excitement mirrored by the uniformed officers stationed ceremoniously around the boat, their postures like royal guards.

Above, a few early fireworks burst in brilliant colours between the two ships, the booming explosions timed perfectly to Wagner's *Ride of the Valkyries*. The captain had selected the piece - perhaps the only one present who fully appreciates its tale of warrior sisters ferrying fallen heroes to Valhalla.

On the Blue Sky and Blue Ocean, pool decks and balconies are packed with guests pressing against rails for a better view. The combined weight displacement briefly brings to mind the tragedy of the *Vasa*, but these modern vessels, even with stabilisers retracted, remain steady.

The upper forward sun deck, adorned with elegant lights and festive decorations, awaits the ceremony. CSCI security teams remain on high alert, ready for one final act of sabotage. Over seventy foiled amateur plots embolden their confidence, but the elusive 'Father Christmas' remains a wildcard. Ronni has her suspicions, though the CSCI security team watch everything that moves. They remain on high alert, ready for one final act of sabotage.

In the forward stairwell, only one elevator ascends to deck seventeen, the ceremony location. Dogg and Raul, tasked with securing it, await the bridal party on deck five. On the landing platform at sea level, Kieron and a few officers prepare to receive the boat. Access to deck seventeen's twin external metal staircases has been restricted, while Zack watches over the port side with the crowd facing the other ship, the fireworks and the tender. Billy secures the blind side, but he knows, as Zack has locked the doors to the port side stairwell exit, his blind side is the only side anyone can access the top forward decks.

In the security room, Ronni monitors the numerous security camera feeds with Marisol Navarro. Their attention is fixed on the brig, where the last locked door conceals Wanda, Carol, and Abi. The other two women had been released as innocents.

"This is recording, right?" Ronni asks, her eyes narrowing.

"Yes," Marisol assures her, pointing to the blinking red light. "That camera is live."

"Good."

On the monitor, Nick and Craig unlock the cell. Wanda emerges, scanning her surroundings. With a smirk, she cups Nick's face, planting a mocking kiss on his nose.

"I knew it," Ronni mutters, watching Craig lift a backpack.

"The two other Santa suits were for Nick and Craig," she explains. "They're the sleepers we've been searching for."

Onscreen, Wanda retrieves a snowball from the pack. "Are these the real ones?" she asks.

"I pulled the bag from evidence," Craig replies with a laugh. "Marked for court."

Wanda tests one against the wall, watching it explode with a mess. "They deserve this," she sneers.

"Do we arrest them now?" Marisol asks.

"Not yet. Let them lead us to their target," Ronni replies with a sly grin.

They watch and listen to the scene escalate below as Wanda issues orders. "You have the cans of paint? You four, trash the buffet. When security shifts to handle that mess, I'll move in on the wedding."

"Marisol, protect the buffet," Ronni instructs. "Film them. Arrest them when ready. My team will guard the wedding."

Marisol departs, leaving Ronni alone. Switching cameras, Ronni tracks Wanda's movements. The would-be saboteur grows visibly frustrated when the only forward elevator of the three that goes to deck seventeen is taken out of service.

"Billy come in. I'm sending you a Christmas present," Ronni says. "Arriving on deck sixteen forward, a heavy weight in her backpack. Be careful."

"Ten-four."

On the sun deck, the ceremony proceeds.

Kieron stands like the lead officer of a close protection detail, watching every move the wedding party makes under the nervous watchful eye of Candice.

"Ladies and Gentlemen, ships, guests and crew, we are gathered here with Blue Cruises Chief Operating Officer Mister Daniel Creedon, to join together, on this Christmas Day, this man, Winston Crocket, and this woman, Prisha Nah, in matrimony," the Captain says.

There is tumultuous applause from both ships. The ships horns blast and it looks like the wedding of the century.

Prisha beams as she reaches to touch the outstretched hands of her groom. She is so happy her wedding is to take place that she does not have a care in the world. She is marrying Winston Crocket and carrying his baby. There is no better Christmas present exists.

Billy can hear the words bellow out of the address system and all he can think of is that on the other side of the ship; someone else is getting married when he has just lost the woman that he may have had a strange but wonderful future with.

Zack holds the wooden doors closed on the port side of the ship, the side facing the other ship where both crowds cheer after Prisha says, 'I do."

Wanda cannot open the port door from inside the forward stairwell. She rushes to the starboard side and throws the door open, bursts onto the deck, her face twisted with fury as she clutches a snowball. She rounds a corner and freezes - standing before her is Billy, calm and unyielding. His gaze cuts through her bravado.

"You and Grigory killed the woman I loved."

"The Russian woman?" she says. "She could have stopped our mission."

"She could have. Single handed. But we did. We did because you are a pathetic, ill guided, confused, ignorant, amateur."

Wanda raises her hands and steps forward to throw the ball. Billy grabs her wrist and uses her own momentum to pull her up off her feet, swinging her around, legs in the air as she twists. She screams as her shoulder is yanked out of joint and she becomes airborne as Billy lets her fly in a white powder cloud of her own making. She sails over the rail freely, then drops down. Billy watches as she hits the seas thirteen decks below and she sinks, under the weight of the bag strapped to her front.

Ronni walks in and stands next to Billy.

"The trouble with putting a backpack on back to front," Ronni starts.

"Yeah. Can't get it off by yourself," Billy says. "Do you want to jump over and help?"

"No. I'm late for a wedding." They walk away talking.

"'You think she was misguided?" Ronni asks.

"Well, that wasn't the way to the buffet Unless she wants sea food."

"You know what I mean."

"Are you going soft, Ronni?"

"She was following orders."

"You are going soft. We all follow orders," Billy says.

"None of us know where the orders come from, or if they are good, or if they are true."

"We chose what we follow. What we believe in. And we suffer accordingly," Billy says.

"Amen to that."

A flower girl traditionally precedes the bride down the aisle throwing flower petals. It is a centuries-old tradition that has changed over the years, and here at sea is very different. The ship is not allowed to throw anything over the side, so the tradition has gone full circle back to the times when wheat, herbs or garlic were used to symbolise fertility and ward off bad spirits. The children toss grain in the air and some petals now the wedding is over, and as Kieron sees the smiling faces of Billy and Ronni on the other side of the deck, he knows the act of terrorism is over.

Ronni puts her arm around Billy. "You know you're special, Billy. Very special."

The wedding ends to tumultuous applause as Dwight is pulled up on a winch and the bird pulls away as the final explosion of fireworks lights up the Christmas sky. The cheering guests on the Blue Sky and Blue Ocean celebrate not just a wedding, but the triumph of love, unity, and resilience.

ABOUT THE AUTHOR

Having spent a remarkable career working across the globe in the movie industry, Stuart has seamlessly transitioned into what he calls the perfect retirement job - being a celebrity guest on cruise ships. With a background that includes financing, Executive Producing, Directing, and Producing, Stuart brings a wealth of knowledge and insider anecdotes to his talks, captivating audiences with his unique perspective on the journey from script to screen.

One of his key insights is that the entertainment industry, at its core, is a business - one focused on filling seats and drawing audiences. His candid reflections on A-list films, award-winning television shows, and working alongside Hollywood's brightest stars are as entertaining as they are enlightening. From on-set triumphs to narrowly avoiding disasters, his stories balance drama with humour, keeping his audiences riveted.

Stuart's engaging speaking style can be traced back to his early career, where he spent a decade as a live radio DJ on several UK stations. This experience honed his ability to connect with listeners in real time, a skill that now shines in his lively, unscripted presentations.

When he's not captivating cruise audiences, Stuart enjoys documenting his travels. Armed with his smartphone, he films informal guides at many of the ports he visits, capturing the local flavour and hidden gems. Occasionally, though, he prefers a quieter moment, dropping anchor in a seaside bar to enjoy the view. His YouTube channel, *Doris Visits*, boasts an impressive library of around 500 port guide videos, a testament to his ongoing passion for storytelling and exploration.

It's clear that Stuart's love for travel and filmmaking hasn't waned. In fact, his storytelling has evolved further with his successful series of cruise crime thrillers. His latest book, the eighth in the series, continues to enthral readers with the most gripping plot to date vividly inspired by his global adventures.

Stuart's wife, Jean, often joins him on his travels, co-hosting their video guides and sharing in the adventure. Their son, Luke, is forging his own path as an entrepreneur, ambitiously launching a new bank. Meanwhile, their daughter has made her own mark in the entertainment world, recently portraying Dyan Cannon in the Cary Grant biopic.

Through his life and work, Stuart exemplifies a passion for creativity, storytelling, and exploration, proving that retirement is just the beginning of a new and exciting chapter.

WITH THANKS

To fellow cruise commentators who have read and edited this.

Jean Heard, presenter of the Doris Visits YouTube Channel of port guides.

David Withington of How To Cruise.

ABOUT THE AUTHOR

Having spent a remarkable career working across the globe in the movie industry, Stuart has seamlessly transitioned into what he calls the perfect retirement job - being a celebrity guest on cruise ships. With a background that includes financing, Executive Producing, Directing, and Producing, Stuart brings a wealth of knowledge and insider anecdotes to his talks, captivating audiences with his unique perspective on the journey from script to screen.

One of his key insights is that the entertainment industry, at its core, is a business - one focused on filling seats and drawing audiences. His candid reflections on A-list films, award-winning television shows, and working alongside  Hollywood's brightest stars are as entertaining as they are enlightening. From on-set triumphs to narrowly avoiding disasters, his stories balance drama with humour, keeping his audiences riveted.

When he's not captivating cruise audiences, Stuart enjoys documenting his travels. Armed with his smartphone, he films informal guides at many of the ports he visits, capturing the local flavour and hidden gems. Occasionally, though, he prefers a quieter moment, dropping anchor in a seaside bar to enjoy the view. His YouTube channel, *Doris Visits*, boasts an impressive library of around 500 port guide videos, a testament to his ongoing passion for storytelling and exploration.

THE BOOKS

Cruise Ship Heist is the inaugural novel in Stuart St. Paul's *Cruise Ship Crime Investigators (CSCI)* series, introducing readers to a world of maritime mystery and suspense. The narrative centres on Commander Kieron Philips, a retired military officer who embarks on a cruise aboard the MV Lady Diana. His journey takes an unexpected turn when he is thrust into a complex heist, compelling him to employ his military expertise to restore order and ensure the safety of all on board.

Cruise Ship Serial Killer is the second instalment in Stuart St. Paul's *Cruise Ship Crime Investigators (CSCI)* series, following the formation of a specialised unit led by Commander Kieron Philips and Hunter Witowski. The narrative unfolds aboard a cruise ship two days out of Panama, deep into the Pacific Ocean, where a series of murders begins to terrorise passengers and crew. With the vessel beyond helicopter range and unable to turn back, the cruise operators enlist the expertise of Philips and Witowski to apprehend the perpetrator. Goodreads

Cruise Traffic: Human Laundry is the third novel in Stuart St. Paul's *Cruise Ship Crime Investigators (CSCI)* series. This instalment delves into the harrowing world of human trafficking, focusing on a criminal network that exploits cruise ships to smuggle women from Albania to major Mediterranean coastal cities. **Amazon**

The CSCI team is discreetly enlisted to investigate the systematic theft of high-value art pieces from the ship's collection. Unlike traditional law enforcement agencies, their anonymity is crucial; any indication that the thefts are under scrutiny could cause the perpetrators to disappear, taking the irreplaceable art with them. Google Books

St Paul delivers a romance wrapped crime. *Solo Cruiser: Deadly Romance* is the fifth novel in Stuart St. Paul's *Cruise Ship Crime Investigators (CSCI)* series. Originally titled *Disastrous COVID-19 Cruise Romance*, this reworked edition shifts its focus from the pandemic to the psychological state of a solo traveller emerging from lockdown. **Goodreads**

Blood Diamonds is the sixth novel in Stuart St. Paul's *Cruise Ship Crime Investigators (CSCI)* series. The story begins with a whistle-blower alerting authorities to an open gem safe aboard the cruise ship MS Aerwyna, suggesting a significant security breach. This incident propels the CSCI team into a complex investigation involving the illicit trade of conflict diamonds, commonly known as "blood diamonds." Amazon

Cruise Ship Murder Reunion is the seventh novel in Stuart St. Paul's *Cruise Ship Crime Investigators (CSCI)* series. The story follows Commander Kieron Philips, who is grappling with the recent death of his partner and the demolition of his office. Amidst his grief, he receives an invitation to a school reunion aboard a cruise ship in Asia - a poignant setting due to past events. Initially reluctant, Philips is drawn into a complex investigation when a murder occurs during the reunion, compelling him to confront his past and navigate the intricacies of the case.

4 Murders, A Wedding, and A Cruise - is an electrifying blend of humour, cultural insight, danger, and philosophical depth, wrapped in the intrigue of a high-stakes mystery. When the CSCI team receives a cryptic tip from a mysterious informant, they find themselves chasing shadows with nothing but their instincts and the haunting suspicion that a luxury cruise could become the stage for a catastrophic attack.